Sonny's Place
Whiskey, Women, Parkinson's Disease, and The Blues

SEAN MICHAEL DANEHY

ISBN: 9798395926609

Book cover created by Christine Lucey Meagher

Research by Al Wood

In memory of Dick Pleasants
and my "Papa Bear" Charles Williams.

Contents

ACKNOWLEDGEMENTS

Thank you to K.T., Jay, Mike, Spider, and Dominique for sharing.

Kathleen Rys, thank you for your companionship, and your encouragement of this story many years ago, when it was just a thought in my head.

Richard Demers, in appreciation of your support of this project, and for the time you spent reading my many rewrites.

Dr. Harte Weiner of CambridgeEditors, for your insightful criticism as well as your enthusiasm for this story.

Tom Sullivan of Sullivan Wordsmithing, for your keen eye, and for getting me to the finish line.

JoAnne Nowak, for all you bring to our table.

AUTHOR'S NOTE

Dear Reader,

Hello, and welcome!

Thank you for taking this book into your hands.

Sonny's Place is written in the much critically maligned voice of the omniscient Narrator. I feel free to jump inside the heads of any of my characters at any given moment because they don't exist without me.

Besides, that's where the fun is!

I wish you a most excellent read.

Best to you and yours,

SMD

1: A HAND IN THE COOKIE JAR

Early August 1973

The Pinecrest Motel

Old Route One

Saugus, Massachusetts

Having finished his business, Sonny Bolla washed up and checked his look in the mirror. Turning off the bathroom light, he walked out into the naugahyde nestle he had rented for the evening at the Pinecrest Motel, Old Route One, Saugus. Doreen, his date for the last seven Wednesdays, sat on the edge of their love bed, pulling back on her nylons.

"Doreen, you kind of resemble Mrs. Robinson in that fucken movie there."

"You mean *The Graduate?*"

"Yeah, that one."

"And who are you supposed to be? My nineteen-year-old lawn boy?" she retorted.

Sonny just shrugged.

Doreen stepped into her heels and rose up. Sonny gazed at her as she buttoned up her blouse. She still looked good after a couple of runs around the track, and he had half a hankering.

"You're gonna forget the rose I bought you?"

Doreen smiled, picked her rose off the mantel, and gave Sonny a kiss on the cheek.

"You wanna go out for a nightcap?" he asked.

"I gotta get back to where I'm supposed to be."

"Yeah, me too."

Sonny opened the motel room door to greet the night, when a flurry of popping flash bulbs blinded him. The voice of his wife Marie Bolla cut to the quick.

"Sonny Bolla, you slimy, cheatin', no good fuck bastard! And who's this whore you're with?"

"Who are you calling a whore?" Doreen wanted to know. She took in this scene for another three seconds, tossed the rose on the ground, and exited stage left.

"You bought that whore a rose? A fucken rose?"

Marie lunged forward to gouge his eyes out with her long, painted nails. Instinctively, Sonny grabbed the photographer by the nape of the neck, converting him into a human shield, much like drunken Americans are known to do at the Running of the Bulls in Pamplona.

The rage of Sonny's charging she-bull wife landed several inadvertent blows. Blood streamed from the photographer's eyebrow. A thick heel intended for the Bolla family jewels missed, cracking the kneecap of his flesh and blood armament. A mournful cameraman cry sliced the warm summer night in two.

As the threesome danced their venomous tango, Sonny held on for dear life. Finally, Marie, frustrated at not being able to inflict pain upon her intended target, stepped back and began to sob.

"I'll see you in court Sonny, and I'm taking you for every penny you've got!"

So with that, Marie Bolla stormed off, her wounded photographer limped and bled a few steps behind. Soon they were down the hill and out of sight. Sonny still had some huffing and puffing to do. He bent over and rested his hands on his knees like a gassed, out of shape linebacker.

Once his respiration leveled off, he reached for a smoke. In his mind he replayed the scene that had just taken place. By mid-Camel he had managed to make an assessment, quickly realizing that there would be no way back home from this.

"Now I've gone and done it. I've really fucken gone and done it."

The rest of his evening would be spent stewing over this in Room Forty at The Pinecrest Motel. Nothing left to do but wander down the hill, buy a bottle and a pack of smokes to help pass the night.

"I wonder if the Sox are on T.V. tonight?" he asked aloud.

2: FACE DOWN IN THE GUTTER BLUES

The Next Day

Early August 1973

New Orleans, Louisiana

The sky had cried all day long in Louisiana, tempering the brutal summer heat of the Crescent City. In Orleans Parish, the waters rose up from out of the gutters to curb level in the streets. Patrick Phelan had started the party alone at Igor's on the Avenue about noon. The couplet of Jax beer and Old Forrester's Bonded Whiskey put the wind in his sails.

A day of heavy lifting, and the last thing he remembered was holding onto the tailgate of his '63 Dodge Dart as the world spun around him. Then somebody turned out the lights. He crashed to his knees as if he'd been shot, falling face first into the rain filled gutter.

The night sky was clearing, and the reflected light of the yellow moon shone on his body, lying face down in a half foot of rainwater. He had collapsed outside the home of his mentor and Bacchanalian role model, Lester Reardon. It was the second Thursday of August, the night of Lester's monthly rent party.

Wisps of brown hair, the seat of his pants, and the bottoms of his boot heels to be wandering were all that rose above sea level. Having extended his arms to break the fall, he lay there motionless. Patrick Phelan woke to the burning of rainwater in his nasal passages, then to the grinding of sand in his teeth.

He tried to get free by willing his shoulders to rock back and forth, but to no avail. Panic quickly set in. It is said that when a man faces imminent death, his entire life can flash back in front of his eyes. Yet Patrick's flashback was very selective. It went back only as far as his arrival in New Orleans on the previous New Year's Eve. It was as if the nineteen years spent growing up in Cambridge, Massachusetts hadn't occurred, or as if his life had truly begun upon his arrival here.

As his cortisol levels skyrocketed, Patrick felt a physicality awakening within and the imposing paralysis began to lift. He found the strength to raise his head upward. Gasping, coughing, and wheezing, he fought off the Reaper. Raising himself up on one knee, he reached for the tailgate of the Dart, his head pounding ferociously. A nauseating dizziness possessed him, as if he'd rolled down a steep hill in a beer barrel.

The Dart held him up as he gathered his bearings. Thoroughly drenched, he might as well have fallen into the Mississippi. The lights were shining from inside Lester's house, the party rolling on without him.

"Can't go back in there" he thought. "Too embarrassing."

Patrick climbed into the Dart, intending to make his way home, but glancing into the rear-view mirror, he nearly passed out again. There was nothing but raw flesh from the bridge to the tip of his nose. Just above his hairline there was an ugly cut the size of a silver dollar. His curly brown hair was matted back, and the dried mud and blood speckled his face with two toned polka dots.

The realization of what had just happened shook him to the core. It took all he had to manage the ride back home. He stumbled up the stairs to his place, not wanting to be seen. Stripping down, he took a painful shower. Carefully, he dried himself off and laid his aching head on a pillow. There were no curtains on his windows, and the Louisiana moon shone freely, casting the dizzying shadows of an undulating magnolia tree on the far wall.

Soon it became evident that the mercy of sleep would not be intervening. He got up for a drink of water and rested his elbows on the kitchen sill. Staring blankly out on to Napoleon Avenue, an important realization came to him slowly but surely, as he spoke it out loud.

"I've got to get out of this town."

3: BILL RUSSELL WAS AGAMEMNON

It was late morning when Patrick Phelan awoke to the sounds of birds chirping outside his apartment window. A few merciful hours of sleep had intervened around daybreak. A trip to the bathroom, and a look in the mirror, assured him that last night had not been a bad dream. There was no hiding from this. He lay back down on his bed. Staring at the ceiling, he reviewed the journey that had brought him to this place in time.

****

One unhappy semester in the Zoo at UMass, Amherst and he decided that college was not for him. Liquidating the five hundred dollars of paper route money he had accrued through his teens, he packed up his 63' Dodge Dart, yearning for an adventure of his own volition.

He had no clue where he was headed, but when his mother Mildred inquired about his destination, two words came out of his mouth.

"New Orleans."

"But we don't know anybody there!" she cried.

"It's about time we do Ma."

Mildred did her best to chip away at him. Her powers of control and manipulation were considerable, but in this instance Patrick Phelan had made up his mind. Departing a few days after Christmas, with no promises of a quick return. He'd drive as far as he could on the first day, pull over and grab a room for the night. Then he'd wake up and set his sights on the New Orleans city limits. If things went according to plan, a New Year's Eve arrival was in store.

But three hours into the journey, fear and uncertainty bubbled to the surface. The New York City skyline soon rose in the west as a menacing presence. "But we don't know anybody there," a familiar voice reminded him at marked intervals.

This sudden appearance of doubt had not been anticipated. Somewhere in his child mind, Patrick Phelan had figured that getting out on the open road would be straight up bliss—heroin without withdrawal. But fear was front and center, staring him square in the eye. There was simply no place to hide.

Knowing that he must get to the other side of it, he pushed through New York, Philly and Baltimore all the while dancing with his demons. He scooted around the nation's capital, jumping on Highway 81. An hour into Virginia and he was level again, but as the sun fell, giving way to the darkness, his demons danced back into the picture.

Confronted with a thick loneliness, he found himself wishing that he'd traveled with a friend. In one uncertain moment, it felt as if he could just slip out through the top of his head and disappear into the black of night, never to be heard from again. It frightened him.

Driving on until he couldn't, Patrick Phelan pulled over outside of Wytheville, booking a cheap room on the Virginia side of the Tennessee border. In his frazzled state, hunger and thirst weren't dominant. He just wanted to close his eyes and disappear for a time. He turned the light on in the room, locked the door and curled up on his side in the bed. Then he fell into several hours of wretched sleep, waking up a little after midnight, feeling scared and lonely.

He reached into his bag, pulled out his Sylvania radio, and plugged it in. Then he searched on the am dial for Larry Glick's all night talk show out of WBZ Radio in Boston. The BZ signal was a strong one, but Patrick feared he was just too far from home. Yet he found that when he held the Sylvania up at a certain angle with the antenna touching the metal of the bed frame, he could bring in the broadcast.

There he was—"The Commander" of the early morning, midnight till dawn hours of the Boston radio airwaves. Fun and frivolity were the order of Larry Glick's show. His minions, called Glicknicks, were a loyal crew of third shifters, insomniacs, and assorted crackpots. Patrick Phelan had proudly been amongst their ranks for years. Wake up at two in the morning, get some milk and cookies and listen to "The Commander" till you fell back to sleep.

Larry was talking in studio with Charlie DiGiovanni, his cab driver friend who always brought him a nightly cup of coffee. Soon after that a regular caller known as The Champagne Lady checked in from Providence to talk Larry up.

"Hi Larry doll, how are you?"

"Hey Champagne Lady. Let me Check! Ahhh, molto bene!"

Never had Patrick Phelan valued Larry Glick's show more than on this night. The late-night radio from home calmed him down like a shot of magnesium and provided companionship, when he so badly needed it. Eventually, he fell sound asleep with the Sylvania wrapped up in his arms.

The next morning got him up early—breakfast and back out on the road. Crossing over into Tennessee, he put Chattanooga and later Birmingham, Alabama in the rear-view mirror. A long, long day of driving finally brought him to Canal Street, downtown New Orleans. He parked the Dart and got out to explore the French Quarter. It was New Year's Eve, and the Crescent City was buzzing.

Quickly he discovered "to-go cups," poured a Dixie beer into one, and began to wander down Bourbon Street, breathing in its decadent intoxication. He opened to the myriad of sounds, smells, and sights; earthly delights promising to satisfy the appetites of any man or woman.

It all seemed to say, "Don't be afraid. Take a chance. Bite into that apple!"

It was overwhelmingly exotic to the Catholic kid from Cambridge. Patrick Phelan was no stranger to the streets around the "Combat Zone" in Boston. But this was different. It was warm, festive, and unashamed. He reveled in it as he ducked to avoid the legs of the female mannequin, dressed in fish net stockings that swung out through the sidewalk window of a Bourbon Street strip club.

"Come right in! Come right in! Lovely ladies for your viewing pleasure!" barked the barker.

Patrick took a right on St. Peter, passing the front door of Preservation Hall as the band played "Muskrat Ramble." Finally, he came out on to Jackson Square, where the people were teeming in anticipation of midnight and the fireworks on the river. As the countdown started a pretty girl came out of nowhere and threw her arms around him, administering a desperate kiss that went from five to four to three to two to one. She smiled, then turned and vanished into the crowd as quickly as she had appeared.

The fireworks reflected off the façade of St. Louis Cathedral, and Patrick took it all in as the City of New Orleans eased into the year of our Lord, 1973. The magical glow of midnight sustained him for some time until he felt a need to touch base with his mothership, the Dodge Dart. He walked up Royal, crossed Canal, and looked over to see her resting safely, right where he had left her. He yawned deeply and began to think about sleep. Looking up he saw a sign that read:

"See Ed for a Bed"

That didn't feel quite right, so he drove the Dart uptown, and found a quiet street off Prytania. He had never imagined being cold in New Orleans until he slunk into his sleeping bag, where he commenced to freeze his ass off in the back seat.

Morning finally arrived and he found his way over to "The Friendly House" on Magazine Street. A hearty breakfast and a pot of coffee helped to thaw him out.

Perusing the *Times Picayune*, he noticed his Boston Celtics were playing the New York Knickerbockers on national television at one o'clock. His waitress suggested that he would enjoy watching the game over at the Maple Leaf on Oak Street. Once there, the Fates directed him to an empty barstool in front of the television. Little did Patrick Phelan know that the City of New Orleans was about to smile on him.

The sight of the parquet floor of the Boston Garden brought on a feeling of deep tribal connection to home that made his pulse quicken. He watched on as his boyhood hero, number seventeen, John Havlicek, stood at the foul line for two free throws.

Havlicek planted both feet, looked at the rim and measured; his face placid, his eyes almost gentle, which belied the summa competitive nature that propelled him into relentless motion. His broad shouldered, angular frame was sinewy, long and lean like a branding iron. Gary Cooper's jaw line coupled with the bright, twinkling eyes of a country boy, who flat out lived to play ball. Equal parts heart, soul, and tenacity—wrapped in a demeanor of soft-spoken decency. Celtic fans had long since come to lovingly call him "Hondo."

In Boston it was sometimes said that there were three things you could count on: death, taxes, and John Havlicek giving you *everything* he's got. A few angst-filled teenage years had passed since Patrick Phelan had last pretended to be him on the Cambridge hoop courts. But now, alone and so far from home, just seeing him up on the television screen made Patrick feel whole and connected for the moment.

John Havlicek was Patrick Phelan's guy. That went back to the spring of 1962 when his dad, Jim Phelan, took him into the old Boston Garden for his very first Celtics game. It was the all important Game five of the NBA Eastern Conference Finals against Wilt Chamberlain and the Philadelphia Warriors. The seven-game series tied at two a piece.

Jim Phelan parked his Oldsmobile just off Causeway Street. He took his son's hand as they walked beneath the hissing, grinding whine of the elevated Green Line train above them. Into the chaos of North Station they entered and up to the Celtic Ticket Booth they marched, where Jim Phelan laid down a $20 bill that he had tugged and percussed from his bill fold and asked for "the two best seats you got!" Jim gathered up his two tickets and change, grabbed Patrick's hand and walked him through North Station to the far wall where they found the ramps that would take them up four flights to where the magic happened.

The climb to the Boston Garden Concourse brought on a vibrating state of anticipation as the muffled echo of the vendors barking out their wares teased them from just above. Upon arrival, Jim took the change from his $20, bought a soda pop, a bag of peanuts for his kid, and a cold beer for himself. Now fully armed, they made their way to the tall promenade doors and the young kid's first glimpse inside. That first glimpse inside was a spectacle of brilliance that could just never

ever be forgotten. The billows of blue tobacco smoke rising up to caress the lights in the rafters, where four World Championship Banners hung proudly.

They found their way to their seats, and they were in fact "the best seats in the house." Midcourt about seven rows up. A tall young man with a crew cut sitting on the aisle seat rose up to let them pass, and they took their seats right next to him.

Everything jumped out at the kid and he just couldn't contain himself.

"Dad! The Championship Banners! Dad, there's Wilt Chamberlain!"

Jim noticed that the young man seated next to them was smiling to witness the kid's joy.

"It's my son's first Celtic game" Jim explained.

"I get it. It's my first Celtic game too!" The young man added.

Then the public address announcer called out—"Please welcome your World Champion Boston Celtics!" and the three of them rose to their feet to watch the Celtics come out of the tunnel on their right and on to the parquet floor.

"Dad! There's Bill Russell and Bob Cousy!" The excitement would not abate.

They rose for John Kiley's National Anthem, then just before the opening tap, the p.a. man made one more announcement. "Ladies and gentlemen please give a warm Boston Garden welcome to the Celtic's First Round draft pick, from Ohio State—John Havlicek!"

Just then the tall young man with the crew cut sitting next to them rose to his feet to acknowledge the crowd. Celtic rookies were traditionally welcomed warmly by the fans. However there wasn't a soul in the old barn that could possibly have imagined what this rookie would come to mean to them.

Jim Phelan reached out his hand, "John, welcome to Boston!" and Patrick did the same. They shook and partook of this game together.

It was the much-remembered battle in which Celtic guard Sam Jones got into the rebounding action and tattooed Wilt Chamberlain with an elbow to the solar plexus. As Wilt's respiratory system came to a screeching halt, the sound of the oxygen shooting from his lungs emitted an utterance that frightened everyone within earshot. Wilt recovered quickly and came after Sam with the bad intent of snapping him in two. But Sam kept the Giant at bay with a photographer's stool he had snatched up off the sidelines.

This, seeing Cousy at the height of his powers, along with the ever-epic battle between Russell and Chamberlain, provided a Celtic initiation of the highest order. It felt to Patrick like he and the new rookie were beginning their Celtic journey together on this very day. So just like that, John Havlicek became Patrick Phelan's guy. And as he grew up, that was who he wanted to be, and when he shot hoops with the neighborhood kids that's who he said he was.

The Celtics prevailed, winning the all-important Game Five on their way to another title. Jim and Patrick Phelan said good bye to their friend for the afternoon, and wished him well.

"All the best John. We'll be watching and rooting for you."

The Phelans did exactly that. They watched, rooted, and emotionally invested in that young man from then on. It was like getting in on the ground floor of IBM.

Now eleven years later, Hondo's busy hands had been all over six more World Championship banners. Since the departure of Russell and the Jones boys, he had become the inexhaustible, unquestioned leader of this, the smallest team in the NBA. Amidst that apparent limitation, they were pushing forward, their eyes on the mountain top—an unprecedented twelfth NBA Title for the Boston Celtics and their fans.

Patrick watched on as Hondo drove the base line on a fast break dish from Jo Jo White, which he laid up off the glass. Dollar Bill Bradley of the Knicks stepped in, planting his two feet in the paint like the Pillsbury Dough Boy. Flopping on his back, he drew an offensive foul, as the ball passed through the net. The Boston Garden crowd howled in outrage at this theft of a Celtic hoop.

"I hate the fucken Knicks!" growled the fellow to Patrick Phelan's left.

"I hate 'em too," chimed in Patrick. "They win one ring and New Yorkers are calling them "the greatest team ever."

"Greatest team ever my ass!" he proclaimed making eye contact. "I'm Lester Reardon," the fellow spoke, extending a hand. He was lean, dark eyed, a few years older, and seemingly happy to share this game with a fellow hooper.

"I'm Patrick Phelan."

They shook.

"Where you from, bub?"

Patrick Phelan pointed to the television and the parquet floor.

"Boston?"

"Actually, across the river in Cambridge. You're a Celtic fan, Lester?"

"Always."

"How so?"

"My father was stationed in Boston for a time in the late fifties. He worked out of the Charlestown Naval Shipyard."

"No shit?"

"Yeah, I was seven. He took me in to see the Celts play a bunch of times. We were there for Game Seven of the Finals in '57."

"You were in the Garden for Game Seven against the Hawks in '57? The double overtime?"

"That's right. We walked right in off the street and bought tickets before the opening tap."

"What do you remember?"

"I remember Cousy and Sharman, the best backcourt in the NBA, couldn't put the ball in the fucken ocean. But a 22-year-old rookie from Holy Cross named Tommy Heinsohn pours in thirty-seven, and grabs twenty-two boards before he fouls out, and players were fouling out all over the fucken place. Then with five seconds left in regulation and the game tied, the ball ends up in the hands of Jack Coleman of the Hawks for an open shot that could win the series. But the other rookie, Bill Russell swooped in from nowhere like a bird of prey, like a fucken pterodactyl and blocked the shot, pushing the game into overtime."

"Then with seconds left on the clock in the second overtime and the Celts up by two, the player/coach of the Hawks, Alex Hannum, puts himself into the game to inbound the ball, and he hadn't played a single second the whole fucken series! Hannum takes the ball out from behind the Celtics backboard and heaves a length of the court, desperation inbounds pass that ricochets off the St. Louis back board, where the great Bob Pettit of the Hawks -- Louisiana's own, swats once, then swats again at the offensive rebound that hung on the rim forever, leaving no time on the clock. The horn sounds, the ball falls out, and the Celtics win their first by a deuce in double O.T. of Game Seven!"

"That's right," concurred Patrick, who was too young to have been there, but had heard his father's stories.

"The place," pointed Lester up to the parquet, "turned into a mad house! I saw grown men crying, jumping up and down like children. Such joy, I still haven't seen anything that could compare with it."

"Wow!"

"The next year my dad got transferred down here, but we're Boston Celtic fans through and through. You ready for another one, bub?"

"Sure."

"Order 'em up," said Lester as he polished off his Mary and dropped a sawbuck on the bar. "I gotta put my laundry in the dryer."

"Laundry in the dryer?"

"Out back," he pointed.

"A laundry in a bar?"

"Yeah man. Down here we get shit done while we party."

Aside from the kiss, this conversation was his first human exchange in days. He'd lived exclusively between his ears from Cambridge to Louisiana, kind of like Papillon in the black hole. He ordered up another round. Soon Lester returned from his laundry, and Patrick Phelan shared.

"The Celtics used to practice at the Cambridge YMCA. It was their home base all through the sixties. We used to skip school, and hide out in Central Square just to see Bill Russell walk down Mass. Ave."

"No shit? Did you ever talk to him?"

"Nah, I was afraid to bother him. But I loved to witness his presence."

"Yeah, regal presence."

"Yup."

"Shit, Russell, The Cooz, Sharman, Ramsey, Heinsohn, Hondo, Satch, Siggy, Nellie, Lusky, and the Jones Boys—K.C. and Sam. Think about it. The greatest basketball team that the world has ever seen, walked the streets of your hometown as if they were mere mortals. Hey man, you didn't need to study Greek Mythology in high school. Bill Russell was Agamemnon."

"Agamemnon? The God of War?"

"Fuck yeah! Two NCAA titles, an Olympic Gold Medal, eleven World Championships in thirteen years! Never lost a deciding Game Seven!"

Lester was preaching to the choir. Boston took this one. The Knicks had no answer for Celtic center Dave Cowens—the highly combustible, undersized, redhead torched the Knicks inside and out. He had some Agamemnon in him as well.

By game's end, these two were fast friends. Lester offered Patrick the couch at his place on Willow Ave. until he could get situated with employment. Within a week he found work as a roustabout on the oilrigs outside of Morgan City. The pay was decent, and he secured a small efficiency uptown on Napoleon Ave.

His work routine on the Gulf ran seven days on, seven days off. Seven bone dry days of endless Gulf Coast toil, followed by seven nights, running the streets of New Orleans—searching for the Nightbird with Lester Reardon.

Patrick Phelan knew he had to get off the merry-go-round. It was time to head back home.

Just then he heard a rat-a-tat-tat on his apartment door.

"Patrick, it's me Lester."

He sat up in bed, wishing he didn't have to open the door.

4: AFTER THE FLOOD

"Patrick, open up. It's me, Lester." Rat-tat-tat on the door.

He rose out of bed, pulled on his shorts and opened up.

"Hey, I was worried" Lester spoke until he got a look at Patrick's face. "Woah! What the fuck happened to you?"

Patrick turned away to avoid the close inspection. Finally, he took a breath and gave Lester a gander at the damage. The tone of brackish red had not quite manifested yet, but it was on the way. Patrick felt Lester's cool fingertips gently touch his forehead and saw him wince as he examined the damage up close.

"What happened?"

"After you pushed that bong on me for the third time in your kitchen, the walls started to close in. I went outside for some air. The last thing I remember was holding on to the tailgate of the Dart. Then I fell face first into the gutter. When I came to, I was paralyzed, breathing in the rainwater. I couldn't move a finger."

"You passed out in the gutter in front of my house?" Lester capsulized.

"I felt like I was gonna die, and my life started flashing back at me."

"No shit? Like snapshots?"

"No. More like the movie in my head. But the strange part is the movie only went as far back as my arrival here in town. As if the first nineteen years of my life didn't matter."

"What did you see?"

"My first walk through the Quarter on New Year's Eve ... Jackson Square at midnight ... Meeting you at the Maple Leaf. Then I was being pushed off a hovering helicopter onto an oil platform in the gulf

… Early Mardi Gras morning—dancing and drinking through the Irish Channel with the Buzzards."

"Then seeing the Wild Tchoupitoulas in full dress at the Festival, Bongo Joe at a Gazebo … Clifton Chenier burning down Stage Four … Irma Thomas melting hearts on Stage Three … Then the whole crowd came down to Stage One to see Fats Domino close the show. "

"Five songs into his set, he breaks into 'Blueberry Hill.'" Everything slowed down at that moment, and I could feel a huge wave of shared joy roll out from the stage across the whole fairgrounds. I realized that I'd never been so happy in my whole life. Then my body woke up, and I managed to pull my head up for air."

"Jesus Christ, Patrick! Where had you been before you got to my house?"

"Drank my way up the Avenue—Igor's, The Polka Dot, Fat Harry's."

"Food?"

"None."

"Why were you hitting it so hard? Something to do with what happened the night before with Sylvia?"

"You know about that?"

"Patrick, she's my girlfriend's roommate. They're women. They discuss everything."

"Does this mean I'm still a virgin?" he asked with a modicum of shame.

"From what I heard, you're not a virgin anymore. Now you're a two-pump chump."

"Great! Did Suzie tell you that Sylvia threw me out of the house?"

"Yes. Rather harsh I'd say. Is that why you were hitting it so hard?"

"I felt so low, I didn't know what else to do. After I stumbled back here last night, it was clear that it was time for me to head back home."

"Yeah, well you aren't the first cowboy to get chewed up and spit out by this town."

"This town doesn't tell you when it's time to go home. Some of us need that."

"Patrick, I know that you love New Orleans, but you aren't 'of it.' And another thing, what happened with Sylvia? There's not a man alive who hasn't experienced that moment. Don't overthink it."

"It's happened to you?"

"Hey bub, we're not machines! Women can have sex anytime they want" proclaimed Lester, licking his fingertips and feigning a rub between the legs. "They can have sex with a man they find repulsive if they've got proper motive. They can just close their eyes and go somewhere else. We're men. We gotta be kickin' on all cylinders to get the job done."

Patrick wished he had that part of his life straightened out, but it hadn't gotten resolved in New Orleans. It was going to have to happen somewhere else down the road. A quiet filled the room as he thought about the journey ahead, and what awaited him there.

"I talked to my mother a week ago. She said my father's getting worse. She says he's been falling down a lot lately."

"Him too?"

"Funny, Lester."

"Patrick, we gotta get some food in your stomach. Let's go down to Parasol's for a Po Boy."

"I don't feel quite ready to meet my public."

"I'll get takeout. Roast beef loaded up with a Barq's?"

"OK. Sounds good."

Lester drove down Magazine to the Garden District, parking on Constance. He felt sad to think of Patrick leaving town. He was the little brother he never had. Lester saw who he was immediately, and took to him right away—opening up his home, helping him get started.

Sometimes friends become family. The previous Easter Sunday, Lester had brought Patrick to his folks' house for the lamb feast. The men watched their Boston Celtics go down in bitter defeat to the hated Knicks in Game Seven of the Eastern Conference Finals.

Hondo had dislocated his right shoulder early in the series and was unable to raise his shooting arm over his head, so he couldn't go in Game Four. He comes out in Game Five and rings up eighteen with one arm en route to a big win. Left-handed free throws and a succession of slashing, lefty spinners in the lane that rose up from his hip with high arcing beauty and grace to kiss off the glass. Run, run, run—run them till they drop. Any other player in the league would have watched the conference finals from the bench in street clothes. But Hondo played with one arm, keeping the Celtics alive, never rolling over.

The magnificent performance that he extracted from himself that night was singular, and not replicable. It took everything he had. His powers and production were greatly diminished in the following games.

By the middle of the fourth quarter of Game Seven, the Celtics could no longer hold back the tide with their Captain so encumbered. Down by twenty, Coach Tommy Heinsohn called time out and took Hondo out of the game. Head bowed in defeat, he walked to the bench and buried his face in a towel. The Boston Garden crowd rose to its feet out of love for him. The only dry eyes in the house belonged to the contingent of B.U. kids from New York and Jersey, who reveled in their triumph as they watched Walt "Clyde" Frazier raise one finger to the sky as he walked off the parquet floor.

"That's the gutsiest performance I've ever seen" spoke Nick Reardon, his eyes welling up. They all felt the same way, commiserating in defeat. Lester Reardon, a twenty-three-year-old son of Jefferson Parish. His Father Nick, a tough Irishman, who worked the docks of New Orleans. His Mother, Sophia—a dark eyed Italian beauty.

Mildred and Jim Phelan had taught their son some manners. He showed up with a nice bouquet of flowers for Sophia, and that was that. She took him in like he was one of her own.

"Lester there's a sadness about him. Why?"

"His Daddy ain't right. He got the Parkinson's."

"The Parkinson's huh?"

"Yeah, got it when Patrick was a little boy. "

"There's a despair about him. It's palpable. It needs to be dispelled. He's such a nice kid. Does he have a girlfriend?"

"No."

"No, of course not. Lester, bring him to Sunday dinner when he's not off shore. That's an order.

"OK Ma."

And this he did. For the next few months, Sophia doted on him. "You're a handsome young man, Patrick" she'd remind him regularly. Patrick would look down at his feet. Sophia would put a finger to his chin, raising it slightly to make eye contact.

"But you need a nice hair cut from a real barber, and you need to buy some new clothes."

5: A GIRAFFE'S ASS

Three Days Later

The Woodland Golf Club

Newton, Massachusetts

Sonny Bolla stood nervously on the first tee of the Woodland Golf Club. He had reached out to his personal lawyer and lifelong friend Moe Venti for counsel, and Moe suggested they talk out on the links. Sonny wasn't much for golf, but didn't bicker. He needed Moe's help in a bad way. Along with the gallery, Sonny watched Moe address his Titleist.

His tall, broad-shouldered presence was an amalgam of arrogance, entitlement, and good looks. A perfect mane of black wavy hair above piercing eyes that warned one and all of his intolerance for anybody's bullshit.

Dressed in matching black polo shirt and slacks, a gold crucifix shining around his neck—Moe was stylin' like Paladin in golf shoes. Sonny's tension rose considerably when his tee shot flew off the club, long and fair down the middle of the first fairway.

Squatting over to tee up his ball, Sonny felt the eyes of the gallery on him. A couple of practice strokes brought no certainty. He stood a micrometer below 5'5", and there fermented much of the issue. A pencil thin mustache etched upon his upper lip was surrounded by ruddy cheeks, and a chin that was slightly pock marked. A close inspection of his scalp revealed the genesis of a slicked down rake job.

Sonny lined up to face the little white ball, and the moment of truth. On his downswing, he prematurely lifted his head, grazing the top third of the ball, which trickled off the ten foot elevation of the first tee like a wounded pigeon, dying some thirty feet away below the laurel incline.

"Your sister's ass!" he bellowed loudly for all to hear.

The gallery was dead silent, not a snicker. Sonny's ashen pallor glowed raspberry red. Grabbing his clubs, he stomped off the tee to find his ball at the bottom of the ridge. Toe tapping it out to a preferred lie, all he wanted was to get the little white ball down the road a piece to avoid further embarrassment. His jaw line and face were taut with tension.

Sonny took a deep breath as the perspiration squirted from his armpits. Another man might have eased up on his swing, just to make contact. But that's not how he rolled. A furious stroke and the ball left the ground with a huge hunk of sod close behind- miraculously traveling a respectable distance. Sonny grabbed his clubs, marched past the enormous divot without concern, and met Moe for the stroll down the first fairway.

"Nice shot, Sonny!"

"Jesus, Mary, and fucken Joseph," whined Sonny, who lit up a smoke in search of his composure. He swooshed the ashes off the gold Ban-Lon shirt that covered his burgeoning potbelly.

They played their way quietly through a few holes until Sonny felt like talking. There's nothing like a beautiful day and a round of golf to rekindle the connection between two old friends.

They were nine years old when they'd met on a baseball field in East Boston. This was back in the day when the neighborhood boys just showed up at the park to play ball. No uniforms. No schedules. No umpires. No teams, and no goddamn parents around to fuck things up.

If there weren't enough kids to field two teams, they'd play rotation ball with players moving from position to position after each batter. No winners, no losers; just the joyful crack of the bat, the sun shining down, and the color of the sky-blue sky.

By eighth grade their paths diverted. Moe jumped on to the Triple Eagle fast track: Boston College High, Boston College undergrad, and Boston College Law School. Sonny maintained the public school route, kept up with Moe on the weekends, and graduated from East Boston High. His formal education concluded after a semester and a half at Boston State. It just wasn't for him.

Sonny and Moe always did a good job of maintaining their connection. By Friday night Moe would tire of keeping up the Triple Eagle façade. He'd loosen his tie and find himself back in the old neighborhood spa, where Sonny would be doing his "Big Bopper" imitation and the corner boys would give Moe the business about slumming back in the old barrio.

Moe didn't mind any of that. He rather liked it and loved being amongst his own. But everyone in the neighborhood could see that Moe Venti was a young man on the rise.

Sonny went to work full time for his father, Sal Bolla, who was the proprietor of The Cosmo Demonic Towing Company of Chelsea, Massachusetts. Sal was a hard edged, humorless, don't spare the rod kind of dad. Sonny manned one of his seven tow trucks.

Sal's discontent ended with a heart attack back in '68, and Sonny took over the family business. But now everything was in jeopardy. As they strolled down the fifth fairway, Sonny looked Moe in the eye and began to open up.

"Moe, we've known each other for as long as I can remember. You're probably the only person in the world I trust."

"What's the matter, Sonny?"

"It's Marie. She's throwing me out. On top of that she's taking me for every penny I got."

"Christ, what happened?"

"You remember a few months back I told you I met a broad at The Hilltop Steak House?

"Yeah. You said you met her in the Carson City Room, correct?"

"Correct. We had a couple of those huge Manhattans. Got a room. Had our fun. Then she went her way, and I went mine."

"Yeah, the old hit and run."

"Well yeah, I hit and ran, but then I ran back again. We started to get together every Wednesday night. Things started to heat up. Moe, I couldn't put this broad down. It was all too good. You know what I'm sayin'?"

"Yeah, I know how it can get that way. So, what the fuck happened?"

"Well last Wednesday night, we meet. Do our thing. Then as we're leavin' the motel room, Marie's outside the door with a photographer to record it all for posterity."

"Oh Christ!" spoke Moe as he shook his head, gazing up at the heavens. "Sonny, for openers, you've got to be thinking more clearly. If you're gonna be screwing around on your wife, you can't be sinning in a rhythmically consistent manner like that. Same time? Same place? Every week? No! You gotta change the night. You gotta change the venue. You gotta know when to take the week off. You gotta be unpredictable. Capiche?"

"You're right Moe. You're right. I was thinkin' with my dick."

"That's it! Your nightstick got hard, and your brain got soft. Now you're in a fucken pickle."

"Hey Moe, if it wasn't for our daughter, I'd have her run over with a fucken milk truck. And even now as we speak, she's poisoning my little princess against me."

"Where are you staying?"

"Well, I'm not out of the house yet. Just out of the big bed. I've been sleeping on a couch in the cellar. I got my own door to come and go by."

"Home sweet home! But you never did want to marry Marie anyway."

"Christ Moe, you were with me the night I decided to dump her. I drove over to her father's house with my mind made up. As soon as she saw me pull up, she came running out of the house all hysterical, screaming, "Sonny I'm pregnant!" She wouldn't stop crying till I told her I'd marry her."

"Yeah, one night you tell me it's over, then a month later I'm standing up as your best man."

The truth of that remark struck a quick blow to Sonny's psyche. His stomach flip flopped, and his knees got rubbery. Moe saw the blood leave his face, so he reached into his golf bag and pulled out a shiny flask. They both took a hearty belt. Then they marched down the fairway until they came upon their balls lying side by side about thirty yards from the pin.

Sonny employed his nine iron, but got under the ball too much. Soaring high into the air, it plopped down well before the green.

"Sonny, that's what's known as a giraffe's ass—high and shitty!"

He grumbled as Moe launched his approach shot perfectly. The ball landed behind the pin with a healthy backspin that brought it rolling toward the cup.

"Come back Little Sheba!" beamed Moe.

"How am I gonna get out of this mess?" pleaded Sonny.

"I'm thinking."

They finished the front nine in relative quiet, parked their bags off in front of the club, and headed in for cocktails. Alone at their table, quaffing away, Moe broke the silence.

"How are things going with your business?"

"The business? It's going great guns."

"How much cash you got coming through there that you can hide?"

"Not much. The fucken jackals that work for me won't take anything but cash. Then most of what's left over goes into an envelope for the worm that oversees the towing contracts at the Chelsea Town Hall."

"So your take is mostly on the books. That's a problem. How do you feel about the work?"

"The work? Are you shittin' me, Moe? Towing cars? I'm a fucken viper. Despised by all humanity. Imagine every person you do business with hating your guts."

"Sonny, I'm a lawyer. I know a little something about that."

"Well, I have to put a layer of protection around my aura just to endure all the hate."

"Protection around your aura? Where the fuck have you been spending time? California?"

"Nah, I read about it in a magazine at the dentist's office."

"Yeah?"

"Yeah. We all have these force fields around us that protects us from evil entities."

"Evil entities?"

"Yeah. Evil entities like cancer, syphilis, psychic possession. If one is weakened, the aura gets permeable, and one of these entities can get in there and take you the fuck out!"

"Hey! Captain Kirk!" Moe snapped his fingers three times, pointing to the table between them, "Back here! Back to the Planet Earth!"

"OK, OK."

"So, the work itself has no importance to you?"

"Moe, if I could make the same dough poolside, drinkin' sidecars in Miami, I'd be there."

"Well, you could always sell the towing company and invest in a long-term project. Something where you could hide the profits, some kind of a cash business."

"You got something in mind?"

They stared into each other's eyes until Moe began to grin.

"You son of a bitch. I can see those wheels a turnin'!"

"Sonny, I'm thinking about buying another barroom."

Sure enough, aside from being a lawyer, Moe was the primary investor in a couple of watering holes in town. "A real fine business to hide your money in" he liked to say. As an attorney, he'd take care of all the legalities, setting up a system of management where the establishments would run smoothly without his presence. Then once a week he dropped in on the joints to look over the books and have a drink.

Moe knew that he was being nickel and dimed by some of his bartenders and managers, but he accepted that as part of the situation. They'd take him for a few bucks here and there, but he was still padding his wallet in a big way. He surely never trusted the people working for him, but if the books were up to a certain standard, trust was an insignificant commodity.

And things had been running quite smoothly. Moe was hauling in bags of cash from a source he barely had to watch over. He was a firm believer in the Don Corleone concept that a good lawyer could pile up more money than ten hoods with machine guns. The only impact on his lifestyle was the need to protect himself from potential victimization. Who knew what the lowlifes in his joints were capable of?

Moe was inclined to think the worst. So, he went out and bought a gun, a Luger nine-millimeter. He'd been packing for the last four years and rode her bareback in his right pants pocket. As of yet, he'd found no occasion to use it, but he felt secure knowing that hot piece of metal was breathing in his pocket.

"Whereabouts you lookin' Moe?"

"I've been eyeballing this place over in East Cambridge, a little neighborhood called Inman Square."

"Inman Square? Never heard of it."

"What a surprise. We get you out of East Boston and you're lost. It's not a bad neighborhood. It sits at the crossroad of a six-street intersection, so you can get there from six different directions. I drove all around there last week, and the square looks like a completely different place depending upon which road you approach it by. It's got a big Portuguese population."

"Portugee huh?"

"Yeah, it's far enough away from the trash in Central Square, and far enough away from those pompous high rent assholes in Harvard Square. It's a nice neighborhood. It's got a beautiful fire station in the middle of it."

"So, what kind of a joint are we talking about?"

Moe leaned forward in his chair and got that serious look on his face that serious men get when they're talking about a serious way to make a serious buck.

"This pal of mine in New York runs a booking agency, and he tells me there's a real market for a Blues club in the Boston area."

"Blues? That's mulignan music, isn't it? You want to do business with a room full of shines every night?"

"Relax Sonny. We won't have to. The booker tells me these Blues fans are 99 percent white! The mulignans aren't into the Blues anymore. They think it's Uncle Tom music. They're into this "Super Fly" shit now."

"Yeah?"

"Yeah, and I hear that there's so many of these Blues musicians competing for the work that they play for peanuts. And to beat all, the booker says these Blues fans drink like they're on the bow of a burning boat! I've got my uncle in Venice lining up a chef to come over and cook up "our food," the right way. No greasy burgers and fries like my other joints. This is gonna be class."

Sonny heard the distant ring of a cash register, triggering the vision of a more glamorous lifestyle; Sonny Bolla, Nightclub Owner. Closing his eyes, he imagined sitting at a table in a comfortable chair, sampling a few bottles of vintage red wine, surrounded by a staff of squeezable, ready to please waitresses bringing him samples from the kitchen.

Moe was delighted to see his friend feeling better and so obviously indulging himself in this brand-new vision. Sonny smiled and stared off into the distance until their waitress returned to the table.

"Anything else, gentlemen?"

"Yeah, another round, beautiful" chimed Sonny. He leaned forward in his chair and said, "Moe, I must admit, I'm intrigued by this possibility."

"It could work out fine, Sonny. Just fine."

The waitress returned with their drinks. As she put them down, she felt the cold clammy hand of Sonny Bolla move up the back of her leg, giving her more than a friendly tweak on the rear end. She shifted her tray, wound up, and gave Sonny a crack to the face that was heard throughout the lounge.

"Asshole!" she barked.

Sonny winced and held his jaw. Moe covered his face with restrained laughter as he looked at the bright imprint of the waitress' hand on Sonny's left cheek. The two got over that, and planned their first visit to Inman Square with the intention of hiding income and securing future prosperity.

6: LOU LOPES AND THE OLD SPORTSMAN'S TAP

The next morning Sonny and Moe met in Inman Square, stopping at the S&S Diner. They sipped their coffees and perused the front page of the Boston Globe, which spoke of the trouble entangling the Vice President of the United States.

AGNEW ASSAILS "DAMNED LIES"

BRIBERY REPORTS "FALSE, SCURRILOUS, AND MALICIOUS"

"Hey Moe, is Agnew goin' down?"

"Nah. Spiro's covered," spoke Moe with cocky assurance. "He's tight with Sinatra."

Sonny gave an understanding nod. They paid up, left the Double S, and walked down Cambridge Street toward the firehouse. It looms big in the face of Inman Square, emanating a strong sense of security and competence. Moe stopped at the corner to admire the structure. It was across the street from him but felt so close that he could almost reach out and touch it.

"What a gorgeous edifice. Look at the arcs, the Moorish and Florentine influences, and the tableaus of the old firehouse."

Sonny looked up at the façade, then back at Moe, then back up at the façade.

"Moe, it's a fucken fire station."

"Pearls before swine, Sonny. Pearls before swine."

They hooked a left and headed down Hampshire Street. "The joint's right down here" spoke Moe. It's sandwiched between the Tortoise Café and a Chink restaurant called The Golden Dragon. The old bird that owns the place is named Lou Lopes. I hear he's all crippled up with arthritis and just aching to unload the joint. Just let me do the talking Sonny. I think we can hit this chump up hard and fast."

Sonny obliged. He felt lucky to have a heavy hitter like Moe Venti there to talk turkey for him. Quickly they came upon the humble façade of The Sportsman's Tap—a stout stone building with two large squares of glass block that allowed diminished light inside.

They walked from the sunshine into the darkness. Momentarily blinded, their eyes adjusted to see a twenty-stool bar directly in front of them. A small contingent of patrons were gathered, doing eye openers. Monty Hall was on the television offering a contestant the opportunity to choose what was behind Curtain Number Two. Off to their left a spacious room extended fifty feet to the back of the house. The room appeared dusty and lifeless. On the far wall a giant moose head stared back at them.

"What a dump", whispered Sonny.

Moe raised a quieting finger to his lips and motioned Sonny to follow him to the end of the bar. They bellied up and stared down at old Lou Lopes. Slowly he made his way toward them, bracing himself with his left hand on the old oak bar. His shoes scuffed the floor with each step. Lou gave Sonny the creeps. He looked like Marley's ghost without the chains. Vacant eyes shone dimly from a tired old face, whose neck hung over slumped shoulders.

"What'll ya have?"

"Are you Lou Lopes?"

Lou nodded in the affirmative.

"Lou, I'm Moe Venti, and this is my business associate, Sonny Bolla."

They all made the obligatory handshakes, but Lou looked on at them with suspicious eyes.

"Lou, I understand this place is for sale" pushed Moe.

"I've been thinking about retiring, but business is still good" he said with an inclusive wave toward his breakfast club down the bar.

"How long have you been here, Lou?", asked Sonny.

"I opened up in '48'"

"Do you use the kitchen anymore?"

"Not in ten years."

Just then one of the regulars called down for another drink.

"Lou, is it alright if we take a look around?" asked Moe.

Lou nodded. They watched him hobble back toward the front of the house. Sonny looked down at his feet and felt overcome by a tidal wave of doubt. Suddenly all of this sounded preposterous, as if he might as well become a cliff diver in Acapulco, his battered body served up as food for the sharks.

"Moe, this place is a shit hole. Maybe we should forget this whole thing."

"Don't worry about the appearance. We could fix this place up in a week.

They walked out into the room to the percussion of their shoes sticking to the filthy beer-stained floor. An extensive network of cobwebs hung from the old, corrugated tin ceiling. It had been many years since Lou Lopes used this space. Right now, he struggled to serve a half dozen patrons.

"Sonny, the stage could be right there against the wall, and a dance floor out here."

"Where's the kitchen?"

"Over there."

They walked over to it and opened the swinging doors. Moe fumbled for the light switch, found it and flicked it on, illuminating a burnt-out shell of a kitchen. A pair of six burner stoves sat idly next to a decrepit fryolator. A couple of mice scurried across the kitchen floor in a desperate search for cover.

"Moe, this place is a fucken dump. Let's get the hell out of here!"

"Sonny, listen to me. This is the best situation possible. Look, we really put the lean on this guy Lopes, and croak him for a steal of a price. We buy this place for a song. Then we bring in some carpenters and give it a facelift. Trust me Sonny. I've been through this a few times. Before you know it, you'll have Marie on a reasonable stipend, and we'll be piling up cash in our island accounts."

"Alright Moe" shrugged Sonny. "I'm sorry. You know I trust you."

"That's better Sonny. Now look. I'll lay a price on him, and when he balks, we walk right out the door."

They took one last look around the slime pit of a kitchen, turned out the lights, and headed back to the bar. Lou Lopes limped toward them.

"Lou, we'll give you $28,000 cash for the place."

Lou Lopes put his weather-beaten hands on the bar, and tried to summon up the strength to make a stand. Sonny watched on nervously. Moe took one look at Lou's tired old face and knew he had him.

"I can do a hell of a lot better than that!"

"OK Lou," spoke Moe as he stood up to leave with Sonny following suit. "This is my business card. Call me if you want. And Lou, the offer drops to $26,500 in 48 hours."

Moe put his card in his hand, smiled, and got up to leave. Scanning the card briefly, Lou Lopes watched the two strangers head for the door. The bright morning sun blinded them, and Moe Venti squinted as he spoke.

"Sonny, I'd bet half my empire that we hear back from Lou Lopes within 24 hours."

7: LOU LOPES GETS PIPED

Sonny Bolla hovered in the catbird seat at the Cosmo Demonic Towing Co. of Chelsea, Massachusetts. The only smooth things here were the wheels under his office chair. They rolled facile from telephone to file cabinet to the key rack on the far wall to the floor safe in the corner. Sonny only got out of his chair if he needed to hit the can.

A less than subtle layer of grease covered every square inch of this workplace. The construction that served as hearth and home for Sonny and his crew was better described as a shack. Not much had changed here over the years, except back in '65, when Sal Bolla had fortified the catbird seat after an assault from a local bad guy whose car had been towed. He installed a bank teller style iron grate. That would keep them out. Slide your payment under that railing, thank you. You'd have to be Atom Man to get in there and make a direct hit.

Sonny took a hard drag off his Camel, then heartlessly crushed it out in an ashtray overflowing with a couple dozen other victims. He ground it out like he was eliminating an enemy and exhaled a thick cloud of smoke as he gazed out at what was his, then at the picture of him and his Pops. Sal Bolla was smiling, not a common occurrence. Sonny felt a knot in his stomach tighten when the telephone rang.

"Cosmo Tow."

"Sonny, it's me."

"Moe, what's up?"

"Are you ready for a career change?"

"You heard from Lopes?"

"Just like I told you. We had him right by the balls."

"Holy shit!"

The immediacy and immensity of this call was truly frightening. His heart pounded like it might jump out of his chest. Sonny's first impulse was to back out. Yet he feared maintaining the status quo would only put him in the poor house. The ire of his wife was festering by the day. Marie Bolla had a mind to wring him dry as a dishrag.

"Sonny, the quicker we move the better. How soon can you unload the business?"

"Christ Moe, I don't know."

"Look Sonny, I'll front this whole deal—renovation and all, till you get Cosmo sold. But I want you around from day one."

Sonny took a deep breath then exhaled.

"Alright Moe, count me in."

"We're signing the papers at seven tonight down at The Sportsman's Tap."

"I'll be there, Moe."

Sonny hung up the phone and felt his internal organs grinding against one another.

****

That night they met up at 7 p.m., down in front of the Sportsman's Tap in Inman Square. There were Sonny, Moe, and Moe's carpenter, Benny Felice. Together they entered the darkness of the old dive, walking past the regulars to the far end of the bar.

Lou Lopes limped down and stared at the trio with icy eyes. It was as if he knew all along that he was going to get piped, and now he was staring at the strangers destined to do the piping.

"Here's the contract and your bank check, Lou", spoke Moe. "Look it over and sign right here. But first Lou, I think you should get us some drinks, and Lou, pour one for yourself too."

Lou Lopes stared back, picked up the pen, and signed his life away.

"Pour your own fucken drinks" he told them.

Moe peered down the bar at the regulars, as if they were a filthy bathroom that needed cleaning. "We'll be moving these low lives out of here. They need to find a new home."

Sonny nodded in agreement as he watched Lou Lopes empty out the register. Then he threw the keys down, grabbed his coat and hat. Limping out from behind the bar and into the empty room, he faced the moose head and seemed to be whispering something to it. Sonny took note. Lou donned his coat and hat then slipped out the front door without his regulars noticing. It was the not so ceremonial end of an era. Moe got off his barstool and addressed the remaining clientele.

"'Scuse me folks, but we've just purchased this fine establishment, and as of right now, we are closed for alterations. So, bottoms up. It's time to go!"

Their faces took on the betrayed shock of the newly disenfranchised. They grumbled and groused, but within a few minutes, Moe had them out on the sidewalk with the dead bolt locked.

"Christ, that wasn't so bad. Benny, remember the last spot we cleaned house on? We had to bring in the big boys from the old neighborhood to disinfect the joint. Those sons of bitches didn't go down easy. They banged that place up real good too. Some of those stew bums had been hanging for so long that they had their mail forwarded there! They got to thinking they owned a piece of it. We were forced to clean house."

Benny smiled and nodded in remembrance. Sonny wandered behind the bar to pour three cocktails. A little taste awoke his confidence, and he began thinking that this deal just might work out after all.

"Hey Sonny, you better start thinking about what we're gonna name this joint."

Sonny smiled and nodded in agreement. "Yeah, we'll have to think of something appropriate." He took another belt of his drink, and with a gleam in his eye, contemplated a name that would do justice to this vision.

8: WHITE LINE FEVER

Patrick Phelan laid low in his apartment for a week, doing appropriate penance. His wounds were healing up while the notion to leave New Orleans grew fertile in his mind. He'd called his employers down in Morgan City to let them know. Then he wrote a thank you letter to his boss, Captain Gino, on whose rig he had toiled for the last six months. Out on the gulf it's as easy to lose a finger as it is your arm, or your life. Captain Gino always kept a watchful eye on the rookie, and he appreciated it.

On this, his last night in town, Lester offered to spring for dinner. That sounded like a good idea, so they headed right over to the La Caridad on Magazine Street. As always, El Abuelo came over to the table with menus, bread, and water. They ordered up a tortilla española to split, the paella for two, and a pitcher of sangria. As was his ritual, Patrick dropped a quarter into the jukebox and played Count Basie's "St Louis Blues," and Randy Newman's "Louisiana 1927."

The two pals had the best meal and talked over all that they'd shared for the last eight months: Mardi Gras morning in costume, marching with the Jefferson City Buzzards through the Irish Channel, and then down St. Charles Avenue to open up the parade. Preceding them was a flatbed truck with kegs of beer and a live band. Patrick carried a walking cane full of pipe cleaner flowers, to be traded for kisses from pretty girls along the way. Pagan tradition once again raised its delirious head to have a moment in the sun, providing an alternate reality for the Catholic boy from Cambridge.

Springtime brought on The Jazz and Heritage Festival for multiple weekends. They'd meet up early at Lester's house on Willow to prep up coolers full of food and drink, transported on a kid's red wagon for easy mobility. Music played simultaneously on a dozen stages throughout the racetrack from late morning till dusk. The unknown talent was often as amazing as the known. They were kids in a candy store.

"Yeah, those kinds of moments happen here at a regular clip," assessed Lester. "Like being in the Warehouse at 2 a.m., thinking it's time to head home, when the front door opens up, and Professor Longhair and his band make their unannounced entrance and take over the stage."

"Yeah, and then you know you'll be watching the sun rise."

"And what worth did sleep have at that moment?"

"Had none!"

"This is New Orleans. It's not America. It's a place apart," Lester appraised.

"You're right. It makes me sad to leave. I love this place so much, but I can't live here."

"Don't feel bad Patrick. Like I said, you aren't 'of it.'"

"I know I'm not. But I wish I was."

"Sure, you don't want to stay through the weekend? The Meters are playing Audubon Park on Sunday, and I think you need to funkify your life."

"Maybe I do, but I got white line fever. I'm out of here."

They paid their tab, thanked the family for another great meal and headed for the Magazine Street sidewalk.

"A cup of coffee before you hit the road, bub?"

"Yeah, sounds good."

Lester drove them down to the French Quarter for one last cup of chicory at the Café Du Monde. The patio was packed, so they grabbed a small table inside. The lively clatter of the operation joyfully abounded. A posturing young waiter appeared to take their order.

"Two coffees with milk" spoke up Lester.

"No beignets tonight my friends?" he asked with a coy smile.

"There are no beignets after paella." declared Patrick.

"Paella?" he purred. "From La Caridad?"

"Yes, from there."

"Oh! The best!"

This perked their waiter up into delivering a curtsy, a wiggle, and a sashay as he headed off to fetch their coffees. They had front row seats to watch the Du Monde crew do their thing. Moving slowly along the conveyor line, servers packed their trays with coffees and hot, deep fried beignets with powdered sugar.

"Slide it up, honey!" called out their waiter with a wicked grin. "Sliiiiide it up!"

"Great coffee, and no cover charge for the floor show." said Patrick.

"My man" began Lester. "Have you considered the pyramid of diversity that is the spine of the Du Monde wait staff?"

"Well yes professor, I have considered this. I see a three-tier lineup. We have the older homosexual men, the young effusive homosexual men, and then you have the Vietnamese refugee women."

"Correct! And our waiter of course is one of the young effusives. What a world of difference between the old timers and the young bucks."

"Yeah, the young bucks are out there proud, struttin' their stuff. The old timers are ..." Patrick searched for the word.

"Tortured," offered Lester.

"Yeah."

"The hard lines carved into their faces. Being a Queen Bee in the '40s and '50s? Can you imagine? Like being black in the Jim Crow South, but maybe worse. Ostracized by family and friends. Either they live a lie, run away to San Francisco, or come down to old New Orleans, where you can be what you are. Those old timers walked a hard mile for all these young rumps," assessed Lester.

The coffees arrived, and they partook.

"Any plans when you get home?"

"Oh, find a job. Live with the folks for a while."

"Are you gonna go back to school?"

"No. School doesn't do it for me. I like working."

They finished their coffees and headed out. Patrick gazed one last time across Jackson Square, and up at the façade of St. Louis Cathedral. They drove past the Jax Brewery and headed uptown to Napoleon Avenue. Climbing the stairs and unlocking the door, they entered the cave that had been Patrick's home for the last seven months. He had all his belongings bagged up by the door.

"You travel light Phelan. I admire that."

"Hey, you never know when you're gonna have to throw all your shit in a car and get the fuck out of town."

In a couple of trips, they had everything in the back seat of the Dart. The Louisiana sun was sinking low. Patrick and Lester stood on the sidewalk. It was time to go.

"Well, I guess this is it."

"Yeah, this is it. Thanks for everything, Lester."

"Patrick, it was my pleasure. Stay in touch. Let me know how things are going."

"I will."

Then, as if on key, Patrick handed over an envelope. "Can you give this to your mom and dad for me?"

"Of course."

Lester had a bon voyage present. It contained a cassette of taped music, a small bag of herb, and a couple of little white pills in case he wanted to drive straight through. They gave each other a bear hug squeeze goodbye.

The slant six engine of the old Dart kicked right over. Patrick said a silent prayer that she would take him home safely. Then he waved goodbye to Lester. Sitting at the corner of Napoleon and St. Charles, he watched the streetcar chug by one last glorious time.

A half a mile down the Avenue, he took a left up the ramp. He'd hook on to Highway 55 North bound for the road through Jackson followed by Memphis. Then on to Highway 81 through Nashville and on into Virginia. He'd drive as far as he could, then book a room.

Slapping Lester's cassette of traveling music into his tape deck, he heard the opening chords of Kristofferson's "Just the Other Side of Nowhere." A magical shiver of aloneness shot up Patrick Phelan's spine as he turned the page of this adventure. One last look over his shoulder at the New Orleans city lights, and he pushed on into the night ahead.

9: WE BOTH FALL DOWN

Patrick Phelan had driven as far as he could. Fully frazzled, he pulled over outside of Roanoke, Virginia at the sight of a roadside motel. Finding a store next door, he purchased a six pack of Stroh's and a ham sandwich. Then he booked a room for the night. Just outside the motel lobby he saw a payphone. He dropped a dime in and requested a collect call home. The operator negotiated the reversal of charges, and the line was open.

"Hi Ma."

"Patrick, where are you?"

"I'm in Virginia."

"Well hip hip hurray" she turned on him quickly. "It was no time for you to be gallivanting all across the country. You quit school. You leave me here alone with your father!"

"Having a bad day, Ma?"

"Well, if you're asking, I've been having plenty of them. I came home from shopping today and found your father on the floor between the sofa and the coffee table. He'd fallen and couldn't get up. When I got home, he'd been lying there for an hour. He refuses to use the walker. I haven't had a decent sleep in months. All hours he's got me up; rolling him over, walking him to the bathroom."

A silent moment passed, as Patrick Phelan felt all the wind come out of his sails.

"Ma, like I said, I'm in Virginia, but I'm on my way home."

"Do you have enough money son?"

"Yeah, I'm all set."

"When should we expect you?"

Patrick knew what awaited him and decided to buy a little more time.

"Ma, I've got a few stops to make. I'll be back in a week or so."

"Drive safely, son. I love you."

"I love you too, Ma. I'll see you soon."

"OK son. We'll see you in a week."

"Bye."

"Bye, bye."

He hung up the phone, grabbed his belongings and trudged off to his room. The beer was cold, but the sandwich was dry and tasteless, leaving him to dream of a muffuletta from Acy's Pool Hall.

Just like that, New Orleans felt so far away.

He smoked up some of Lester's herb and drew himself a hot bath. Stripping bare, he climbed into the tub with another cold beer. The medicine, in concert with the hot bath, granted him a reprieve. Sadness, for the moment, was an arm's length away. Then the bath cooled off, the beer was finished, and the moment passed.

Patrick climbed out of the tub, toweled himself dry, and stared into the mirror. His mother's eyes and his father's jaw line looked back at him. Gently he touched the healing wounds on his face. He hoped they'd be gone by the time he saw his mother.

"He fell down. I fell down. We both fall down." he spoke.

Exhaustion and despair double teamed him as he climbed into bed. The return trip home brought him to a place where he couldn't stop thinking of his father. Jim Phelan had run a thriving dental practice out of the family home on Sparks Street in Cambridge, when his hands began to shake. He was only forty-eight. They trembled slightly at first, but dentistry is not the kind of business where one can hide the shakes.

Rumors of alcoholism spread through town. If your hands shake, you must be a drunk. Soon, most of his patients were going elsewhere.

"Parkinson's disease" was the determination of the doctors, who got to the heart of the matter. A loyal group of patients stuck with him until the end. The end being when Jim realized that he could no longer do the work. Patrick was just a little boy, yet he could still remember the sense of doom that invaded their home.

The consequences became more completely understood on the day that the men came over to dismantle Jim's office and haul away his dental equipment. Patrick stood outside his bedroom door at the top of the stairs, peering down at his father in his office foyer. His work place of twenty-three years had just been stripped bare. The tools of his trade carried out the front door, piece by piece.

Patrick Phelan crouched down on one knee, clenching the banister rail as he paid witness to his father's fate. Jim thought he was alone, and never saw his son watching from the top of the stairs, when he broke down. It was a very personal, lost moment that he never would have shared with anyone. The tears streamed down his face as he sobbed, and his hands shook violently.

Patrick witnessed the scene and was seized by Jim's hopelessness, inheriting it as if it was his own. They became Siamese twins of the spirit from that moment on, seemingly locked into the incurable.

They sold the house on Sparks Street later that year and moved into a two bedroom apartment down by the Charles River. The walls were thin and white, offering no place to hide. Money got tight, so Mildred picked up work as a switchboard operator down the street at the Mount Auburn Hospital. Jim got loaded up on L-Dopa, slouched into his Lazy Boy, and stared resignedly into the television set.

Patrick Phelan took a deep breath, thinking about these things until sleep tracked him down.

10: ON OLD CAPE COD

He woke up early in his pitch-black room. The clock on the nightstand read 6:37. Fumbling for the light next to his bed, Patrick flicked it on. The sleep of the dead had taken him away for a good twelve hours. A couple of deep breaths revived him as he tiptoed to the window and peeked out through the curtain at the early morning light. He turned on the television to the local news at sunrise.

"Yesterday President Nixon accused Congress of abandoning Cambodia. And later reasserted his innocence as he decried the nation's Watergate obsession."

The cheap motel room held no allure. He got dressed, packed up his things, checked out, and crossed the street for a solid breakfast, grits included. Patrick filled his gas tank, then he and the Dart headed up the northeast corridor.

The hours of the day rolled by, and it became clear that the old slant six engine could once again be counted on. She was humming like a champ. After all those hours alone in transit, the Dart took on the persona of a comforting, dependable friend. Sometimes he'd find himself talking right out loud to that hunk of metal.

In the quiet moments, he thought about New Orleans and this adventure, which was coming to a close. He felt richer for it. Louisiana was a magical place that filled him to the brim. It had been a challenging journey that he had taken on by himself and made happen. The curriculum hadn't been planned by a big university. There was no faculty adviser to answer to. Patrick made it up as he went along. He went where he wanted to go, read what he wanted to read, and thought what he wanted to think. It simply felt right.

He already missed Lester Reardon. Lester and New Orleans would forever be inseparable in his mind. Lester had an electricity about him and always set the tone, whether at a gathering or a one on one. He was the most alive person that Patrick had ever met. Lester took Patrick in, and the city of New Orleans opened up to him like a flower. When you're out running the streets of New Orleans with Lester Reardon, you make a lot of new friends. It was quite a gift for a quiet kid from out of town.

Heading home, he wanted to take on some of Lester's presence and inspiration—to summon it up and have access to it as he headed down the road. Take the best of a true friend and manifest it in yourself. Always have them with you in that way.

The only thing that the trip had not provided Patrick was a fulfilling resolution to his virginity. At age nineteen it wasn't something he was ashamed of, but rather something he wanted to be rid of, like a bad chest cold. So, matters in the Department of Romance had not gotten off to a great start. He longed for a girlfriend, but in truth he was scared to death of them, the love act itself, as well as the possibility of conception.

Certainly, there were reasons for this slow start. Back in '64, Nanna Phelan had moved into the house on Sparks Street to ride out her last days. Jim's Parkinson's had begun to manifest. Mildred was in such a state that she didn't think to set Nanna up in her own room. She just moved her into a second bed in Patrick's room.

Nanna and Patrick Phelan shared that room for several of what the Wonder Bread people call "the formative years." She would usually retire about an hour after him. Entering into the dark room, she'd drop her dentures into a glass of water, strip bare, and slip on her nightgown. Night after night, his sagging toothless grandmother disrobed in the dim of that room. He didn't really want to look but he couldn't help himself.

She was the first woman he would see unclothed. This peculiar arrangement continued until Patrick awoke one morning to find that Nanna Phelan had turned to stone in the night. It was not enough to neutralize his desire for the carnal, but it surely set him back a few years.

Shortly after Nanna's passing, Mildred somehow figured that this was the perfect time to talk to her son about the birds and the bees. Jim was not invited in on the symposium. The lecture went on for twenty minutes or so, and Mildred spoke of an "internal touch." She was gravely serious. After the discourse, Patrick was left with the impression that the love act must really hurt a lot. Pleasure didn't seem to be on the menu.

This didn't quite jive with the stirring in his pants he felt whenever he looked at his Archie comic books and saw that purple streak in Veronica's black hair. So, it was all a bit muddled.

His last amorous encounter had not been a confidence builder. He worried if this concern would ever straighten itself out, so to speak. Was he incurable like his father? Sometimes he felt that way. The day passed with an all-consuming white line fever as he reflected on all that he left behind as well as all that he was returning home to.

As he approached the looming New York City skyline, he took note that it didn't frighten him this time. This small, personal victory felt fortuitous and hard earned. Now he knew he could take on the Big Apple whenever he chose to.

He flew by all the Nutmeg Inns that Connecticut had to offer, and it was early evening as he approached the Providence, Rhode Island city limits. Home was an hour away. A big part of him felt like he should head straight back to Cambridge, but he'd bought another week from his mother.

"Fuck no!" he shouted out loud and jumped on to Route 195, headed to Cape Cod, where his childhood pal Robby McDougal was passing the summer. Robby came from a wonderful home. He had three good looking sisters and a mother and father that always made Patrick feel welcome. Their home was a haven for him, where people seemed to be well and life was good. Sometimes Patrick wished that he could just live there. Oddly enough, he was doing the same thing now, heading to Robby's to avoid going home.

In a short while he was crossing the Sagamore Bridge, driving through Falmouth Center, and turning up the driveway of the McDougal summer home. He saw Robby's old jeep and leaned on the horn. In seconds he came out the swinging porch door in disbelief.

"Round trip?" he shouted out.

"Yup."

"Holy shit! I can't believe that old eggbeater made it down and back."

"Believe it, brother!"

Patrick had some film in his camera, and the two old friends lined up for a photo in front of the Dart. A little cookout was in progress in the backyard. Robbie cracked open a beer for Patrick and introduced him to his guests.

"This guy just drove that shit box down to Louisiana and back!"

It felt like a proud accomplishment to Patrick. He also felt lucky. Lucky to be hiding out for a week on old Cape Cod.

11: WHO SAID ,"YOU CAN NEVER GO BACK HOME AGAIN?"

Patrick Phelan spent the week kicking back with his old pal. They caught up with each other sharing their adventures of the last year. Clearly their time apart involved with independent explorations further cemented their bond rather than putting distance between them. They were right in tune; Patrick savored the camaraderie.

The days were spent relaxing at the beach, sometimes four wheeling around the dunes in Robby's old jeep. At night they made their way over to The Casino by the Sea, where The Beaver Brown Band had set up shop for the week. They sounded good and were packing the place.

One by one those summer days of sunshine and ocean breezes passed. Labor Day lurked around the corner, and the college kids were busy squeezing all the juice they could get out of their summer vacations. Uncertain summer romances knew that the clock was ticking. Soon long distances and the autumn winds would be changing things. Phone numbers and addresses were exchanged. Future rendezvous were left simmering on the back burner.

September was coming on fast, and for the first time, Patrick Phelan had no idea what he'd be doing. Everyone expressed envy of his carefree situation. But as he packed up the Dart and bid farewell to Robby, a clueless uncertainty took hold of him. He wished he could just hide out for a few more days on Old Cape Cod.

In spite of that, he got back on the road to Cambridge. His great escape was winding to a conclusion. It seemed to take forever to get through the town of Plymouth, but once he did the South Shore, Sister

Corita's gas tanks, and the Boston city skyline were right there for his viewing pleasure. Jumping on to the Mass Pike, he stole a peak into old Fenway Park, then pulled off at the Cambridge/Allston exit. Crossing the Charles River by the big Coca Cola sign, he hooked a left on to Memorial Drive, and drove down to his parents' apartment. He parked his car under an oak tree in the same spot he had left last winter.

Patrick entered the building, climbed the stairs, and unlocked the apartment door. There he found his father slumped into his easy chair—half asleep, drool running down his chin. Mildred heard the door open and came out of the kitchen to welcome him. She reached up to embrace her only child, but quickly pulled back, scowling.

"I'm still very upset with you" she spoke.

"I'm sorry Ma, but I had to do what I had to do."

"Promise me that you won't disappear like that again."

"OK Ma, I promise."

Mildred's unconscious response was the obligatory embrace; out of the corner of the room, her counterpart, Jim Phelan, struggled in vain to rise out of his chair. Walking over, Patrick took his father's hands in his own, pulled him to his feet and hugged him.

"It's so good to have you home, son," whispered Jim. His eyes welled up with tears, and his hands shook uncontrollably. Jim wiped his chin with his handkerchief, and kissed Patrick on the lips. They were very Italian that way.

It didn't take long to realize that Mildred hadn't exaggerated his father's decline. Most notable was the change in Jim's face, which hung over his hunched body like a faded drape. It had become mask like, expressionless. Patrick Phelan had been home for all of an hour when he felt like he'd never left. It was mid-afternoon now, and Jim was slumped back into his chair, staring blankly at the soap opera on television.

"He turns it on in the morning, and keeps it playing all day, and into the night." Mildred confided. "I can't deny him this. It's his only pleasure, but it drives me up the wall", she moaned shaking a clenched fist.

Patrick Phelan stared at his father's face, and drifted back in time to a Sunday afternoon they'd spent alone together in this very room. It was shortly after they'd abandoned the big house on Sparks Street. Mildred was pulling a shift at the Mount Auburn, and they watched a movie, *The Eddie Cantor Story*. He was lying on the floor at his Father's feet, watching Cantor capture a hungry audience with a song.

"Is that what Eddie Cantor really looked like Dad?"

"Yes", he heard in a muted sob.

Looking up, he saw tears streaming from his father's eyes. He was slumped into his chair in a fashion that Patrick could never grow accustomed to. It seemed that the force of gravity had become too much for Jim, or as if the burden, which was his to bear, had been heartlessly delegated.

The hopeless nature of these tears was unnerving. Searching for something to say, he couldn't find the words. While Jim sobbed, Patrick retreated to his bedroom to get his bearings. But Eddie Cantor's voice seeped through the thin white walls of their new home. He could have found a place to hide in the old house on Sparks Street, but the new apartment offered no such reprieve.

Jim's tears were nothing new to Patrick. The first time he saw them was on that cold, grey September day in 1960, when father and son huddled around the radio in the kitchen on Sparks Street, listening as

Ted Williams hit a homerun in his last at bat. He saw him cry again the morning after they had stayed up late to see the Middle Weight Title bout—Emile Griffith versus Benny "The Kid" Paret. When Jim learned that "The Kid" had died in the night from the beating he took, he broke down at the kitchen table.

Jim cried whenever the Celtics won a World Championship, which was almost every year. He could cry over a special memory, or the mere thought of an old friend.

"Yeah, he can turn them on and off like a water faucet," Mildred would say coolly.

But these Eddie Cantor tears weren't relenting, and Patrick retreated to his white room to gather himself. It felt like sink or swim. Instinctively he grabbed his basketball, slipped out the door and dribbled up Sparks Street, crossing Huron and Concord to the hoop court on Upland Road. It became his sanctuary, and he filled in all his free time with this pursuit, shoveling the snow off the courts in winter if necessary. Don't think. Just keep dribbling. Just keep shooting.

"Patrick, would you like to help me with a beef stew?"

"Yeah, sure Ma."

"We need stew meat. Do you mind running to the store?"

"Not at all."

Patrick rose up, relieved to be put into motion. Mildred handed him a five and sent him down to the IGA market in Harvard Square for a couple pounds of stew meat. A light rain had begun to fall, so he grabbed an umbrella.

"And pick me up three packs of King Size Kents."

"You're just poundin' nails in your coffin," Patrick sang that old country song.

"Just pick 'em up, if you know what's good for you."

A strong wind blew off the river as he headed down Mt. Auburn Street. Directly in front of him about fifty yards away, he noticed the tall, sturdy presence of a man walking toward him. There was something familiar about the gait. He too was hiding under a black umbrella, and walking with him was a young boy. A minute later their paths crossed in what was once Henry Longfellow's cow pasture. Patrick stole a peak from underneath his umbrella, recognizing him immediately.

"Rue Morley."

The three of them stopped in their tracks. Rue Morley stared straight on, searching for the name that belonged to the familiar face.

"Patrick Phelan," he spoke.

They shook hands. Patrick gazed at his bearded face and saw it to be pale and puffy around the eyes. Rue introduced his son Arlen, and Patrick shook his hand as well.

"Rue, I haven't seen you since you went to play ball in Carolina. How've ya been?"

"Doin' alright. You?"

"Same."

Patrick Phelan was a fifteen-year-old sophomore when Rue Morley was a senior. He was one of the toughest players in the city that year, leading St. Mary's onto the parquet floor of the Boston Garden. Underneath all those Celtic World Championship banners they stole away the Class B Tech Tourney Title. Rue landed a full scholarship down in Carolina but had a beef with his coach, and his basketball future fell through the cracks.

He was one of those 6' 3" guys with a big man's game. Another three inches, another twenty pounds, and there would've been no stopping him. Patrick sensed a tone of disenchantment about him.

"When did you get back in town?"

"About a month ago. My wife and I decided we needed a change of scenery, so we came back up here to give it a shot."

"I'm sorry things never worked out for you down there."

"Hey Patrick, I don't think about it anymore. It feels like a couple of lifetimes ago."

"You playin' any ball?"

"Nah, you?"

"Nah. What are you doin' for work, Rue?"

"I just picked up a job tendin' bar at this new joint opening up in Inman Square called Sonny's Place."

"How's that goin'?"

"Too soon to know. They're gonna open in about a week. This guy Sonny … I'm not so sure about him, but the music is gonna be top shelf. Chicago Blues, everything out of the windy city. They're serving Italian food till ten. Then the show begins."

Wow! Italian food and the Blues? What a combo platter! Are they hiring?"

"Cooks."

How's the money?"

"Probably not great. But they got a chef coming in off the boat. I'll put a word in for you if you want."

"Thanks… That's an idea. I'll at least be by for a beer."

"OK. Good to see you, Phelan."

"Good to see you too, Rue."

Patrick watched the Morley boys amble off. "Holy shit, Rue Morley's a father," thought Patrick. "Things change, and fast." Seeing Rue again provoked some feelings. Nothing to do with Rue personally, but mostly to do with feeling not good enough.

Patrick had lived for nothing else but to make the high school basketball team. Playing time would not have been a requirement. Merely to be part of the squad would have sufficed. Run out of the tunnel in uniform during Tech Tourney time with his teammates onto the parquet floor of the Boston Garden, where the Houdini of the Hardwoods once made magic happen.

It was not to be. Coach put him on the taxi squad, which meant no uniform. Coach also made him keep the scorebook during games—humiliating. Rue hit a buzzer beater to clinch the Tech Tourney Title game, and the whole school mobbed him at midcourt. Patrick finally got out on the parquet floor, but he was wearing his wing tips.

The next year the coach cut Patrick the day before the first game. "Phelan, you're too slow, and the sophomores are running circles around you." He was crushed. Robby McDougal, who ran cross country, found him clearing out his locker. Robbie walked him all the way home, knowing how much he was hurting. Once more, Patrick felt the depth of his insufficiency. It felt strange to be back home as he made his way down to the IGA. for stew meat and cigarettes.

12: DINNER WITH UNCLE LIAM

By the time Patrick had returned with the stew meat, Mildred had already gotten down to business. As was her style, she lined the kitchen counter with old newspaper, laid down the chopping boards, and pulled two knives from the kitchen drawer. Then they got busy.

"Patrick, you get on the carrots, celery, and onion. I got the potatoes and the garlic."

While in the midst of peeling and dicing, some peace would overtake them. It seemed that whenever they got busy preparing an evening meal, the family's troubles would fall to the wayside for a spell. Mildred was a stickler for detail, but when they cooked together, Patrick genuinely enjoyed her company.

The knife work was complete, and Mildred put her old stew pot on a high flame with a splash of oil. She seasoned and lightly floured the meat. Together they heard the magic sizzle as the stew meat hit the hot oil. After a couple of minutes of browning, she followed with the chopped onions, a spoonful of tomato paste, a pinch of oregano, a bay leaf, and the chopped garlic.

"Stir that well, Son. You don't want the garlic or the paste to burn," Patrick spoke in his best Mildredese.

"How many times have I said that to you?" she smiled.

She added a couple ounces of butter, and another spoonful of flour. Patrick kept his wooden spoon in motion till the flour cooked off, smelling like toasted almonds. Mildred followed with a cup of red wine and a quart of water. She liked to let the meat simmer until tender before adding the rest of the vegetables.

"Your Uncle Liam is joining us for dinner tonight," announced Mildred.

"Great. How've he and Delia been?"

"They've been good."

Around a table full of friends, Mildred often took delight in revealing Uncle Liam's scandalous youth. As a young man he had a nose for the open road. "Sometimes when he'd had a scuffle with Pa, Liam would disappear for a week or two until we'd get a call from the police in Ohio or Pennsylvania after they'd found him sleeping in an alley or a doorway."

At sixteen, lying about his age, Liam joined the Marines. He fought the Japanese in the South Pacific and returned home from the War with a box full of medals and a steel plate in his head that would set off the metal detectors anytime he went through Logan Airport.

He and his wife Delia ran a workingman's bar over in North Cambridge by the town dump. The sign that hung outside the establishment appropriately read "The Kilkenny Pub By The Dump." Seven ounce drafts were thirty cents, two for fifty-five. You could show up with laundry money and get a roll on.

Speaking in a general way, it could be said that Liam didn't drink. For the most part, he managed to run his bar amidst a hard drinking clientele without imbibing. Yet every year, usually in March, when rain and dirty snow become the order of the day, he'd fall off the shelf and go on a roll. It wasn't a festive, social kind of thing. He'd set up shop in the basement of his bar and he'd drink alone for days at a time. If someone tried to talk to him, they'd wish they hadn't. Delia and Mildred knew enough to stay away. They'd let him ride it out, and in a few days, he'd resurface, pulling himself together, apologizing to no one.

"Is Aunt Delia coming over too?"

"No, she's tending bar tonight."

Mildred pulled a piece of meat from the stew, cut it in half, and they both tasted for tenderness. Then she added the celery and carrots, holding back on the potatoes for a bit because they cook quicker. While Patrick hovered transfixed over the pot, gently stirring the swirl of vegetables and meat, she began picking up the mess.

"Ma, tell me the story about the mayor again."

"The mayor? You mean Mayor James Michael Curley?"

"Yeah, that Mayor. Tell me about him again."

Mildred finished wiping down the sink, then lit a cigarette, and retold the story that Patrick loved to hear.

"Well son, like you know, when I was twelve, I had to leave school and get a job in a factory to help out the family."

"That's where you had to pull the threads off the drapes, right?"

"That's right son. It was a drapery factory, and they'd have a bunch of us young girls seated at a table, and we'd pull all the loose threads off the drapes as they came down the line.

"Did you have any fun there, Ma?"

"No sir! We were all teenage girls, real young. We should have been in school or out having fun. We worked sixty hours a week in the same room, and we weren't allowed to talk to each other. But we were poor, and my folks needed the money."

"But Ma, tell me about the mayor."

"Well, when I became eighteen, I decided that I didn't want to live the factory life anymore. I wanted something better for myself, and I thought I might like to become a nurse. Of course, I never graduated from high school, so I couldn't get in anywhere."

"So what happened then?"

"Well one day I got my nerve up, and I went right down to City Hall, and walked into the mayor's office."

"Wow!"

"That's right son. Don't bother trying that today. So anyway, the mayor was in a meeting, but his secretary told me to take a seat. Fifteen minutes later I was sent into his office, and it was just me and him."

"And what did he say?"

"Well, after I explained my situation to him, he smiled that big Curley smile. [He was a very handsome, stylish man.] He put his arm on my shoulder and walked me to the door. Then he told me, "Mildred, give all your information to my secretary and we'll take care of that for you. But promise me one thing, that you'll study hard and become a wonderful nurse."

"And he made it happen?"

"Well, the next fall I was enrolled at the Carney School of Nursing, and in two years I was an R.N."

"And they never found out about the high school diploma?"

"No, they never did, and Patrick don't you ever mention that to anyone outside this house."

"Oh Ma, nobody cares about that now."

"Don't be so sure of that," said Mildred.

In a short time, the simmering stew came to be. The apartment buzzer rang, bringing on the arrival of Uncle Liam, who greeted his three kin. Soon all four of them were seated, jamming butter on the warm crusty bread, and gently blowing on each spoonful of the hot beef stew. It didn't matter that they were amidst the dog days of August.

"It's delicious, Darlin'," announced Liam after a few delirious spoonfuls. Jim nodded in agreement. A little stew dribbled down his chin as he looked across the table at the brooding eyes of Liam Kilkenny.

"Patrick helped me with it."

"Keep cooking with your mother, sailor. It's a good thing for a man to know.

Dinner passed in a most amiable way. Uncle Liam asked all about Patrick's Louisiana adventure; working in the gulf, the characters he met, the nightlife in the Crescent City, the music, the food. Liam posed all the questions that Patrick thought his parents should be asking. He wanted to know all about the adventure, and made Patrick feel happy that he'd had it.

As dinner ended, Mildred cleared the table and retreated to the kitchen. An intuitive wave of warning came over Patrick. He heard the strong running of tap water, then the opening of the cabinet door below the sink. If the tap ran for a while, you knew that she was having a second shooter, which she chased down with a glassful of water. Mildred drank socially, but like Liam she wasn't opposed to the private ritual if the spirit moved her. Then there was a good reason to think that trouble might be festering.

She brewed a pot of coffee and served some up for Liam and herself. Patrick knew that he was about to be put on the witness stand and grilled. He'd been home for about four hours and hadn't heard a word of it yet. Sometimes when Mildred was gearing up to make a stand, she'd bring Liam in for support. Patrick hated to see that pouting whiskey look on his mother's face. She lit up a smoke and began her interrogation.

"Well, son, what are you planning on doing with your future?"

"My future?"

"Yes, son, your future. Are you planning on going back to school?"

"No, I'm not planning on that."

About twenty seconds of silence passed until a disgusted Mildred redirected the flow of conversation through Liam. "You see? This is what I don't understand. He's a bright boy with a world full of opportunities. Opportunities that we never had!"

Liam was quiet. He couldn't possibly enjoy being dragged into these scenes. Yet he would never sell out Mildred. Patrick resented that his mother would bring him in for an intervention.

"Don't you have any plans, Patrick? Any career goals?"

"Yeah Ma, I got some career goals."

"And just what are they?"

"Well Ma, I got three goals. First, I never want to take another test. Second, I never want to fill out another job application. And third, I never want to go through another job interview."

She asked for it. So, he gave it to her. Then he felt the tension rise in the room as Liam looked straight through him. He wasn't going to stand for any disrespect directed at his sister. Patrick wisely decided not to lay it on any thicker.

"Patrick, you can't go through life with this attitude. You'll be left out in the cold!"

Patrick glanced over at his father. Hands shaking at a frantic clip, Jim stared off at the far wall.

"Well, you say that you're not going back to school. Are you planning on getting a job?"

"Of course, I'm gonna get a job, Ma."

"And doing what?"

"I'm not sure, but I ran into an old friend today. Dad, do you remember Rue Morley, the ball player I used to tell you about? Took St. Mary's to the Tech Tourney Title?"

"Morley, the mortician's son from Porter Square?"

"Yeah, that's the one. Well, I ran into him today, and he told me that there's a restaurant opening up in Inman Square, and they're looking for cooks."

"It gets mighty hot in those kitchens, sailor," warned Liam.

"No hotter than it got on that oil rig in the Gulf."

Patrick decided that he had had enough. He asked to be excused and left the three of them to worry about his future.

The evening sky had cleared. Patrick took a stroll down Memorial Drive to catch the last hour of light. He smoked down the last bit of Lester's herb and tried not to be bothered by his mother's harassment. Planting himself down on the Boylston Street Bridge, he looked toward the Boston skyline.

He felt no certainty about becoming a cook. It's true that he liked to putter around the kitchen with Mildred, but cooking as a way of making a living had to be another thing altogether.

September was almost here. Patrick thought about the tension brought on by the ninth month of the year. September has always spoken of beginnings. The years don't begin in January. They begin in September. He could just feel the influx of the Greater Boston student population. Young people with big plans were coming in from all over the world.

Patrick longed to feel certain about something, but he just didn't, and he was incapable of pretending. He stood up to shake off the feeling.

"Tomorrow, I'll go down to Inman Square and at least talk to this guy, Sonny. It can't hurt to talk," he figured. Then he got his feet moving and ambled into Harvard Square to have a few beers at Cronin's.

13: A MICK BASTARD COOKING ITALIAN FOOD?

Patrick Phelan was half awake when he heard the familiar sounds of Mildred on her knees, scrubbing the bathroom across the hall. He'd woken up an hour earlier, took a trip to the can, and came back to find his bed made. Mildred was relentless in her own special way. Someone might say that all that cleaning kept her from going crazy, but that would have been a lie.

If you can't control anything, you can clean. In fact, "Mrs. Clean" is what he sometimes called her. You know—the woman married to the muscular, bald guy with the earring. Then he heard five sharp knocks on his door.

"Patrick, time to get up."

"OK Ma."

He reached over to his radio dial and tuned in WCAS, the local Cambridge station, and out warbled the voice of Desmond Decker off of *The Harder They Come* soundtrack. Having just returned last night from seeing the midnight show down at The Orson Welles Cinema on Mass. Ave., it put some good wind in his sails.

Jimmy Cliff, simply revelatory in the role of singer Ivan Martin, who crosses the line of no return. The movie had created such a buzz around town that The Welles let it move in and take up residency. Reggae music was making its presence felt in a big way.

Patrick Phelan got dressed, poured a cup of coffee, and joined a shirtless Jim Phelan at the breakfast table, where he had just finished his cornflakes with bananas. Several layers of flab hung wistfully over the waistline of his jammie bottoms, as he engaged himself in the morning ritual of consuming his medication that Mildred had laid out for him.

He shoveled the pills a small handful at a time into his mouth and chased them down with a tall glass of orange juice. Having finished, he put down his empty glass and let out a gasp of air. He was most lucid during the morning hours before his medication had sunk its claws into him. It was the best time to converse. Patrick caught him sad eyed as he read the top fold of the sports page, which read

"SOX WILT, HOW DO YOU SPELL COLLAPSE"

"Dad, you've lived here your whole life, and you still make an emotional investment in that team?"

"Call me a fool."

"Thankfully, we've got the Celtics."

Jim Phelan looked up at his son with a shimmer of light in his eye, nodding in agreement. It was true that a trip to Fenway Park was magical and dreamlike. There was no questioning the Big Bad Bruins or the greatness of Orr. Yet for the Phelan men, it was always about the Celtics. A trip to the Boston Garden to see them play was a journey to the Cathedral of Hope.

"I say we win it all this year, Dad."

"I still say we need a big man. You know I love Cowens, but if Red can find a true center, preferably a colored one, and we move Dave out to power forward" he gesticulated with trembling hands.

"Dad, we would have won it last year if Hondo hadn't ripped up his shoulder. We can do it with Cowens in the pivot. We can do it because we got Paul Silas. Silas is the key."

Before Jim got sick, he brought his young son in to see many games. They saw all the great players of the day—Oscar Robertson, Elgin Baylor, Jerry West. There was nothing Jim Phelan would rather do. But somewhere in the winter of 1966, they had to stop going. It had become a kind of claustrophobic crisis for him.

Jim found that a loud, crowded arena could trigger a round of the shakes that just wouldn't quit. Having to take his son home at halftime was heartbreaking. More fixedly he stared into his television set. Jim Phelan began to check out. Patrick never pushed him when it became apparent that he couldn't make the trip. Though deeply, he missed the part of Jim that the Parkinson's had taken away.

Their conversation was interrupted as Mildred began vacuuming up a storm in the living room. Patrick got himself ready to leave and inquire about work in the kitchen at Sonny's Place. He said goodbye to his folks, and Jim offered words of encouragement as he headed out the door.

"Maybe this cooking job will be right for him, Mildred" spoke Jim, his eyebrows twitching with hope.

"He gives up a college education for that?" she shook her head in lament.

******

Patrick drove down Cambridge Street to Inman Square. He parked the Dart on Antrim and walked around the front of the fire station, down Hampshire, past the Shamrock until he could see the humble façade of the old Sportsman's Tap across the street. There was a white Eldorado parked out front with vanity plates that read "SONNY." In front of the big white boat were a couple of vans; one an electrician's, the other a carpenter's.

He crossed Hampshire Street and headed on inside, where there was plenty of commotion. Patrick stood still for a moment as his eyes adjusted to the darkness. There he saw Benny Felice, shouting directives at his crew, sometimes over the scream of a band saw. Planks, tools, wires, and sawdust were scattered all about the room.

The renovation was taking on the quality of a psycho-socio-archaeological excavation. One could feel the joy of post-World War II cruising through the fifties until it began to diminish on its collision course with the sixties. What was left now in 1973 was this old stone bar, encrusted with the decades-long presence of lonely drinkers and their thoughts. It left the Sportsman's Tap with a "we had a good run, but now it's time to go" kind of feeling.

Taking it all in, Patrick Phelan stood patiently, waiting until Benny Felice finished the task at hand, and made eye contact.

"Hi. I'm looking for Sonny."

"He's downstairs in his office," said Benny, pointing toward the back stairwell.

"Thanks. Hey, where do you think the ghosts of an old barroom go when you turn a joint over like this?"

Benny Felice looked Patrick in the eye to measure his sincerity before answering.

"I don't know where the fuck they go. But you want them to go. We keep the back door wide open for them while we work. Trust me, you don't want to trap them in here. I've seen what that brings."

That gave Patrick a chill.

"Place is lookin' good."

"Thanks."

He walked the length of the bar to the back of the house, found the staircase down to the office, and knocked on the half open door. Sonny was on the telephone.

"Look Sam, I can get my veal from Liberto's for $2.75 per pound. Can you better that, or do I do business with him? Yeah? OK then, well why don't you go shit in your hat!"

Sonny slammed down the receiver and growled. He looked up to see Patrick standing in his doorway.

"Who are you?"

"Well, uh, I'm Patrick Phelan. I was referred here by my friend, Rue Morley."

"Morley? My bartender?"

"Yeah. That's him. We're old friends. He told me you're hiring cooks."

"Yeah, that's right we are."

"I'd like to apply."

"Patrick Phelan, huh? A mick bastard cooking Italian food?"

Patrick shrugged and chose not to be offended.

"Here's an application form, Irish," gestured Sonny motioning him off to a desk across the room.

The application for employment was one of those two-sided deals that wanted to know the name and address of every school you ever went to, the name and phone number of every boss you ever had, as well as the reason why you left the job. Patrick felt sick at the mere sight of it, and suffered through a couple of minutes, trying to fill it out.

Then he chose a different tact. He approached Sonny, who was adding up some numbers on a calculator. Beads of perspiration shone on his forehead, a cigarette dangled from his lips, his eyes squinting in avoidance of the smoke. The ashtray in front of him was overflowing.

Important looking legal documents were scattered about his desk. Sonny looked up.

"You finished, Irish?"

"No. I was just hoping we could talk about this?"

"Talk? Talk about what?"

"Well, the job here. What it's about? What you're looking for? You know, that stuff."

Sonny stared back at him blankly. This brand of employee relations was new to him. He understood all the ins and outs of the towing business. Unleash your jackals on the world. Pray they don't strangle anybody after a bitter exchange of words and hope for the best. But this restaurant thing, the hospitality industry, it felt a bit more subtle. Sonny Bolla was not acquainted with subtle, but he wanted to be certain to get things off on the right foot. Of course, that meant be the hammer, not the nail.

"Tell me Irish, have you got any experience?"

"Well no, but I cook a lot with my mother."

"You cook with your mother?" Sonny announced bursting into laughter. "Look Irish, we're opening a serious establishment here. We're looking for experienced people. We've got a chef arriving tomorrow from Venice. Do you think he's gonna be impressed with your credentials?"

"Hey, maybe he started cooking with his mother too. Wasn't there a time when every great chef had no resume? Everybody's gotta start somewhere. I'm a hard worker. If you give me a chance, I'll pick things up fast."

Sonny leaned back into his chair. He'd spoken to a lot of experienced cooks in the last few days, and they were all looking to get paid. Moe's policy was to pay the chef and fuck everybody else. But they still needed a pair of hands, and Sonny figured maybe he could squeeze some work out of the kid.

"Irish, I'll tell you what we're gonna do. I'm gonna give you a shot as a prep cook, and we'll see how it goes. You'll be working under our Chef, Guillermo Vitello."

"Thanks Sonny. I promise you; I'll work my butt off. When do we start?"

"Friday morning at nine. We're having a meeting of all employees. After that, the kitchen crew will work through the day, preparing dinner for a private party for our friends and the media. Then after dinner, the music starts, and we open to the public."

"Great! But oh, Sonny, how about money?"

"Money? Well Irish, let me tell you, you'll be working with one of Italy's finest chefs. So as far as we're concerned you should be paying us for the experience. But graciously I might add, we'll start you off at $2.50 an hour."

"Minimum wage?"

"That's right, Irish."

Patrick hesitated a moment. He'd gotten used to making pretty good money down in the gulf, but he decided to seize the opportunity. Once he'd proved himself, he'd ask for more.

"OK, Sonny, I'm in."

"Welcome aboard, Irish. I'll see you back here Friday morning at nine," said Sonny, extending a hand, which Patrick shook firmly.

"Thanks Sonny. Do I still have to fill out this application?"

"Nah, don't bother. Just fill in your name, address and phone number."

This, Patrick did gleefully. He bid Sonny adieu, scampered up the stairs, and ran into Benny Felice having a smoke by the front of the house. Patrick reached out his hand and Benny shook it.

"Thanks for the directions. I just landed a job. I'm Patrick Phelan."

"I'm Benny Felice. Well, I'd say congratulations Patrick, but you'll be working for Sonny. Let me know how that goes." They both laughed.

"Everybody happy with the renovation so far?"

"Yeah, everything except the moose head. Sonny wants to get rid of it, but his partner Moe's not budging. He loves it."

"What's his issue with the moose head?"

"Sonny thinks it could be a portal."

"A portal? A portal to where?"

"Who the fuck knows?"

Patrick looked back up at the tapestry of cobwebs entangled in its antlers. He stared at it for a long minute, wondering what Sonny saw.

"Nice to meet you, Benny."

"My pleasure" he spoke with a nod.

Patrick headed for the street, feeling genuinely thrilled to be employed again. He walked back to the Dart, got inside and spoke to her. "The pay sucks, but at least I'll be learning something. And I didn't have to fill out the job application!" he cooed triumphantly.

14: THE DAY OF OPENING NIGHT

Rue Morley left his Oak Street apartment to head over to the meeting of all employees. The commute was a one-cigarette walk from home. He crossed Cambridge Street and turned left on Hampshire, passing by a small group of old timers laughing and chatting in Portuguese. Looking down at his new place of employment, Rue discovered that a glowing neon sign had been erected.

SONNY'S PLACE

FINE ITALIAN FOOD

HOME OF THE BLUES

The old Sportsman's Tap was now officially a memory. Rue opened the front door and entered the dark tavern. Inside he found twenty people milling about, drinking coffee, and talking. He noticed Sonny Bolla standing at the far end of the bar. He seemed anxious as he spoke to a tall, dark, impeccably dressed fellow, who happened to be Moe Venti. They seemed to be hashing over some last-minute details regarding this meeting. Rue felt a tap on his shoulder and turned around to see Patrick Phelan.

"He took you on, eh Phelan?"

"Yeah, he did. Thanks for the lead."

"No problem, man. It's nice to know somebody here."

Rue and Patrick sat quietly, taking in the newly reconstructed interior. The joint looked good. The corrugated tin ceiling had been repainted, and new overhead fans installed. The wood floors were sanded and shellacked. All the furniture and chairs had been replaced and upgraded. They glanced around the room at all the new faces, realizing that soon they would be working side by side, probably getting to know each other's business a bit too well.

Across the bar sat three young women who appeared to be sisters. The oldest was a dark, moody, stunning presence—more handsome than beautiful. She projected a suspicious world weariness, an indefinable air of intolerance. It was as if she had heard a lifetime of insufferable crap from men in pursuit. The middle sister was less majestic, yet more open. Patrick Phelan's eyes met the youngest. She smiled at him, and he smiled back. She had a long, narrow face, and a cute gamine look about her. He felt like he knew her from somewhere.

Shortly thereafter, Sonny and Moe took their seats on the stage underneath a smiling moose head that appeared delighted by all the action. It felt like the virgin year of 1948, all over again, when Lou Lopes opened The Sportsman's Tap.

"Good morning, everybody. I'm Sonny Bolla, and this is my business associate, Moe Venti."

Moe gave the newly hired staff a silent, confident nod. A list of the house rules regarding the do's and don'ts of employee behavior were distributed. Sonny read through the dictum, occasionally fielding questions regarding insurance, uniforms and work schedules, and all the other basic nut and bolt concerns of restaurant life.

Patrick glanced over at Rue Morley and saw him surveying Sonny as if he were piecing together a jigsaw puzzle. Sonny kept up his parade of smokes, and whenever he would stumble over a question, Moe would pick up the slack and respond with an aloof arrogance.

"What a smug bastard" thought Rue.

"If there aren't any more questions" spoke Sonny, "I'd like to introduce our chef, who just arrived here from Italy, Guillermo Vitello."

Guillermo, dressed in whites, stood up in proud posture, hands folded behind his back. His presence provoked a spontaneous round of applause from his fellow workers. Patrick looked closely at him, knowing that he would have to make this man happy with his work.

"So that will bring our meeting to a close. The kitchen crew will get to work, and we'll see the rest of you at five o'clock to get ready for tonight's opening party."

The folks from the front of the house got up to leave. The cooks followed Sonny, Moe, and Guillermo into the kitchen, where they were handed uniforms and aprons. Then one by one, beginning with Patrick Phelan, the cooks were introduced to the Chef.

"Guillermo," said Sonny, "this is one of your prep cooks, Patrick."

Patrick Phelan offered his right hand to shake. Guillermo responded with his left, so he adjusted and firmly shook it. Then suddenly in mid-shake, the chef pulled his right hand out of his pocket, resting it on his chest. The hand was missing its index and middle fingers. Patrick felt the chef's eyes burning a hole straight through to the back of his head. He glanced from his eyes to his stubs, then locked into his eyes.

In those few seconds, Guillermo had seen what he needed to see. He knew that Patrick Phelan was alright, and that he could fit into his kitchen plans. Guillermo liked to disarm new acquaintances in this manner. People's defenses would turn to dust, and for a few brief moments he believed that he could look right inside them and see what they were all about. He based his character judgments upon these insights.

"Pahtreek," spoke Guillermo, smiling. Patrick smiled back and felt the tension dissipate. Stepping back, somewhat dazed, he watched on as the rest of the kitchen crew went through the chef's baptismal initiation rite. It left the room thick with tension, but Guillermo found only one bad apple in the whole lot, Sonny Bolla's cousin Freddie DiSavio. Guillermo looked into Freddie's eyes and saw nothing but trouble, an accident waiting to happen. He would have thrown him out of the kitchen right then and there, but unfortunately Freddie DiSavio was family.

Guillermo wasted no more time on evaluations. He proceeded to put his new team into motion. Tasks were assigned to all the new cooks, spreading them into workspaces throughout the kitchen. Patrick Phelan found himself between Guillermo and the only woman in the kitchen, Helen Beach. Helen was cherubic in appearance, and a bit older than the rest of the young crew. She'd spent the previous afternoon with Guillermo learning how he prepared the fresh pasta. Now she ran the sheets through the cutters, which she adjusted to make tonnarelli, fettuccine, and linguine.

Patrick Phelan was set up with a bucket of onions to skin and dice. It didn't take long for his eyes to tear up. This, coupled with his inexperience and desire to keep pace, led to the index finger of his offhand slipping under the angle of his blade. He gasped, and dropped his knife to the board as the blood surfaced, and quickly covered his dangling fingernail.

"Oh Pahtreek!" exclaimed Guillermo, who motioned him to the sink to clean out his wound. Guillermo handed him a clean paper towel to dry it off. The Chef sprayed on some disinfectant, then applied a band-aid and a finger cot. While Guillermo administered first aid,

Patrick gazed once again at his mutilated hand, and realized an apology wasn't necessary.

As Guillermo tended to Patrick, the kitchen seemed to stop for a moment. Freddie DiSavio took that as a cue. He put down his knife and wandered over to his stash by the ice machine. He lit up a smoke, uncovered his tape deck, inserted a Deep Purple cassette, and proceeded to crank it up nine notches.

Guillermo was all over him in two shakes. He ripped the plug out of the wall in mid-"Smoke on the Water." Then he grabbed the butt out of Freddie's mouth and stomped on it.

"No rrradio! Worrrk!" he bellowed.

Freddie DiSavio tucked his tail, turned cherry red, and retreated to his chopping board.

Guillermo then took Patrick Phelan's knife, and showed him how to use it, curling his off hand fingertips inward and away from the blade. He ripped through a couple of onions, then handed the knife over to Patrick, who made the adjustment and searched for his proper rhythm.

The Chef stepped behind him and rested his hands on his shoulders for a moment. They dropped and his neck uncoiled. Then Guillermo came back around to Patrick's side and put his good hand to his own chest, took a deep breath and let it out slowly. He nodded for Patrick to do the same, and they took three deep breaths together, then went back to work without a word. It was a priceless, nonverbal culinary lesson for the rookie. Begin at a place of calm repose.

Patrick glanced over on Guillermo's chopping board to see his boning knife unravel a leg of veal like a good mystery novel. It was shocking to see him handle that knife with just his ring and pinky finger. So willful.

Helen Beach dumped a pile of spinach fettuccine on her table, busily fluffing and separating the strands.

"Is this your first time in a kitchen, Patrick?"

"You can tell?"

"Oh, you just look a little green, that's all. We were all virgins at one time," she winked assuredly.

"Have you been cooking a long time, Helen?"

"Oh, about five years now. I started working in kitchens just after I broke up with my second husband, Wally. What a piece of shit he was," she evaluated in hindsight. "So anyway, Guillermo's got me making pasta and he's breaking me in on the desserts. We got some tortas de chocolate coming out any minute."

Just then the timer bell went off. Helen and Patrick stood side by side as Guillermo opened the oven doors and touched the tops of the tortas for doneness. Then he reached in with his bare hands and began pulling out the cake pans one by one and gently laying them on a rack to cool. Patrick and Helen looked at each other in shock as Guillermo removed the final pan unscathed. He glanced at the two and gave them a wink of the eye.

"You gotta be fucken nuts," spoke Helen in a whispered hush. "That oven is 350 fucken degrees!"

The entire crew paused to take this in.

"Are you for real?" inquired Helen.

Guillermo just strutted back to his leg of veal. Patrick reached over to touch the pans. They were "red mad" as Mildred would have said. Guillermo looked up from his veal leg to find everybody staring at him.

"Bizzy, Bizzy," he shouted.

The day passed quickly. Guillermo had his crew boning chickens, deveining shrimp, pounding veal medallions, and chopping vegetables. Patrick quickly noticed that there was no wasted motion to the chef's style. Every move had purpose. He never stood by idly without a task at hand. The nature of his challenge was that there was always something to be done. A passionate energy emanated from him. As Patrick worked at his side, he felt as if he was standing next to a warm fire.

A variety of stocks and sauces simmered away on low flames, filling the kitchen with aromas that had the crew salivating. Guillermo was an old school chef, but he knew it was essential for his crew to experience his food firsthand. So as midafternoon approached, he pulled together a sampling of the menu, and the team sat down in the dining room for a tasting.

The homemade pasta was served in a variety of ways: baked stuffed cannellini with spinach and ricotta, lasagna Bolognese, tonnarelli carbonara, linguine with white clam sauce, and fettuccine with hot oil and garlic. Patrick Phelan never knew pasta had so many faces. Occasionally, Mildred would serve up spaghetti with a red meat sauce, but that was the extent of her Italian repertoire.

One of the cooks, Frankie Pope, began extolling the virtues of homemade pasta.

"It's a small miracle—flour, eggs, salt and water! It's peasant food but fit for a king."

Next, Guillermo brought out a sample platter of various proteins; chicken, veal, beef, and shrimp all prepared in different ways. The next ten minutes passed to the sounds of forks scratching plates, and the sighs of happy palates. Amidst the quiet contentment, sulking Freddie DiSavio let loose with a vile belch that he made no attempt to restrain.

"Did I get any on you?" he asked Patrick with a laugh, while pretending to brush carrots off his shoulder. "Not a bad meal," he blurted out as he lit up a smoke with no concern for anybody still eating. He flicked the ashes into what remained of his dinner. Upon finishing his smoke, he stomped it out in his plate. The sight of a crushed filter tip rising up from a bowl of half-eaten pasta was the logo by which Patrick Phelan began to identify Freddie DiSavio.

15: THE OPENING NIGHT JITTERS

Tension percolated within the inner sanctum of Sonny's office. The restaurant's namesake was in the grips of the opening night jitters. His mind swung like a pendulum to everything that could possibly go wrong.

"Moe, I'm nervous as hell."

"Relax, Sonny! Everything is under control. We're running smooth like silk. You're gonna relax tonight, have some fun, and just play host."

"I guess I'm nervous because I haven't broken the news to the old lady about selling the business."

"Sonny, remember one thing—she's the ex-old lady."

"You got a point there."

"You've done the best you could trying to please her, and the first time she catches you fucking up, she wants to cut your heart out. From now on you worry about your daughter, and you worry about us. Sonny, there's no room to be worrying about anybody else."

"You're right Moe. I know you're right."

"Tonight's important. We've got people coming in from the press, some of the Cambridge town honchos, and a few of the more influential cops in town. We get enough of these people on board, and things'll run smooth for us."

"I got it Moe."

"Tonight, just hang loose and have fun with it. This is the start of a whole new life for you. The place looks great. You should feel proud of what we've done here."

"I do, Moe! I do," he stammered, trying to pull himself together.

"Sonny, you need a drink. Let's head upstairs. It's almost show time anyway."

The two restaurateurs checked their looks in the mirror, tightened up their ties, and headed upstairs to greet the night. There they found the place to be a beehive of activity.

Rue Morley and a lean, dark, mustachioed Latino named Miguel were setting up the bar for action by stocking beer, stacking glasses, cutting lemons and limes, and generally getting ready for the onslaught of opening night. The trough was set up with the necessary brands of bar liquors. The juices and mixes were all iced down and ready to go as the two owners bellied up to the bar.

"Morley, Mr. Venti will have a Chivas on the rocks with a splash, and I'll have a Manhattan straight up with a cherry."

"Would you like to start a tab?"

Sonny looked back at Rue a little funny, then at Moe. "Fucken guy thinks I bought a barroom to pay for my drinks?"

"Just being engaging, Boss."

Sonny and Moe chinged their glasses "to a long and prosperous future."

The wait staff had begun setting up the dining room for the party. There was a baptismal excitement in the air. Sonny polished off his Manhattan in a hurry, put the glass down firmly and motioned to Rue for a refill.

Just as his drink arrived, the front door opened, and in strode the three sisters accompanied by an older man. He was dressed in a greasy blue mechanic's suit. Rue noticed immediately the serious look he wore as he glanced about the room, sizing things up. Then the sisters pointed down to the end of the bar, where Sonny and Moe sat. He marched down to them and the sisters followed.

"Mr. Bolla, I'm Enrique Madeira," he spoke with a thick Portuguese accent. "I have come home from work tonight to find that my three daughters have taken jobs here without asking my approval. I don't like the idea of them working in a barroom to begin with, but they insist that this is a respectable family restaurant, and that I shouldn't be alarmed."

Miguel, Rue, Stella, Tisha, and Elena Madeira all looked on. Rue stole a couple of glances at Stella, and her dark eyed, full-bodied presence. Her mouth was ample and sculpted, and her beauty went flying off in every direction. Stella Madeira was simply cinematic.

Sonny stared back at her father. This was his first public relations concern, and words would not surface. Moe saw that it was time to intercede.

"Enrique, my name is Moe Venti, co-owner of this business." Moe rose off his stool and extended his hand for a shake. "I want to assure you that we are running a respectable establishment. My partner, Mr. Bolla and I both have daughters, and we understand your concern. Rest assured that your girls will be safe and watched out for here."

Enrique Madeira postured silently. His eyes shot back and forth between them like searchlights. He was cinematic too—in a blue collar, Omar Sharif kind of way. Stella hadn't fallen to earth from outer space.

"Alright gentlemen, I'll accept your assurance. But I'd like you to know that I live and work here in Inman Square. I'd also like you to know that I enjoy a couple of beers after work, and from now on I'll be having them here with you, just to make sure of your words."

And with that, Enrique about faced, found a stool halfway down the bar, and ordered a beer. His three daughters surrounded him, expressing their thanks. He gazed back and forth at them.

"Get me an ashtray" he commanded, which Tisha did. "If you're going to be waitresses, be good waitresses. Now go to work."

They turned and did as they were told. Rue followed them to the end of his bar, watching Stella's backside. Miguel gave him a nudge with his elbow and whispered.

"Fine! Eh?"

"Man, I'd like to sneeze in her suitcase," Rue confessed.

Sonny, not liking the tone of Moe's exchange with Enrique asked, "Moe, why did you kiss that grease monkey's ass? Do we want him drinking here every night? He smells like fucken gasoline."

"He's obviously from the neighborhood, and there's no profit in ruffling the feathers of the neighborhood tonight."

Sonny surrendered and refocused on his Manhattan. Rue served up a cold beer to Enrique.

"You can't be trusting your precious cargo to just anybody."

"I've been listening to bullshitters my whole life. Spare me."

This being his first customer, Rue introduced himself, and extended his hand. Enrique shook it but kept his edge, gazing back at him with his "who the fuck are you?" eyes. Being a Dad himself, Rue understood the concern. It's a mean old world, and no man who has come this far raising his daughters has a well of trust to hand out to strangers, not in dark taverns anyway.

Back in the kitchen, Guillermo had things well under control. An enormous stuffed sow with an apple in its mouth was rotated in the oven one last time. Just then a knock came from the back door that led from the stoop to the back alley and dumpster.

Patrick opened the door. There stood a tall, handsome black man of mountainous proportion, sporting a ten-gallon cowboy hat. He made his presence known.

"Howdy son. We're the Alabama Al McGuirk Band at your service.

"Are you Alabama Al?"

"Why yes, chef, I'm the one and only. Here for a reason, not just a season!"

He smiled a big smile that revealed a shiny gold filling in his front tooth in the shape of a star.

"I'm Patrick," he said, and they shook hands.

"Man, somethin' sure smells good in here!"

Patrick propped open the back door for Alabama and his boys. They began to unload their equipment, hauling it through the kitchen on their way to the bandstand.

Guillermo was not thrilled with the intrusion, but he didn't react. The sight of a black man wearing a cowboy hat derailed him. He wandered over to get a closer look at the black cowboy. Al McGuirk felt his gaze, and they locked eyes for a brief moment. Al couldn't sense friend or foe, so he said nothing and headed to the front of the house.

Guillermo wandered out to the back stoop, disappointed to see that Alabama Al had arrived in a Ford van, and not on horseback. He'd never seen a black cowboy in any of the old Bonanza episodes dubbed in Italiano. Not one riding the Ponderosa or walking the streets of Virginia City for that matter. Then Guillermo thought of Hop Sing, Ben Cartwright's Chinese cook. How the hell did he end up on the

Ponderosa? Guillermo took a moment to think of his family an ocean away, and realized he had a lot in common with Hop Sing.

Alabama Al made his way out to the bar, where he introduced himself to Rue, Miguel, Sonny, and Moe. Rue came around the bar to lead him to the stage.

"Nice place y'all have here, Rue."

"It's our first night, Al, so be easy with her."

"Rue, we always be gentle the first time through till the last set. Cuz that's when we scratch all our itches!"

Back at the bar, Sonny turned to Moe. "So now I gotta start bein' friendly to all these crows?"

"Just be friendly enough to get a night's work out of 'em."

"Or enough of a prick to get it out of them."

"There you go."

Moe and Sonny didn't know anything about the Blues. If elevator music would have brought serious drinkers into their bar, they would have piped it in. Soon they were off their stools, playing host to all the invited guests. Along with town officials and off duty cops, the bar people that ran Moe's other establishments were in attendance as were an assortment of shady associates and business acquaintances. It was a thirsty, "free lunch" kind of crowd. Rue and Miguel were pouring drinks aplenty as they learned how to dance with each other behind the busy bar.

Rue found it strange that he didn't recognize anybody in the room, but he'd been out of town for a while and things change. Just then an old face appeared. It was more jowly and ruddier than he remembered, but sure enough it was Officer Milligan of the Cambridge Police

Department, dressed in street clothes, apparently there to conduct some "personal business."

Officer Milligan had developed a fertile hatred for Rue Morley through his high school years. Anytime Milligan saw Rue's old Rambler cruising about town, he'd follow behind waiting for any kind of infraction to pull him over and search his car. If nothing materialized, he'd confiscate Rue's Haffenreffers, of which he drank many.

Milligan popped Rue for the big one his senior year—a couple of roaches down by his gas pedal. His basketball scholarship was put in jeopardy, and his father had to put some cash in an envelope to make it all go away.

Rue planned revenge but waited a couple of months for the dish to cool. Then one night as Cambridge slept, he tiptoed up Milligan's driveway on Appleton Street and poured a five-pound bag of Domino's sugar down his gas tank.

That morning Milligan's station wagon sputtered and died halfway to work at the Central Square lockup. He sat down and wondered, "Who could have done this?" But he had such a way of creating enemies that he could only narrow the list of suspects down to a couple dozen. Rue enjoyed that caper immensely, and he savored the memory of it as the good officer ordered up a drink without recognizing him.

"Compliments of Sonny, Officer Milligan."

"That's Sargent Milligan," he said as he searched for a name to fit the face.

"So, it's Sargent Milligan, now. Did they send you down to pick up the envelope?"

"Morley? You're back in town? And you haven't changed a fucken bit. Have you? Still a two-bit fucken punk."

"Congrats on the promotion, Millie. I knew you had it in you."

"Hey Morley, I heard your basketball career shit the bed down in Carolina. You probably thought you'd be playing with the fucken Celtics about now!" he laughed.

"Maybe so Millie. But it's better to be a has been than a never fucken was."

They stared at each other with a shared focus based on mutual hatred until Milligan broke the clinch.

"Where's your boss?"

Rue pointed Sonny out to Milligan. He was in the middle of the room surrounded by three stout, cigar smoking Italians and their lady friends. The women hung from the arms of their wide men like candy canes off a Christmas tree—far too lovey-dovey to be anybody's wife.

Rue watched Milligan wade into the crowd and disappear. The thought of the sugar sliding down his gas tank left the trace of a satisfied smile on his face.

Meanwhile the steady flow of medication had settled Sonny's nerves. He felt reborn—no more tow trucks, and now he was surrounded by the smiling faces of people having fun. Yes, he was born again—Sonny Bolla, Restaurateur/Night Club Owner! The guests crowded around him and Moe, offering congratulations and best wishes.

"Moe, we're gonna knock 'em dead here!" announced Sonny with a clenched fist and a greedy grin.

"That's a fact," chimed in Moe as they toasted once more to their future prosperity in the Land of Veal, Barolo, and the Blues.

Back in the kitchen, Guillermo Vitello opened his oven door one last time, and with the touch of his hand to the hip joint, knew the sow to be perfectly cooked. He pulled it out, covered it with foil, and let it repose. Then he sent out the word that dinner would now be served.

Sonny jumped up on a chair, let loose a shrill whistle, and requested the guests to make their way over to a table. They all grabbed their drinks and made their way over to dine.

Guillermo started things off with a cup of minestrone. Antipasto came next, followed by a variety of pastas that were served family style to each table. By the time the pastas were tasted, Guillermo had won his war.

"Almost as good as Mama's" was the refrain that echoed throughout the room.

Bathed in vindication, Sonny postured proudly as the proverbial peacock, beaming arrogantly as if he had prepared the feast himself.

"More red wine!" he shouted at the Madeira sisters, pointing to a nearby table.

Soon Guillermo was carrying the roast pig through the swinging doors and out into the dining room to the oohs and aahs of the crowd. He set himself up on a table and began to carve. In a short time, full stomachs and empty heads prevailed. Once again cigar smoke began rising to the ceiling.

Alabama Al and his boys enjoyed a plate of food at Rue's bar and Al assessed the festivities. "Man, I bin pickin' my guitar in barrelhouses from here to forever, and I ain't seen nothin' like this before."

"Not your typical Blues crowd, Al?"

"Maybe we should be one of them Eye-talian, violin totin', Don Corleone's daughter's weddin' band." Then he leaned forward and whispered, "Can y'all feel the heat in the room?"

"I've felt edgy all night, and didn't know why," confessed Rue.

"The heat appears, where the Blues play. It's a fact. I got radar for that shit. But tonight, these motherfuckers are loaded down!"

Back in the kitchen, the crew began breaking down the workspace and cleaning up. Freddie DiSavio made a beeline for the cheap, room temperature sauté wine. With no apparent superior in sight, he filled a water glass to the brim and knocked it down. Helen Beach pulled a shred of the pork from the sow's carcass and had a taste. "Not bad" she determined.

Back at the front of the house, Sonny took the stage to read a statement prepared by Moe Venti for the benefit of the media in attendance.

"Thank you all for coming to the opening party of Sonny's Place. Remember, nobody's got the Blues like Sonny's. Seven nights a week we will be bringing you the finest live music indigenous to the American Negro, along with the finest in Italian cuisine. Right now, Sonny's Place is proud to present to you from Montgomery, Alabama—The Alabama Al McGuirk Band."

The crowd greeted them warmly.

"American Negro?" questioned Alabama Al. He looked out into the crowd, and turned to his bass player Moody, "Once again, not a Brother or Sister in the whole fucken house. Who the fuck are we? Stepin Fetchit?" Alabama Al decided to take his mood out on the guitar as was his custom.

The band kicked into a solid twelve bar blues, and the room filled up with that sound for the very first time. The moose head above the stage glowed in delight at this new day that had arrived. Any dormant, depraved spirits of the past were chased out into the Inman Square night. It was a brand-new ballgame.

The music marked the end of the evening's formality. Many of the invited guests bid good night and good luck to Sonny and Moe. Outside the front door a solid contingent of Blues fanatics waited patiently for entrance.

Moe Venti had lined up a couple of intimidators from Revere Beach known as the Lugg Brothers to handle the door. As patrons forked over the cover, thoughts of questionable behavior or shenanigans of any kind evaporated as they were confronted with the immensity of the two. Their reputation preceded them; the Lugg Brothers knew how to put out a brush fire.

In a short time, the kitchen was clean. Patrick washed up, changed and punched out. He and Frankie Pope grabbed stools at the bar and ordered up a couple of cold ones.

Alabama Al had taken over the room and was well into his set, when he employed the long extension cord on his guitar, jumped off the stage, and wandered out into the crowd, which was howling, stomping, swaying to his Blues.

In addition to eliminating any distance that existed between performer and audience, his guitar playing was reaching a tumultuous level. Alabama Al made his way right up to Rue at the bar, calling out for "somethin' sweet." Rue quickly reached for the Dr. McGillicuddy's and poured him three fingers worth.

Alabama picked up the shot glass while still pulling the bluest of notes out of his fretted left hand. He gestured a toast to the audience, fired down the drink and slammed the empty shot glass on the bar. Looking across the room at his band, he gave them a nod of his head, which brought the song to a decisive conclusion punctuated by the crash of cymbals and drums.

The silence lasted a brief second before the crowd erupted. Alabama Al made his way back to the stage grinning—ear to ear. His front tooth shimmering like the North Star.

"Coming through, coming through" shouted Elena Madeira as she bobbed and weaved her way through the patrons, balancing a tray full of empties. She leaned on the service bar, discarded the ice and swizzle sticks, then racked her glasses as Rue made his way down to her.

"Whadya need sweetie?"

"Three Schlitz, a Heineken, a rum madras, two stingers on the rocks, and a Johnny Walker Black with soda."

She shuffled her checks around and watched patiently as Rue shook and poured his way through her order. Elena looked over to her right and saw Patrick.

"Hey, you're one of the cooks, aren't you?"

"Yes, I'm Patrick."

"I'm Elena. Nice to meet you," and she extended her hand and gave Patrick a shake. Just then her two sisters arrived at the service bar with their trays stacked to the hilt.

"Patrick, these are my sisters Tisha and Stella." The three acknowledged each other with a nod.

"Great dinner tonight, Patrick," offered up Tisha.

"Yeah, by the way Patrick, when are we getting married anyway?" Elena laughed, rubbing her tummy.

Her playful words made Patrick smile. He watched the sisters scurry about the service station, garnishing drinks and moving adeptly in and out of each other's way. Then looking up, he saw Sonny and Moe heading downstairs with Sargent Milligan in tow.

"Rue, isn't that Milligan the cop with Sonny and Moe?"

"Yeah, but he's Sargent Milligan now."

"Isn't he the cop that tried to take you down?"

"Yes."

"What's he doing here?"

"What do you think he's doing here?" asked Rue as he rubbed two fingers against his thumb, gesturing payola. "Patrick, how many people would you say are in this room right now?"

"Maybe two hundred."

"Well, the legal capacity is 110," spoke Rue pointing to the liquor license taped above the cash register. "So, they have no choice. They have to play ball with Milligan. And suppose some night the Lugg Brothers have to take on more than they bargained for. If you aren't throwing Milligan a few crumbs, the cops take their time coming over here if they get a call. Maybe stop off for coffee and a slice of baklava along the way, and in that time the joint could be destroyed. It's just the way the game is played."

Patrick considered this as Rue went back to pouring the whiskey, wine, and gin. Just then an attractive redhead entered with a young boy that Patrick recognized to be Rue's son Arlen. Patrick gave Rue a shout and pointed toward the door, where the redhead was negotiating with the Lugg Brothers. Rue motioned them down the bar to a couple of stools next to Patrick, where Rue introduced his wife, Leslie.

"It's a little late for him, isn't it?"

"Yeah, but he just wouldn't take no for an answer. He had to come down and see where y'all were working."

"Well tomorrow's Saturday, no big deal. "

"Rue, they called me in to work on Monday."

Leslie Morley had been a schoolteacher down south and found that the only way to break into the local teaching market was to start out substituting.

"What school?"

"Dorchester High, sophomore social studies."

"Dot High? Holy shit."

"Is that bad, Rue?"

"Not if you're wearing a football helmet."

"Rue?"

"Sorry Honey. It's a little rough, but you'll be alright," he hoped.

The band kicked into their second set, and Arlen Morley's face lit up. His view of the stage was impaired, so he swiveled around on his stool to get a better look. Rue reached over the bar, grabbed Arlen and lifted him on to his shoulders for the best view in the house. Arlen stared in amazement at the wild black man, who had launched into song, storming about the stage, playing his guitar with a purposeful fury. It took Alabama Al all of a minute to bring up the heat in the room.

"The circus doesn't make a kid any happier than that," commented Patrick to Leslie.

But a nod and a smile couldn't mask her obvious disenchantment with all this. She wasn't really sharing in any of it. She made Patrick uncomfortable. So, he returned his focus to the music as Alabama brought the song to a powerful conclusion. The crowd exploded and Rue delivered his giggling son back to his seat.

"OK pal, it's time for you to go off to bunko land."

"Aaawww Rue" complained Arlen, who never called his father Dad.

"No noise," he was told.

Arlen and Leslie Morley said their goodbyes, headed down the bar past the Lugg Brothers, and out into the Inman Square night. As they got to the corner of Cambridge Street and Hampshire across from the fire station, they could still hear the muffled sound of the Blues.

"Mommie, when I grow up I wanna be a bartender in a Blues Club like Rue."

This remark stopped Leslie Morley in her tracks. She knelt down on one knee and grabbed her young son's hand.

"Arlen, there are many better things to grow up to be in this world than a bartender. Just because your father aspires to be nothing more than that, it's no reason for you to be shooting so low."

His mother's words silenced the youngster and drained the joy out of him that the trip to Sonny's Place had brought. Satisfied that she was heard, Leslie got off her knee and walked Arlen back home down Oak Street.

16: TUCKIN' IT TO MA BELL

Alabama Al broke into his final number. "Ladies and gentlemen, we want to thank y'all for comin' down to opening night of Sonny's Place. We're the Alabama Al McGuirk Band saying goodnight, and we'll see y'all next time. Remember there's good news tonight. Cambridge, Massachusetts' got a new Home of the Blues."

The crowd howled its approval as Alabama Al brought his set to a close. Opening night was a grand success. Both the food and the music had delivered on its promise. The Luggs turned on the house lights, and the fans found out quickly that it was time to bottom it up and go.

"Drink up! Drink up!" they barked. "You don't have to go home, but you can't stay here."

The Luggs worked the middle of the room turning chairs upside down on tables. The place emptied out quickly and was filled with the intolerable silence that takes hold of a room after a good Blues band has had its say. Sonny and Moe came up to deal with the cash box.

"Good night, everybody," whispered the Madeira sisters.

They left and made their way home through an Inman Square that had become quiet and still.

Rue and Miguel gave the bar a final wipe and called it a night. They headed out the front door with Patrick Phelan and the band following suit. The Luggs locked the door behind them.

"So, Al, when do you boys grace us with your presence again?" inquired Rue.

"Sometime 'round Thanksgiving."

They all shook hands with each other and said their goodbyes. Rue gave them quick directions to the Mass Pike for tomorrow's show in

Syracuse. The band piled into their van, and Alabama Al hollered out with a big starry smile.

"We git it on! We git high! And we git outa town!"

The boys watched the van sail down Hampshire Street, clean out of sight.

"You gringos wanna come over my place for a smoke?" inquired Miguel.

They did, so they jumped into the Dart for a quick ride around the corner to Miguel's place on Antrim Street. They parked and followed him up a flight of stairs where he unlocked the door and led them into a tiny apartment. The place reminded Patrick of his efficiency in New Orleans. The furnishings were sparse; a sleeping bag on the floor, Safeway Supermarket milk crates for seats, and a cardboard box that served as a table. Miguel tossed a bag of herb and rolling papers down in front of Rue and went off to his fridge to grab three beers.

"You just passin' through here, hombre?" inquired Rue as he surveyed the scantiness of the abode.

"I don't know, man. We'll see what happens."

Rue did the honors and they smoked one down. Quickly the rigors of the day and night were put at arm's length. A certain calm filled the room. Rue became inquisitive.

"Who are you? Where do you come from? And where have you been?" he wanted to know.

"I'm a rollin' stone, son of a wheat farmin' Chicano Shaman from four corners, Colorado. And I've been everywhere, man. If I haven't been there, I'm goin' there," he smiled. Miguel felt good to share some company. He'd been floating around the last few months pretty much on his own and didn't mind explaining himself to them.

"What town in Colorado?"

"Alamosa. Beautiful place, man. Craaazy Chicanos," he smiled warmly to think of home.

"How did you end up here?"

"I was headed up to check out the Maine coast, but I pulled off the highway looking for some breakfast, and somehow ended up in the Tortoise Café. I overheard talk about them looking for bartenders next door. So, I stopped in to see Sonny, and he hired me. Then I walked around the neighborhood and stumbled into a for rent sign. If I hadn't found this place, I would have just driven on. It's been a real trip."

"Whadya think of Sonny?" Patrick asked.

"Sonny's a fucken nickel dick!" said Rue.

Miguel laughed, not needing to confirm or deny. They breathed in and out, processing the night for a minute, when Miguel made a proclamation.

"Hey man, tonight's the night!"

He jumped up off his milk crate, went into a closet and pulled out a brown paper bag. Inside was a telephone that he proceeded to plug into a jack. Miguel grabbed a wrench and put it in his back pocket. "Follow me," he spoke, putting a finger to his mouth, asking for quiet. He led them down the stairs and out into the street.

Squaring off with the telephone pole, he took three running steps and leapt, grabbing onto the lowest iron rung that protruded from the pole. He shimmied and pulled his skinny body up the pole till he managed to get a foothold. Then he climbed without hesitation up to the cable box, took the wrench from his back pocket and began making adjustments.

In minutes he was back down, scampering up the front stairs to his apartment with Rue and Patrick on his heels. Miguel made a beeline for the phone. He picked up his receiver, holding it out for all to hear, and out poured the delicious sound of an illegal dial tone.

"Holy shit!" shouted Rue. "Tuckin' it to Ma Bell! I love it!"

"Make a call brother," offered Miguel as he handed the phone to Rue.

Rue dialed up his Carolina amigo, Buddy Ray, and got him out of bed.

"Buddy Ray! It's Rue! I know it's late but listen!"

Miguel and Patrick wandered out to the kitchen to give Rue some room.

"Where did you learn that trick?"

"I learned it from my cousin Manuel. He works for the phone company in Alamosa."

Soon Rue wrapped up his call, "Say hi to everybody for me Buddy Ray!" Then he handed the phone off to Patrick, who dialed up Lester Reardon's number without hesitation.

"I won't be waking this guy up. That much I know. … Lester! Phelan here!" he shouted. And the two quickly got into catching up on the news of the last three weeks. Miguel and Rue hung in the kitchen to give Patrick a minute. And as Patrick wound down his conversation with Lester, he could be heard saying, "Lester, think about coming up here for a visit. We'll get you back in the Garden and you can get an up close and personal look of that wild look in Dave Cowens' eyes. Stay in touch. Goodnight, Lester!"

Then Miguel took the phone and placed it on his cardboard table between them. "Who do we call now, hombres?" he asked. They all looked at each other in silence until Rue reached for the phone and dialed up long distance information.

"Hello Operator, give me the number for the White House."

Patrick had been leaning back on his milk crate, but promptly fell on his ass for dramatic effect. Miguel gave a clenched fist, "Yeah man, get the big dog on the line!" Rue pulled a pen from his pocket and jotted down the number. His eyes had a glassy look of purpose as he dialed the phone number of the palace on Pennsylvania Avenue.

"Do you think he's awake?" giggled Miguel as he pointed to the clock that read 3 a.m.

"We'll get him up." Answered Rue. "I've got a few things to discuss with him. It's ringing."

"Good morning, the White House."

"Yes, good morning. I'd like to speak to President Nixon please."

"I'm afraid that's not possible, sir."

"Well, what's the problem? Is he home?"

"Yes sir, he is, but he's asleep at this time, and I'm afraid it's not his policy to take these calls anyway."

"How about the Vice President?"

"No sir."

"Kissinger?"

"No sir."

"I don't get to talk to anyone?"

"Just me, sir."

"Do you get many calls like this, Ma'am?"

"All night long, sir."

"Well thank you for your time, Ma'am."

"You're welcome, sir. Good night."

"Hey, we gave it the old college try, boys."

"Good effort, Rue"

"Rue, you sound pretty angry at our President," spoke Miguel. "Makes me wonder if you might've done some time way down yonder in Vietnam?"

"Nah. They wanted me, but they didn't get me. They called me in for a physical after I dropped out of college. I ate about a dozen blueberry pancakes before I boarded the bus to go to the base for my physical. As soon as the doctor put the stethoscope on my chest, I puked all over his white coat. Then they just threw me the fuck out of there."

"Lovely. How 'bout you, Patrick?"

"Nah, I'm a couple years younger than Rue. I had Lottery number 146. Didn't look safe, but the war was winding down, and they never called my number. But I wasn't going anyway. I'd have headed to Canada if I had to. But something funny happened. My Uncle Liam called me up to meet him at his bar. He lined up a doctor friend to meet us there. This doctor wrote up a history of asthma for me. Liam was a Marine Sargent in the South Pacific during the Big One, a Purple Heart. But he told me he wasn't letting me go over there. He just wasn't gonna let it happen. This was just a little while ago. If it had been '69, he'd have driven me up to the fucken gate. But he saw enough of these guys coming back, hanging out in his bar. He saw how fucked up they were. It didn't take him long to figure it out."

"What about you, Miguel?"

"No man. I wasn't as smart as you guys. I did my time down in Hell's half acre."

"Were you on the ground?"

"No man, I didn't see any action at all. They stuck me in a clerk's office in a Saigon Hospital, pushing papers. I don't know why. Maybe I was the token spic. I'd enlisted with my cousins Pablito and Esteban, as well as my best friend, Glen "

"They'd promised to keep us together, but as soon as we got over there, they sent us in four different directions. Everybody else got sent right into the fields. Glenn stepped on a land mine and came home in a bag. Pablo and Esteban survived the war. But Esteban couldn't handle it. He drank himself to death. Pablito seems to be hanging in there. He's got a good woman and a couple of kids. I think he's gonna be alright. He's tryin' hard to put it all behind him. Now when we see each other we don't even talk about it."

"Is it hard for you to talk about it?" asked Patrick.

"No, not really. But I wasn't in the thick of it over there. But those guys, man it was so hard for them to talk about it, even with me. Poor Esteban, after he got home, he couldn't relate to anyone. If someone told him they were bummed out about their job, or because their car broke down, he'd just hit the fucken roof. They didn't know what down was, and he couldn't handle that."

The room was quiet for an appropriate while before Miguel continued.

"They got sent to the War. I got sent to the party. And that's what Saigon was man, one big party. Women, booze, drugs. All you can imagine of that. Still, guys were getting popped around you just enough to make you wonder if you were gonna get home in one piece. When I got word about Glen dying, I flipped out for a while. Went AWOL. I was gone for a week, shacked up with a Vietnamese woman in a hotel. One night about three in the morning, we were asleep in bed, when the door came flying open and three Viet Cong are pointing guns at me. They started interrogating the chick, bantering back and forth for two or three minutes. I figured it was the last round up for this Chicano. Then it seemed that they got the answers they wanted. They shut the door and left. I turned myself in that morning, and they put me in the hole for a month."

Patrick and Rue looked at each other shaking their heads.

"You remember Nickie Dunn?" Rue asked.

"Of course, I remember Nickie Dunn."

Nickie Dunn was the point guard on Rue's Tech Tourney team. His eyes used to light up when he'd land Patrick Phelan in the one-on-one drills at practice. Nickie would go by him as if he were an open turnstile. Patrick dreaded the matchup. Nickie's first step was lightning, then gone.

Rue turned to Miguel, "Nickie and I fell out of touch when I left town. But I ran into him last week for the first time, and aahhh, he's just a shell of himself. He did his time over there, and I couldn't get out of him exactly what happened."

"Figure the worst, man. If he's your friend maybe, you can get him to talk. He needs to talk about it whether he knows it or not."

The hour was late, and the mood was somber, so the boys called it a night. Miguel walked them downstairs to the street and they said their goodbyes. Rue turned down a ride home, preferring a quiet walk through Inman Square. Patrick kicked over the engine of the Dart and made his way back home.

It had been a long, eventful day that he played over in his mind. Most notably, he found he possessed an effortless curiosity about cooking. Not once all day did he have to remind himself to pay attention. Time passed quicker in Guillermo's kitchen than it had ever passed before. Patrick knew that he'd stumbled on to something. It was a brand new feeling.

He made it home, quietly entered the apartment, and tiptoed into his bedroom. Then he stripped down and took a quick shower. He dialed in "The Commander" on WBZ then took the band-aid off his cut finger to let the air get at the wound. Patrick stared at it for a good minute. It felt like a culinary rite of passage. A little blood must be spilt.

He toweled himself off and went to bed. Just as sleep was about to overtake him, he heard his father struggling to get out of bed. Shaky, uncertain steps made their way down the hall. These old sounds filled Patrick with the fear that Jim might crash to the floor. Nevertheless, he made it down the hallway, grabbing the bathroom doorknob for support. It rattled in his trembling hand.

Jim flicked the light on and shuffled into the bathroom. He lifted up the seat and stood there for a long time. Then Patrick heard the trickle of water hitting water. Jim flushed the toilet, and Patrick listened to the shuffling of his untrustworthy feet taking him down the hallway, back to bed.

"Who said you can never go back home again?" he asked himself one more time.

17: PROSPERITY IN BLUES HEAVEN

The trees of Cambridge began morphing into fiery flowers as the month of September passed by. A slight chill emerged to accompany the afternoon breeze on the river, turning the fashion into sweater weather. The beauty of the days heightened by the fact that the real cold weather was just around the corner.

Down at the Home of the Blues, Sonny and Moe were perusing the accountant's report for their first full month in business. The numbers were off the charts. They had struck gold. Word spread throughout Inman Square, from the barber shop to the haberdasher to the fire station. The talk was about the two strangers from out of town, who opened up a club that had the white kids standing in double file to see the black legends of the Blues.

Sonny and Moe offered up the pure product. They were the unknowing keepers of the flame. There was no denying that. The music had always pushed forward relentlessly. In the early days, the music paddled its way up the muddy Mississippi from New Orleans through the Delta, just like mercury rising on a hot, sweaty day to its apex in Sweet Home Chicago.

All the way up the great river, the music spilled out on either side. It roared down the highways and byways to parts all over, miraculously finding the back door of Sonny's Place seven nights a week. Once inside, the fanatics witnessed and paid testimony to the power of the Blues. Those searching for a spark in their life could find it here.

"Moe, pinch me! I'm afraid this is a dream. I feel like I'm in heaven."

"You are, Sonny. You're in Blues Heaven!" he cackled greedily.

A local rag, *The Reality Paper*, had covered the opening night festivities and puffed up a piece about "Sonny Bolla—Patriarch of the Blues." They quoted his opening night speech word for word along with photographs of him and Alabama Al McGuirk, who put his arm on Sonny's shoulder for proper effect.

In a truly unpremeditated fashion, Sonny had become a wanted man. The Blues fans sought him out to thank him for building a home for the music. Lily white liberals sought him out to congratulate him on his humanitarian work for Black artists. Then there were the women that take delight in bedding down a guy whose name is in neon.

Sonny's plate was full. There was so much money generated that he moved into a bachelor pad on Fairfield Street in the Back Bay. Marie Bolla had officially filed for divorce. Sonny and Moe began the process of hiding as much revenue as possible. In accordance with their belief in creative bookkeeping, each night at 10 p.m. they changed the typeset roll of the cash register. The last four hours of business were off the books. The skids were well greased. There was only one thing that bothered Sonny.

"Moe, I haven't minded putting in the long hours to get this thing going, but I'm getting one endless headache from listening to the racket these baboons are making every night. Moe, I need to be able to escape from time to time while that music's playing."

"I can understand that. Why don't we give someone the responsibility of closing down at night? We'll make a manager out of somebody. How about your cousin, Freddie?"

"Freddie's a fucken pea brain."

They bantered back and forth till Rue Morley's name came up. They weren't sure of him either, because he certainly had a mind of his own. Yet he appeared to be the only candidate in the house. They decided to make him an offer.

"If we catch his hand in the till, we'll cut it off and send him packin'," declared Sonny.

"Fair enough," confirmed Moe. "But let me tell you—Morley is an asset. He pours more liquor than any bartender I've ever seen."

That was a fact. Rue was a two-fisted pourer, a real volume man. The busier things got, the faster he poured. He was sitting barefoot and shirtless at his kitchen table when the phone rang.

"Morley residence."

"Rue?"

"Yeah."

"Sonny here."

"What's up?"

"Rue, can you come in a half hour early today? Moe and I wanna talk to you."

"Somethin' wrong?"

"Nah, everything's fine. We gotta deal to offer you."

"Alright, I'll see you in a bit."

Rue wondered what this could be about. Then he returned to Ryan's column in the Globe, happy to learn that an old school baller like Art "Hambone" Williams would be making the Celtic roster for another season.

Then the front door opened, and Leslie Morley entered, loaded down with books. As soon as she saw Rue, tears began to fill her eyes.

"What's the matter?" Rue wanted to know, peering over the top of his newspaper.

She dumped her books on the kitchen table, sat down and sobbed.

"Rue, I can't take this job anymore. I can't control these kids. They make fun of my accent and they're walking all over me."

"What happened?"

The whole day was a disaster. I had the ninth graders today, a group I hadn't taught yet. The kids in the first class all sat in the wrong seats so that I couldn't follow the seating plan. Then someone shot a paper clip at me, when I was writing on the blackboard. Rue, I hate it up here. This whole move was a mistake. A terrible mistake."

Leslie Morley burst into tears again and retreated to the bathroom to compose herself.

****

Patrick Phelan changed into his work whites and punched the clock. Things had been going pretty well, and he was feeling comfortable in his role. But more than anything, he was enjoying the good feelings of belonging to a team that really stood for something. Right from the get-go, Guillermo had brought great food to the kitchen of Sonny's Place. He had set the standards high, and through word of mouth he was establishing a solid reputation around town.

When Patrick Phelan told people where he cooked, he felt proud.

As he passed by the walk-in fridge, the door opened up and out walked Helen Beach.

"Hi Patrick."

"Hi Helen. What's up?"

Helen had a naughty grin on her face. She was holding an enormous cucumber in her stubby fingers. "My date for tonight," she giggled.

Patrick set up shop next to Frankie Pope, who was pounding veal medallions. The sound of his hammer, delivering in a rhythmically decisive manner filled the kitchen as Helen began letting out climactic moans and shrieks after each slam. Her howls rose in volume and intensity until she burst into uncontrollable laughter.

"Oh Johnny! Oh Johnny!" mimicked Guillermo as he called out the name of Helen's beau.

The Chef was in the process of skinning a huge slab of salt pork with a boning knife. He cut off one of the pig's protruding nipples and ambled up behind Patrick as if he were offering a taste of something wonderful from his hand. Patrick opened his mouth to taste what was being offered. The cold, rock hard texture of the pig's nipple gagged him, and he spit it out in disgust. Guillermo roared as did the rest of the crew.

"That's why kitchens have swinging doors," laughed Frankie. "Because what goes on inside just ain't fit for public consumption."

****

Rue Morley left home and his sobbing wife to make the short walk over to the Home of the Blues. He tromped downstairs to the office, where he found Sonny and Moe holding court.

"Come on in Rue. Take a seat," spoke Sonny as he leaned into his chair and lit up a smoke. "Rue, we've decided to hire a night manager to shut down the house and close out the register. The job is yours if you want it. We'll give you a $25 per week raise."

"Let's get it up to fifty bucks a week and we're on."

Sonny looked over to catch Moe's reaction. He was unruffled and gave a silent nod that sewed up the deal. They shook hands on it, and Rue headed back upstairs. He ran into Miguel and told him of this latest development.

"Congrats Rue."

"Thanks Pal, but to be honest with you, I'd have taken a pay cut just to get Sonny out of here a few nights a week. Who's playin' tonight?"

"Big Mama Thornton."

"Wow. Get ready for a crankin' night."

Soon the Madeira sisters showed up on the scene for the night shift. Elena grabbed a cup of coffee, said her hellos all around and walked over to talk to Patrick. This had become their nightly custom. Elena was an open book, and they'd talk about all kinds of things. She had a way of drawing Patrick out a bit, and he liked seeing her walk through the kitchen door.

"Patrick, you've got a car, don't you?"

"Yeah, I got a car."

"Whadya say we just leave here?"

"Where we goin'?" smiled Patrick.

"California!" she decided after moderate deliberation. "Whadya say Patrick? I could be packed and waiting at the corner of Norfolk and Cambridge in twenty minutes. They won't even miss us."

Splitting town wasn't in the cards, but Patrick liked the idea of driving to California with Elena Madeira. He felt so comfortable in her presence.

"So, when are you gonna give that girl a break?" Rue had recently inquired.

"What do you mean?"

"What do you think I mean?"

Patrick knew what he meant. But he didn't like Rue getting up in his head like that. It wasn't cool to confess to being afraid of girls. And it wasn't cool to admit to one's lack of experience. Patrick kept that to himself for the most part. He could talk to Lester Reardon about it because Lester never did anything but be caring of him. But Rue was more apart. Imbued with a bit of a mean streak that you wouldn't want to leave yourself open to.

Returning to the kitchen, Patrick served up the staff meal of fettuccine alla panna. The sisters grabbed their bowls of pasta and headed out to the dining room to eat. During the daytime the bar was tended by a recently divorced, painted up blonde by the name of Lil. Moe Venti brought her in thinking that her look might provoke some daytime business. He was right.

She had established a solid three martini lunch crowd that showered her with tips. "Diamond Lil" as Rue had dubbed her, finished up and wandered over to join the Madeira sisters at their table. Soon Helen Beach was off the clock. She grabbed a beer and joined the four of them for a womanly type of chat. It wasn't long before the talk came around to men.

Diamond Lil's bitter divorce had left several cold, hard lines around her eyes. Trust and kindness had been vanquished from her being. Material possessions had become her focus. "Yeah, I'm finished with love," she'd say. "There's only one kind of man I want now. He's got to have plenty of m-o-n-e-y."

"First you look at the purse, huh, Lil?" giggled Elena.

"Jeez Lil, you're too young to give up on love," insisted Tisha.

"Sorry Doll, but love gave up on me," she said glumly. "Yeah, there's only one man around here that fits my bill of sale." Then she perked up noticeably as she heard Sonny's feet shuffling up the stairs from his office. Her eyes followed him into the kitchen.

"Sonny? Lil, you're after Sonny?" quizzed Helen.

"That's right, and I'm gonna get that man. Mark my words!" And with that she got up to close out her register.

"Poor girl," spoke Stella Madeira. "Someone should tell her that Sonny's been humping everything in sight around here at night."

"Yeah, he lures them down to his office," noted Tisha.

"Yeah, down into his den of sin," chimed Elena. "I had to go downstairs to get some bev naps out of the storeroom last week, and he was giving some woman a going over."

"No shit?" queried Helen. She was never around for the action at night, and she loved catching up on the dirt. "Well, I think Sonny's one of the sleaziest bastards I've ever met. Nothing he'd do would surprise me."

Back in the kitchen, Guillermo went over a few things with Frankie Pope before leaving for the night. The line at night had been set up with Frankie in the middle, responsible for sautéing and expediting orders. Patrick handled the pasta station to his left, while Freddie DiSavio grilled steaks and baked off lasagnas and cannellonis. Frankie liked keeping Freddie in that corner "because it's tough to fuck up a steak."

Frankie had become an excellent mentor to Patrick in the first month. He was both an experienced and inspired cook who took great delight in the creativity of his trade. Cooking for Frankie was a combination of alchemy and magic. He fancied himself as a kind of Renaissance man. Food wasn't just food. It was more like the history of the world. He'd spent much of the summer wandering around the Greek Islands. His rap was full of myth and legend. His enthusiasm was contagious. Patrick felt lucky to be working under him.

One of the most consistent problems that the restaurant had encountered through the first month was finding dependable dishwashers. They came and went. It didn't seem to be a gig that anyone wanted until Mouton Duvalier and a fellow who called himself "The Turk" showed up on the scene. Mouton was a Haitian just off the boat with a wife and five children. He latched on to the job as if it was a gold nugget. He was short but thick—built like a fire hydrant. The Turk was a recent transplant into town from the Bronx. He was in Sonny's Place for one reason: the music.

The Turk played a mean Blues harmonica. When the bands would arrive, hauling their equipment through the back door, the Turk would pull out his harp and begin to wail, just to show them what he was all about. Thus, he would receive invitations to jam on stage after his kitchen chores were complete. The Turk had begun to establish a reputation for himself. He was tall and skinny with pale white skin. A long black ponytail hung down his back. He looked a bit peculiar when on stage with a group of Brothers, but when it came to playing the Blues, the Turk could hang with the best of them. In Sonny's Place that was the bottom line.

Together Mouton and the Turk handled the tasks of washing dishes, scrubbing pots and pans, sweeping the floors, and cleaning the bathrooms. They did their dirty, thankless job without complaint, and Frankie always made sure to cook them whatever they wanted for dinner.

"Cheekun! Cheekun!" Mouton would always request.

"It's chicken! Not cheekun! Speak fucken English," screamed Freddie DiSavio, desperate to have a human being on the ladder rung beneath him. Mouton got up in Freddie's face, daring him to say another word. But he didn't. Freddie knew that Mouton could make corned beef hash out of him any old time he wanted.

The dining room filled up, and the crew kicked it into gear. Then they flat out sprinted for the next couple of hours feeding the hungry masses. Around 8:15 the storm subsided for a bit and the three cooks stepped out on the back stoop to catch their breath.

The back porch was their hang, their reprieve. Every kitchen needs that place, where cooks can stop for a few minutes and catch their breath. Fresh off his journey, it didn't take Frankie long to begin an oration about the Ancient World. This was of course no interest to Freddie DiSavio.

But Patrick was all ears when Frankie would rant about Constantinople, the Byzantine Empire, or the ancient city of Ephesus.

"Ephesus, man! The ancient city of Ephesus—the city of 100,000. They only dug it up and discovered it at the turn of the century. Man, you wouldn't believe it. The library, the House of Government, and the brothel all located on the same block, kitty cornered from each other! Then I took a boat ride from Turkey, back to the beautiful island of Samos, and in the town of Kokkari, I took a long hike one day into the hills and went swimming at a waterfall. I dried myself off and tried to take a nap in this big cave by the falls. But I woke up in a panic when I realized that over the last 10,000 years, every act that one human could commit upon another had happened right there where I lay. That notion shot panic through my whole being. I jumped into my boots and the spirits chased me out of those hills. I got back into town and had to fire down a few ouzos just to calm my nerves. Yeah man, the Ancient World!"

They stood in silence on the back stoop for another minute. Then they heard the rattle of a van coming down the alley as it pulled up to the back door. Out stepped Willie Mae "Big Mama" Thornton, and she was aptly named. She walked up the steps of the stoop and Patrick held the door open for her.

"Son, d'yall have a dressing room here for me?"

"I'm sorry Big Mama, but we don't."

She didn't look surprised by that, and she kept on walking out to the bar, where she found a secluded booth to get ready for the show. As Patrick watched her immense world weariness amble into Sonny's, he thought it was wrong that she didn't have a warm, clean room to enjoy a little privacy before her show. But this was the Blues, not Broadway. This was Sonny's Place, not Symphony Hall.

Willie Mae Thornton was a certifiable link in the chain of substantial black women that more than held their own in the rough and tumble world of the Blues. In terms of high voltage vocal power, she took a back seat to nobody.

In the dining room, Elena Madeira spotted Big Mama and reached into her bag to grab her flash camera. She ran up to her booth and snapped a quick photo. The flash went off in Big Mama's startled eyes, and she blew a gasket.

"Fucken white girl! Takin' my pitcha? You wanna take my pitcha, you ask Big Mama. You don't take nothin'!"

Dark, angry light shot out of her eyes, accenting a mean scar on her forehead. Elena froze, mumbled an apology, and quickly retreated. A wave of shame and embarrassment overtook her, and tears came to her eyes. Rue saw the whole thing happen, and when he saw how upset Elena was, he followed her over to the wait station.

"What happened sweetie?" he inquired, putting a hand on her shoulder.

"Oh Rue, I screwed up. I pulled a tourist number on Big Mama, and she almost bit my head off."

"Yeah, I saw. Man, she's tough."

"What should I do?"

"Ask her if there's something we can get her."

Elena took a couple of breaths, and once again approached the booth where Big Mama had set up shop. She had her compact mirror out and was making her face. Elena stood for a long minute before Big Mama acknowledged her presence with eye contact.

"Big Mama, I'm so sorry I offended you. Is there anything we can get you?"

"A tall glass of water, a double whiskey neat, and an ash tray," she solicited without extending forgiveness.

"It's time!" Frankie announced back in the kitchen. Patrick nodded, and headed out to the bar to get beer for the crew. This was an enjoyable nightly stroll through the swinging doors, out to the dining room and up to Rue's bar. Take a moment, look around and see who was in the house. It was like any other night until a woman seated on the edge of the service bar folded up her menu, and Patrick's eyes met hers.

"Hello" she said rather boldly with a killer smile. Her pale blue eyes looked him over, like a tigress sizing up her prey.

"Hello," came out of his mouth as if spoken by someone else.

"Are you the chef?" she asked.

"Well, no, but I'm one of the cooks."

"Honey, if you're cookin' my dinner, you're the chef."

"OK, I'm the chef."

"Maybe you'd like to cook me something special. I'm starving."

"Alright. Is there anything you don't eat?"

"I eat everything. I'm Liza Jane," she said, extending her hand to him.

"I'm Patrick," he managed to say as he took her hand.

Patrick Phelan returned to the kitchen and told Frankie what was going on. He went out to the bar to steal a look at her. "Wow. I think she's heavy on the garlic."

They discussed the possibilities, and Frankie was adamant about going in the puttanesca direction. He tossed Patrick a few shrimp to take the dish up to the next level. "Yeah man, black olives, tomatoes, capers, garlic, and anchovies—that's gettin' down to it!"

So, Patrick went with that. He seasoned and sautéed the shrimp with a little julienned onion, boiled off some fresh tonnarelli, and tossed it all with a generous pinch of parmesan, fresh parsley, and a good ladle of the puttanesca sauce. The dish looked good. Patrick walked out to the bar and delivered it to her. Rue had set her up with napkin, utensils, and a crust of bread.

"Well thank you Patrick. That looks fabulous," she smiled. "Are you getting off soon? Can you join me for a drink?"

"I am getting out soon. Will you still be here?"

"I'll make a point of it," she said, smiling that smile.

Patrick headed back into the kitchen totally under the influence. By this time a handsome, bearded gentleman wearing a leather jacket, a swamp fox hat, and carrying a brief case sat down at the booth where Big Mama Thornton had set up shop. Elena came by and he ordered a glass of wine and a bowl of pasta before the kitchen shut down. It was the last order of the night.

They put out their final orders and began to clean up the night's mess with a directed vigor. The kitchen was spotless in no time, but Patrick had a concern as he punched the time clock.

"Frankie, I can't hang out with her smellin' like sweat, garlic and onions."

"No, you're right. Hey man, it's one of the true hazards of our profession. What you need is a fucken shower. Hey, there's a shower down in Sonny's office. Maybe he'll let you use it."

Patrick got on the intercom and gave Sonny's office a blast.

"Sonny here," piped in the boss.

"Sonny, this is Patrick."

"What's your problem Irish?"

"Sonny, would it be alright if I took a shower in your office?"

"Irish, are you shittin' me?"

"No Sonny, just this once?"

"Jesus Christ, Irish. Every night I have to fight with these musicians that want to take over my office. I'm sick of it. Just this once. Understand?"

"I got it Sonny. Just this once."

"Swing by the bar and pick me up a tall seven and seven."

"Got it."

Patrick went out to the bar, ordered Sonny's drink and told Liza Jane that he'd be right back. Then he headed downstairs to find Sonny immersed in paperwork. He looked up when his drink was served.

"What's goin' on up there Irish? Why are you worrying about how you smell tonight? It's not like you."

"I've got a pretty girl waiting for me upstairs," he confided.

"Well, that's great Irish. But remember one thing about pretty girls. If they didn't have a pussy, they'd be extinct, like the fucken Do Do Bird!"

Sonny hadn't used that line in a while, so naturally he burst into laughter over it. Patrick stripped down and jumped into the hot shower, scrubbed himself up and rinsed himself down. Then he hopped out of the shower and began toweling off. He looked up to see Sonny checking out his machinery.

"Christ, Irish, can you get the job done with a pecker like that?"

Patrick didn't know the answer to that question. So he got dressed quickly, thanked Sonny and scampered up the back stairs. His nervous heart palpitated, but some outside force seemed to propel him forward. His feet took him right over to the bar, and the seat that Liza Jane was holding for him. She put her hand on his shoulder and whispered in his ear.

"That was one of the nicest meals I've ever had. Thanks."

"I'm glad you liked it" he managed to say.

Patrick ordered up a beer from Rue, sat back in his chair, and for a moment, contemplated the power of having something to offer, something to bring to the party. Cooking good food was like finding a new way of talking. A well-prepared meal, when offered to a woman, could be more convincing than an elaborate rap from the hippest of cats. Rest assured that Sonny's Place was full of hip cats with elaborate raps.

The fellow sitting with Big Mama asked Elena for a check. She wrote it up and left it on the table. He quickly glanced at it, handing it back to her with a fifty-dollar bill. Elena reached out for the money.

When her hand got close to his, a golden bolt of static electricity shot out, giving their fingertips a crackle and a snap that could be seen and heard. It surprised them both, and they stared into each other's eyes for a quick moment. Big Mama saw it happen, and she raised an eyebrow too. Elena went to get his change, thinking that it was an odd occurrence.

The house was beginning to fill up, and it seemed that the women were outnumbering the men. Rue called that "The Big Mama Factor." Clearly the women in town were excited about seeing another woman do her thing on Sonny's stage.

"The booker in New York got lots of good ink in the papers for this show," explained Rue. "That brings out 'the Quiche Lorraine Crowd.'"

"The Quiche Lorraine Crowd?" giggled Liza. "Who are they? Am I one of them?"

"The Quiche Lorrainers are the folks who wouldn't ordinarily come to a Blues Club, but when they see a nice write up in a newspaper, they get to thinking that listening to the Blues might be kind of a chichi thing to do."

"Then I guess I must be one of those Quiche Lorrainers!" she confessed with a big laugh. Clearly, she could enjoy a chuckle at her own expense. Serious and sensitive didn't seem to be her way.

Big Mama Thornton's band came to life and started warming up the stage for her entrance. The noise of the band made talking difficult, so they focused in on the music. The Blues was new stuff for Liza Jane, but she found herself slipping right into it. Soon the bass player grabbed the microphone in midstride and broke into a bluesy introduction.

"Ladies and gentlemen, please, please put your hands together, and welcome one of the rocks upon which this church was built! The one and only Queen of the Blues—the Big Mama herself—Big Mama Thornton!"

The room erupted as she made her way from the back booth to the stage. She was big. She was mean. And she was all business, wasting no time before breaking right into "Little Red Rooster." Her voice bellowed from within those huge pipes, letting forth a big, brassy sound full of desperate emotion.

Patrick Phelan glanced over at Liza Jane and a shiver shot up his spine. He sensed that some indefinable, useless pattern in his soul might be unraveling. Sonny's Place was like a kiln: an environment that could melt down the most stifled of human hearts. Unbeknownst to Sonny and Moe, the music that came down in their dark tavern had the power to heal.

People in the crowd were already screaming for "Hound Dog," but Big Mama was in no hurry to go there. Instead, she worked her way through a mournful version of "Summertime," and followed that with a knock down drag out version of "Ball and Chain." More than a few folks in attendance realized that she had to have been one of Janice's musical mothers.

Then in her restlessness, she kicked her drummer off the traps to show everyone what she knew about rhythm. The next number she was back out front blowing a thick harmonica lead. Her versatility was astounding. But the crowd kept calling for "Hound Dog."

"So, you want some Hound Dog, eh?" and she began to bark and wail like a dog before breaking into her set closer that made the King's version sound like it was sung by a white, pimple faced teenager at a sock hop. The song culminating with her entire band howling like hungry dogs loose in the woods.

The crowd roared its approval as the bass player once again grabbed the microphone and showered Big Mama with accolades that followed her all the way to her back booth. Patrick felt the set just wash over him. His nightly involvement with the Blues had become a cathartic ritual. As he watched Big Mama nestle into her seat, he spoke to Rue and Liza.

"I'll bet by the time that Big Mama was fourteen, she had kicked the crap out of every punk in her neighborhood."

"I'll bet she did some damage," agreed Liza Jane.

The lights came back on, putting the full house into a between set never-never land. People got up to stretch their legs, crowding around them at the bar. It became a bit claustrophobic, and Liza was beginning to feel a restlessness come over her. In the blink of an eye, she knew what she wanted. She'd heard enough music for one night. She was ready to make a little of her own and didn't think twice about petitioning for it. Grabbing Patrick by the arm, she whispered in his ear.

"Patrick, do you want to come home with me?"

"Right now?"

"Right now."

He was stunned by her boldness. Was it dinner? Was it the Blues? It didn't really matter. Something was happening here, and it simply could not be avoided. The two of them put on their coats and headed for the door. Liza took him by the hand as they walked out.

Rue was pouring drinks for Elena Madeira, when he saw her face drop, and a lonely tear being wiped from her eye. He turned to see

Patrick and his newfound friend breezing past the Lugg Brothers, and out into the night.

"Christ, maybe I should learn how to fucken cook," Rue muttered to himself.

18: THE BIG MELTDOWN

"My car's over here" spoke Liza, pointing down Hampshire Street. Patrick followed a half step behind her in a daze. She unlocked the doors, they hopped in, and she kicked over the engine. "It's got to warm up a minute," she spoke. Turning to her right, Liza looked Patrick in the eye, and put her arm around his neck, pulling him close. They kissed a kiss that didn't want to stop. Then they kissed some more.

"I think she's warmed up now," smiled Liza as she put her car in gear and began driving away. They rode in silence up Cambridge Street to Mass. Ave. and Porter Square, hooking a left on Upland Road. Up the hill she drove, pulling over across Raymond Street by the hoop courts.

"You live here?" he asked with a smile as he gazed out on the playground, where he spent his younger days.

"Yeah, that grey house over there" she pointed.

I must have dribbled a basketball past your house ten thousand times on my way to that court."

"You were a basketball player?"

"Yeah."

"Were you any good?"

"Nah, I wasn't very good," he sighed as he looked down on the empty court.

"Did you have a lot of fun down there as a kid?"

"I don't think I had a lot of fun as a kid. It was mostly me and a basketball. I was kind of all alone with it."

"Well, you're not alone tonight. Come on in."

They got out of the car, and walked up the stairs, where she unlocked the front door. "My roommate, Emma's, not home yet. Come on in the kitchen, I'll open up a bottle of wine." This she did, pouring a glass of red for each of them. Then without saying a word, Liza took Patrick's hand, leading him down a dark hallway, and up a steep, narrow staircase to her bedroom.

She lit a candle by her bedside, and another on her dresser. Shadows and light flickered off the walls and ceiling as if in a dance. Liza pulled her sweater over her head, kicked off her boots, and began to unbutton Patrick's shirt. He obliged by reaching around and unsnapping her bra. In moments the rest of their clothes were in a pile on the floor, and the two were entangled, skin to skin under the covers.

Naturally, Liza began orchestrating their dance. She pulled him on top of her, directing him to her breasts, which he began to play with in an overly gentle manner as if he were afraid of damaging the goods.

"A little harder honey, I'm not gonna break."

Patrick accommodated Liza's request much to her delight. "Yeah baby, like that, just like that." Then she slid up on the bed a bit, and put her hands on his shoulders, directing him downward. This was new territory—his first sojourn south of the border, down Mexico way. Curiosity coupled with the call of duty followed him down.

"Get your boots on honey. It's gonna be wet down there," she giggled.

She was right. He was slippin' and a-slidin'. She tasted strong and earthy, both sweet and salty. "Put a finger inside me honey. Yeah, just like that." Quickly Liza Jane's engine began to reverberate, letting Patrick know he was on the trail. Still busy at work, he looked up over her short blonde hairs and between her lovely pears. Her eyes were closed, and her head rocked back and forth on the pillow. Soon her panting took on a desperate tone and nonverbal utterances filled the room until she couldn't take another second of it.

She pulled Patrick up to her face, then reached down and brought him inside her. Quickly he felt her inner warmth melt him down to a joyless climax. His heart filled with embarrassment. He mumbled an apology. Not able to look at her, he assumed that this scenario had come to its typically unsatisfactory conclusion.

"You silly boy" she smiled at him. "Don't you know the first one is always a waste?"

She giggled as she rolled him over, climbed on top of him and stared down at him, helpless on her pillow.

"You are a silly, silly boy."

He didn't respond, so she went right for his ribs, knowing that this silly boy had to be ticklish, and he was. She held him prisoner until he begged for her to stop.

"You are a very, very silly boy," she told him again.

She kissed him gently on both eyes. Then a long, slow, motionless kiss on the lips, and Patrick Phelan felt a peace come over him. There was no past. There was no future. There was just right now. They eye gazed for a long minute before Liza began making her way downward, her lips making gentle visits here and there.

Patrick closed his eyes, and by the time she reached her destination, he was seeing pink bubbles exploding out of the middle of his third eye. In a heartbeat she had him fully grown then brought to the edge of pain before delivering him inside her. The effortlessness of this transition was a revelation.

Patrick found himself snugly enveloped, rock hard and going nowhere. Immediately he knew that this was what it was all about.

Liza knelt on top of him, putting Patrick's hands on her breasts, then she broke into a slow canter as if riding a horse bareback on a beach. In time her pace picked up, and she began to drop down on him in a more decisive, rhythmical manner—then, like she was pounding down cross ties with a sledgehammer. She began to really shout about it—music to Patrick's ears, and this disintegrated whatever amused detachment he held on to as he was hurled into total involvement.

They were two sprinters joined at the hip, racing down the track with no finish line in sight. Then out of nowhere Liza Jane found herself breaking into a conclusive, mellifluous cry. She didn't want to jump off the cliff alone, so she flexed her vaginal muscles, hitting a new rhythm and angle that Patrick surrendered to, and they both went flying off into the abyss together.

As they slowly returned to earth, their panting subsided, and they rested in each other's arms. Through the wall Patrick heard the Doc Severinsen Orchestra breaking into their theme, while Ed McMahon read the list of tomorrow's guests.

"Emma's home," she whispered.

Patrick sat up, reached for his glass and took a hearty belt of wine. "Amazed" was the only suitable word to describe his frame of reference. Amazed to be alone with this mysterious woman. Amazed that she had vaporized his fears. Amazed to find out that he was just a regular guy after all. He laid back on Liza Jane's bed as if in a dream. He was warmed inside and out by the mercy of it all.

The shrill ring of a telephone outside in the hallway broke the quiet. Patrick noticed a look of concern come over Liza Jane's face. She didn't move when she heard the sound of her roommate's footsteps coming down the hall.

"It's for you Liza" spoke a voice from beyond the door. She wrapped herself up in a bathrobe and headed for the phone, carrying the extension down the hall beyond the range of his ear. Liza was gone for a while, and upon her return she appeared visibly upset. She searched for a cigarette, lit it up, and sat on the edge of the bed.

"Something wrong?"

"No" she replied, not knowing where to begin, or whether to begin at all.

"What's the matter, Liza?"

"Patrick, that was my ex-fiancé on the phone. I broke off our engagement a couple of months ago. We were due to be married just last weekend. I had the invitations written, and the envelopes were stamped and addressed. Then I called it off. Jack's been hounding me ever since."

"Where's this guy from?"

"He's from Connecticut. Old Saybrook, where I'm from. My roommate Emma is an old friend of mine from back home. When the shit hit the fan, she invited me to move up here. A change of scenery seemed like a good idea. So here I am."

"Well, I'm glad you're here."

"Thanks," she said with a sad smile as she took a drag from her cigarette.

"Would you rather not talk about it?"

"No, I don't mind talking. Do you mind listening?"

"Not at all."

"I lied to Jack on the phone tonight. He asked me if I was alone, and I told him I was."

"There's no sense in torturing the guy."

"I guess."

"Did you love him?"

"I thought I did."

"What happened?"

"Oh shit, he was so fucken controlling. Jack's a lawyer, and he's just so obsessed with getting ahead. He's into politics. He did a lot of work for Nixon's reelection."

"Nixon? Are you shittin' me?"

"No. He's a real tight assed Republican. He used to take me to these parties, and tell me what to wear, and what to say to this person or that. And he'd hit the roof if he ever saw me smoking a cigarette. "Bad P.R.," he'd say. Meanwhile he'd be working up a peptic ulcer trying to buy the right house in the right neighborhood."

"He sounds like a real dweeb."

"A real dweeb?" she laughed. "Well, he's handsome, and comes from a well to do family. My mom thought he was a great catch. I'd just had my heart broken by my first love, and I latched on to him."

"He sounds like a real serious guy. Did you have any fun with him?"

"Well, we had a pretty good sex life, but he could never really make me laugh, and I love to laugh. I knew something was wrong when none of my friends liked him. He's a pretty uptight guy. Whenever we'd go out on the town, I couldn't get him out on the dance floor. Very self-conscious, always thought people were looking at him."

"Doesn't dance? That's a bad sign," Patrick assessed. "I'll bet he never cooked you dinner either."

"Jack couldn't fry an egg."

She put out her cigarette, took a sip of wine, and slipped back into bed. They lay on their sides, facing each other with their heads resting on a pillow. Soon they were entangled again, doing what people do. Another hour passed till they fell asleep in each other's arms.

19: SPIRO'S SWAN SONG

Patrick Phelan awoke to feel Liza Jane's fingers running through his hair. She sat on the edge of her bed in a pink bathrobe, her hair wrapped in a towel. "I've got to leave for work in a little while, Patrick." He cradled a cup of coffee that she had brought him.

"Where do you work, Liza?"

"Oh, I just got some temp secretarial work in Harvard Square. It's nothing I really want, but I just grabbed the first thing I could get when I came to town."

"Could you give me a lift by Inman Square? I left my car down there last night."

"Sure honey, but we've got to get moving so I won't be late for work."

Patrick crawled out of bed and got dressed. He looked out her window and down on the basketball court in the park on Upland Road. The multicolored maples shimmered in the breeze. The cloudless sky looked bluer than he had ever seen it. Liza Jane was still getting dressed.

"I'm gonna meet you out front."

"Alright."

Patrick made his way out the front door, down the steep staircase, and onto the street. The crystal-clear light of the new morning was dazzling. He walked over to the park, and on to the hoop court, where he had passed so many hours. His teenage years flashed back at him in a flood of memories. The court appeared a bit smaller than he remembered, yet every square inch of it was familiar to him.

Liza Jane came strutting out her front door, and Patrick walked back up to the street to meet her. "What a beautiful day!" she declared as the crisp wind blew her hair all about. She shook it from side to side in a display of disheveled perfection.

He couldn't stop looking at her. "Why don't you call in sick, and we can go out for breakfast?"

"Now don't go making me irresponsible."

They hopped into her car and made the drive down to Inman.

"Liza, I have tomorrow off. Can I come over and cook you dinner?"

"Well, I should say you can."

"Seven o'clock?"

"See you then," she smiled.

They kissed each other goodbye. Patrick hopped out of the car, and watched Liza drive down the road and out of sight. He stood on the sidewalk next to the fire station for a long minute. There wasn't a need, thought, or want in his happy little head. Everything felt different. Everything.

Eventually his hunger brought him across the street to the Tortoise Café for breakfast. "Good morning, Chef, and why do you look so happy?" spoke Ted, whose tired eyes hung over the griddle.

"It would take a long time to tell you the whole story, Ted. But I'm dreaming about corned beef hash with a couple of eggs over easy."

"Comin' right up."

Patrick sipped a cup of coffee as a steady stream of customers came and went during Ted's busy morning. A copy of *The Boston Globe* rested on the counter. Patrick read the headline aloud as Ted delivered his breakfast.

"Agnew calls 2 p.m. press conference."

"He's goin' down!" proclaimed Ted with a big grin.

"No shit?"

"It's what they're saying."

"What's he gonna do? Join the effete corps of impudent snobs?"

"I could use a pair of hands around here."

Patrick worked his way through breakfast, amazed at how much could change in one day. There was someone he needed to share his news with—Lester Reardon. He took one of the Tortoise's promotional postcards, addressed it, mooched a stamp off Ted, and simply wrote, "Dear Lester, The blight is over!" Then he dropped it into a mailbox on the corner.

Patrick headed back home to steal a few hours of sleep before work. He parked the Dart, and climbed the stairs to his folks' place. Once inside the apartment, his mother's sleepless eyes glared back at him from the couch. Mildred was still in her nightgown, smoking a cigarette. Her face was taut with tension. Jim leaned forward in his Lazy Boy. His hands shook in expectation of an explosion. Quickly, Mildred was revving on all cylinders.

"Patrick, where have you been all night? We've been worried sick! We called the Cambridge Police, the State Police, and Your Uncle Liam. We were sure your car was wrapped around a telephone pole somewhere!"

"You called the Police and Uncle Liam? What is this? Am I ten years old or what?"

"While you're living in this house, you'll be living by our rules. And if you think that means you can be out gallivanting all night, you're sadly mistaken."

"Ma, I'm a grown man, now!"

"If you live in this house, you live by our rules."

"Yeah? Well clearly, it's time I don't live here anymore."

"Let's not have words", pleaded Jim, whose tremors rose with the anger level of the room. Mildred lit up another cigarette, then headed for her bedroom to let the authorities know her son was found.

"Where were you, Son?" asked Jim in a concerned tone.

"I was at a party."

"All night, Son? What do you talk about all night?"

"Sports."

Patrick paced back and forth, mumbling aloud. "She calls the Cambridge Police, the State Police, and Uncle Liam. I can't live here. I have to look for an apartment."

A sadness came over Jim Phelan. He leaned back in his chair, staring blankly at the television. In a moment Mildred returned.

"Liam is on the phone, and he wants to speak to you," she said sternly.

"Oh great. Call in the firing squad," and he picked up the phone. "Good morning, Liam."

"Good morning sailor. Now why are you worrying my sister like this, staying out all night long? Did you get lucky last night?"

"As a matter of fact, I did" he confessed, turning away from his mom and dad.

"Well congratulations. I figured as much. Who wants to think about your mother when you're all wrapped up in the good stuff?"

"Thanks for understanding."

"Hey, I was nineteen once."

"Yeah, back in the Cro-Magnon Era."

"You got that right. Say, Patrick, can you drop by here sometime this week? I need a pair of hands to help me move a few things around in the bar. I'll drop a couple of Celtic tickets on you for the trouble."

"No trouble Liam. Sounds great."

"OK sailor, now next time you go getting lucky, and you aren't coming home, please give my sister a call and make up a good excuse."

"Alright Liam. And I'll get by this week."

"Good enough sailor. Take care."

Patrick bid Liam adieu, hung up the phone, and retreated to his room. A little shut eye before work was definitely in order. He laid his head on the pillow and closed his eyes. Warm visions of Liza Jane filled his brain along with expectations of their next meeting. Soon he dozed off to a cacophony of Mildred's overworked vacuum cleaner battling against Jim's television set from which an enthusiastic announcer pleaded, "Lucy Watson! Come on down!"

20: HARVEY WALLENBERG

Sonny Bolla sat at his office desk, amidst a pile of paperwork. Yet somehow, the column of numbers and a to do list could not hold his focus. The crawling king snake in his pants had awoken to the notion of Diamond Lil's swizzle stick legs wrapped about him. Sonny had been making himself available to Lil from the get-go, but she preferred to dangle the carrot. Call it control through denial, or simply playing hard to get. Lil wanted to see Sonny's tongue hanging down around his knees.

In truth her tactics didn't bother Sonny at all. He was a genuine lover of the chase—the sweet fruit of anticipation serving as the appropriate appetizer before the main course. The shrill ring of the telephone rudely interrupted his carnal vision.

"Hello, Sonny's Place."

"Good afternoon, is this Sonny Bolla?"

"Speaking."

"Mr. Bolla, my name is Harvey Wallenberg."

"Yeah?"

"Mr. Bolla, as of today I am representing virtually all of the Black Blues performers on the circuit that have been playing your club at this time."

"What? Look pal, we deal with the booker down in New York. If you have a problem, talk to him."

"Mr. Bolla, you don't understand. The booker in New York is out of the picture now. You have to deal directly with me."

"What the fuck are you talking about?"

"I'll make it simple for you. As of today, I represent all the Blues that matter from the East Coast to the West. Be it New York, Chicago,

Texas, or Louisiana. We're calling for a 100% pay raise across the board, beginning this Friday with Hound Dog Taylor and The HouseRockers. If an agreement is not reached by 9 p.m. this Friday, we'll be going on strike."

Sonny's blood pressure rose, and a cold sweat broke out on his forehead. "Look pal, these chumps are lucky to be playing here!"

"Well, speaking frankly, Mr. Bolla, we both know that you and the booker have been pitting these musicians off against each other and underpaying them. That's been the way since the beginning. We both know that you're doing very well by these musicians, and that's why the buck stops here."

"Look asshole, I don't know who you think you are, but if you think you're gonna come in here and muscle me, you just might be lookin' up at the sky from the bottom of the Charles River."

"I'll overlook that remark for the time being. I also know who really makes the decisions in your affiliation. So, I'll call back after you've had a chance to talk to Mr. Venti."

Sonny heard a click in his ear and felt a rage surge upward from within. He slammed the phone down violently on the receiver and muttered a bouquet of profanity. Then he got on the horn to Moe Venti.

"Moe, we got trouble. I just got a call from some Jew lawyer in town, and he says that he's corralled all the Blues musicians into a Union, and they're demanding to be paid double what we bin' payin'!"

"Is that right?" inquired the cool one.

"Moe, this pig's prick is gonna call back."

"Sit tight Sonny. I'll be right over.

There was a bee in Sonny's bonnet, making paperwork impossible. So, instinctively, he tromped upstairs for a drink at Diamond Lil's bar. Nothing could be done till Moe showed up. So, he resigned himself to watching Lil prance, wink, and pour her way through a busy lunch.

Back in the kitchen, Helen Beach had just grunted and cursed her way through the frantic lunch rush that for some reason had mostly gone to her side of the line. Guillermo leisurely sautéed his way through the shift, while Helen dealt with a satchel of pasta dupes that were blowing in the breeze like Mrs. Murphy's laundry line.

Her worktable was a chaotic clutter of essential ingredients, minced garlic, lemon juice, parsley, julienned onions, and matchstick zucchinis. The stovetop was a mass of molten creamed primavera. Guillermo noticed all the collateral damage, and thought he'd give her the business. But she saw him coming and launched an assault of her own.

"Guillermo, the word in English is "slob." That's me Guillermo, a big fucken slob! You got it Guillermo? Me big fucken slob! Now that's your side of the fucken kitchen, and this is mine!"

She took a breath and pushed her thick glasses back up on her nose. Guillermo backed off, sensing that he might get bit. Frankie Pope walked through the swinging doors in time for Helen's tirade.

"Give him hell Shorty!"

"Fuck you, Studly," she growled back.

Guillermo came back from the bar with two glasses of vino bianco in an attempt to placate and indulge his cooking partner, the mercurial Helen Beach. He was feeling pretty good about things. Soon he'd bring his wife and family over from Venice. It was hard to live his life with them through letters and photographs. If everything went well, he thought he might have them here by Christmas. Hope abounded.

Moments later, Patrick arrived sporting the glow of newly found manhood. He strolled through the swinging doors to find Guillermo and Helen giggling as they sipped their vino. Patrick ran into Frankie Pope by the time clock.

"Frankie did you hear about the Vice President?"

"Yeah man, I watched the news conference. Spiro's gone! It's too good to be true."

"Now we zero in on Nixon. It's only a matter of time and we skewer his ass."

"I'm not that hopeful, but it sure is a pretty thought. So, what happened last night? Did things work out for you?"

"Frankie, things couldn't have worked out any better."

"I told you. Heavy on the garlic."

"Yeah, that must have been what turned the tide," smiled Patrick.

"Just remember me when her sister comes to town."

"I don't know if she has a sister."

"Yeah? Well, I think she might have one."

"I'll keep you apprised."

Both cooks got into their whites and headed up to the front of the line, where Guillermo stood over a pot, stirring gently. Frankie took a look.

"Pasta fazool?" he inquired.

Guillermo nodded in the affirmative and continued to stir the pot. Then he put a saucepan with a cup of olive oil on a high flame, adding whole cloves of garlic, a healthy pinch of crushed red pepper, the same amount of dried rosemary, and the peel of a lemon. He let that unlikely concoction sizzle full throttle till the pan and the ingredients were smoking. Then he strained that screaming hot oil into his pot of soup.

The sound cut like a knife. Then he added about a pound of cooked fettuccine, cut into small pieces.

He stirred for another minute, then ladled himself a sample into a cup. Standing tall, blowing on a steamy spoonful, he closed his eyes and tasted as if in a trance. Everything rang—ding, ding, ding off his palate. Guillermo nodded his satisfaction and served his cooks a cupful.

The smokehouse flavor of the soup sent them into a succession of spoonfuls that didn't stop until their cups were empty, and their happy mouths yearned for more. It was a perfect dish for an October night.

"A bowl of this, a piece of crusty bread, a glass of red wine and you're there!" assessed Helen.

Back at the bar Sonny continued to medicate. He motioned to Diamond Lil for another drink. As he watched her sashay on down to his end of the bar a lusty plan was hatched in his birdbrain.

"Lil" he began stroking her hand, "What do you say we have a quiet lunch, and a nice bottle of chianti down in my office? I'll get Guillermo to fix up something special. Lil, you know it'll be fine. We'll be dynamite together!"

Diamond Lil took back her hand and sveltely placed it on her hip, Mae West style. "Well, I'll tell you Sonny, I think my customers, you know, the ones that help me pay my bills, well I think they might really miss me if I were gone. But let me set you straight on another matter. I'm not a cheap date. I have very expensive tastes, and a true penchant for material possessions. And lastly, I have no intentions of getting horizontal on that pullout couch in your dusty office!"

She smiled a coy smile and shimmy shook her bones down to the other end of the bar, where a couple of her regular, midafternoon customers had convened. She had cultivated a nice following for herself. Lil poured a good drink, remembered first names, and from all accounts provided an enticing visual. The customers that came by to pay homage every afternoon practically threw their money at her.

Sonny was left with nothing but anticipation to chew on between sips. It was hardly a problem. He'd had more action in the last two months than he knew what to do with. The rewards of being a cult figure were not to be underestimated.

In time Moe Venti made his appearance and found his business partner holding up the far end of the bar. "You got a little head start on me Sonny?"

"Moe, the Jew that called here this morning drove me to it."

Moe ordered up a cocktail from Lil, and she brought it down to him.

"Thanks Lil, and if you don't mind, would you send Rue Morley down to the office when he arrives?"

"Sure thing Moe," she winked and smiled a flirty smile. Moe gave her a wink back then turned to Sonny.

"Let's go downstairs."

The two were halfway into their descent when Moe inquired, "So what's the story Sonny? You got into Lil's pants yet?"

"All in due time, partner. All in due time."

They nestled down in their bunker, considering how they might deter Harvey Wallenberg and his plans of a Blues Union. It wasn't long before they heard a knock at the door. Rue Morley made his appearance.

"Sit down, Rue. We got trouble brewing," announced Sonny.

He spoke of the phone call from Harvey Wallenberg, or "that fucken Jew" as he was more inclined to identify him. Sonny explained the entire scenario: the dramatic wage increase demands, the unionization, and the threat of a strike.

"That's all very interesting, but why are you confiding in me? I'm a bartender, not a union buster."

"Rue, this move for a union seems to be involving specifically the colored musicians. Sonny tells me there's no shortage of white Blues musicians in town."

"That's right Rue! You can't deny that. I got at least a half dozen white boys a night coming up to me, telling me they got a band and they wanna play right here at "The Home of the Blues," he spoke, tapping a finger on his desk. "Sometimes I get the feeling they'd play here for nothing just to say they did!"

"Well, that might be true Sonny, but I don't think you understand the nature of this beast. This music is Black music at the root. Now I know we don't draw too many Black folks in here as an audience."

"Yeah, and thank God for that," interrupted Sonny.

"But this music is Black music. There's an army of white boys playing it. And some of them are pretty damn good. But you're talking about a picket line here, and you're talking about white boys crossing a picket line to scab on their inspirations. You may as well ask them to piss on Elmore James' grave."

Sonny and Moe looked at each other. Their silence asked the question, "Who is Elmore James?"

"I fear you guys aren't in touch with this thing that's making us all fat. If I were you guys, I'd pay 'em what they want. Let's face it. You two have nothing to complain about. Even if you give them what they want, you're still makin' a killin'."

"Well thanks for your input, Rue," spoke Moe. "We'll keep you posted on what's happening."

Rue nodded, rose from his chair, and made his way upstairs to get ready for the night. Sonny took a fierce drag from his cigarette. "What do we do now, Moe," he inquired as the smoke billowed from his nostrils.

"I say we call the Jew's bluff."

"Damn right!" spoke Sonny with a fist pump.

Rue found Miguel at the bar, cutting fruit for the night, and told him of the impending conflict.

"You got a bad feeling about all this, Rue?"

"Yeah man, I do. It's just that deep down I know they don't give a flying fuck about the music."

All this made sad sense to Miguel, so he reached for the Absolut. "I think I'm ready for a drink," he spoke in a quiet melancholy. He poured up a couple of kamikazes, and they downed the hatch.

Guillermo's pasta fazool had left a dry spot in Patrick's throat so he wandered out to the bar for a soda. It didn't take Rue long to inquire about last night.

"Did things work out alright for you last night, fellah?"

"Yes, they did," spoke Patrick with a goofy grin.

Rue looked closely at his face, turning his chin from side to side while examining his profile. "Yeah, you look different. Like some terrible burden has been taken off your shoulders. Patrick, did you know that sperm retention is the leading cause of hunchbacks in our society today?"

Patrick laughed heartily, delighted that a whole world of humor and innuendo were now at his fingertips since he'd become a viable member of the club. Then Rue spoke again.

"Yeah, well look, I'm glad you got laid last night, but there's one matter I need to mention to you. Maybe you better tend to Elena tonight. She watched that blonde lead you out of here by the hand last night."

"She did?"

"Yup, and I'll tell you what, the sight of you two walking out of here put a real sad look on her face."

"You breaking hearts around here, Patrick?" inquired Miguel.

Patrick retreated to the kitchen in an attempt to run from the feeling that had come over him. The thought of hurting Elena Madeira made him nauseous. Could last night have been a mistake?

"No last night was not a mistake!" he heard a loud voice shout.

Then who was Elena to him? He knew that his feelings for her had a romantic quality, but he never felt secure enough to make a move on it. He just wasn't sure of himself. This cognition brought on an embarrassing dose of shame. It rumbled in his belly. Soon Elena would be coming to work, and he would have to face her. He dreaded the thought of it.

21: ELENA'S BLUES

Meanwhile, back at the Madeira home on Norfolk Street, the two older sisters were tying up some loose ends around the house before heading into work. Tisha finished off the dishes in the sink, while Stella pulled a roast from the oven for Enrique's supper. Drying her hands off with a towel, Tisha shouted up the back staircase toward a closed bedroom door.

"Elena, we're getting ready to leave for work soon. Are you coming?"

There was no answer. The sisters looked at each other—Tisha with quiet concern, Stella with an equal dose of disdain.

"She's your sister for Christ's sake!"

Tisha climbed the stairs and gave a gentle knock on Elena's door before entering. She found Elena lying in bed with her bathrobe and slippers on. She tiptoed over to her bedside and snuggled up to her. Elena rolled over to meet her, letting her sister see her bare face, whose eyes were bloodshot from crying. Elena sniffled and took a deep breath.

"I'm sorry you're feeling so sad little sister," whispered Tisha as she ran her fingers through Elena's hair.

"Tish, do you think anyone will ever love me?"

"Of course, Elena. I love you right now."

"I know you do, Tish," and she cried a little more as she reached out and hugged her sister. "But do you think a man will ever love me?"

"Yes Laynie, I do. I think there's someone just around the next bend waiting for you."

"I thought it might be Patrick."

"So maybe you were wrong about him."

Tisha helped Elena rise, get her work clothes on and generally pull it together. Elena's worst days never required too much of anyone's attention. She was a remarkable combination of fragility and strength. Especially considering the cards that life had dealt her—the death of her mother due to complications at her birth.

Elena's arrival into the world had rearranged the whole familial landscape. Enrique lost his wife. Stella and Tisha lost their mother. Tisha had no memory of her, but Stella knew her well. The loss was wrenching for her.

Enrique's outlook was similar to Stella's. He lost his beautiful wife, and he'd never really been able to process it. His pain lived down deep, locked up inside him. It was known to surface twice a year, once at Christmas, and once again around early spring during the anniversary of the birth and death. Those were the times of the year when Enrique walked closest to the quicksand of his misery. Elena knew enough to tread lightly during these times. She looked into a mirror and gently touched a pimple that had sprouted on her chin.

"I got my period this morning too."

"Jeez Laynie, it's all coming down on you," she spoke as she ran a brush through her sister's hair.

"My insides ache."

In a short time, the three sisters were out the door headed to work. As they walked, Elena began to speak her mind, and as she did her eyes teared.

"I thought about it last night, I figured that Patrick just doesn't find me attractive."

"Oh Elena, you're a perfectly fine-looking girl," spoke Stella curtly.

"Not perfectly fine like you," moaned Elena.

"Yeah, but nobody's beautiful like Stella," opined Tisha.

"Yeah? And a hell of a lot that gets me! All the men I'm interested in are either intimidated by me or prefer that I be unattainable. Then you've got the rest of the idiot men in the world, who can't walk by me in the street without taking a shot. Fuck them all. Every last one of them!"

Stella's declaration brought silence to their walk, until they turned the corner on Hampshire, and came within a stone's throw of Sonny's Place.

"Oh man, I just don't want to see Patrick today."

"See him right now, and put it behind you," admonished Tisha.

Elena took her advice to heart, summoning up the determination to look last night's disappointment in the eye.

Feeling her arrival, a rumble of tension rose in Patrick Phelan's stomach, Soon the swinging doors of the kitchen opened up and in came the sisters. Patrick caught cool looks from Stella and Tisha. Elena didn't acknowledge him. She hung up her jacket, punched in, and went about her side work.

As Patrick cut up bacon for the carbonaras, he realized that she had no intention of looking his way. He approached her as she stood by the coffee machine, stacking filters full of ground beans.

"Elena, could we talk for a minute?"

"I'm busy right now, Patrick."

"Elena, please."

Elena turned toward him, and he felt her stern gaze. She gave him a silent nod to follow her as she headed to the back porch for a moment of privacy. Patrick walked behind her, nervously, not knowing what to expect.

"What's on your mind, Patrick?"

Patrick stammered and stuttered, searching for the lost doorway into this conversation. He couldn't find it and stood mute.

"I saw you two leave here last night. She led you out by the hand. She was beautiful."

Patrick winced and looked away. She put her warm hand on his shoulder, and their eyes met.

"Patrick, I don't think it will come as a surprise to you that I've developed some feelings for you over the last month. But now it's obvious that I was wrong to think you might feel the same way."

"But Elena,"

"Listen to me Patrick. I'm talking now," she firmly established. "I thought we were destined for a romance. I even had a dream about it a few weeks ago."

"You had a dream?"

"Yes, I had a dream. You and I were together, and we were happy. Then last night I saw you waltz out of here with that blonde. I sat up most of the night wondering why I would dream such a thing."

"Elena, I'm sorry."

"Don't sorry me, Patrick. I'm hurt and upset right now, and if we're going to be working together, I'm going to need to keep my distance from you. So don't go expecting me to be the same old Elena Madeira around you."

She turned and walked away. As the screen door slammed behind her, Patrick sat down on a milk crate trying to sort out what just happened. Then he heard Frankie's voice scream from inside.

"Patrick, get your ass in here. We're gettin' hit!"

The dining room had filled up right from the get-go. Patrick bolted back into the kitchen to see Frankie sorting through a fistful of dupes. Then he started barking out orders.

"They're drivin' us to Newark!" proclaimed Freddie DiSavio.

"Bend over and take it like a man!" Frankie advised.

22: HARVEY APPEARS

Sonny and Moe sipped on their beverages and waited on a call from Harvey Wallenberg. The telephone's shrill ring broke the quiet. Sonny took a quick look at his watch.

"Moe, that's the Jew bastard now. Why don't you jump right on him?"

Moe picked up the phone and leaned back into his recliner. "Sonny's Place, Moe Venti speaking."

"Hello Mr. Venti, this is Harvey Wallenberg. I believe you're expecting my call."

"As a matter of fact, Mr. Wallenberg, word has it that you're the new self-proclaimed savior of the poor oppressed Blues musicians of the world. Do you ever worry that you might be pushing them right out of the market?"

"No, I don't fear that, Mr. Venti. In fact, I'm very much in touch with their value in today's market."

"Ah, I see, and you're more in touch with these things than the booker in New York?"

"Mr. Venti, the booker in New York is nothing more than a self-serving pimp. Besides, in terms of the Blues, the booker is out of the picture now. You have to deal with me directly."

"Yeah? Well, I spoke to the booker an hour ago, and he assured me that he'd have a Blues band here, ready to go any time I wanted."

"Look Moe, he's offering you a white Blues band because all of the black musicians are now in our stable, if you catch my drift."

"No, you look Harvey. We aren't running an Afro American relief foundation here. We're running a fucken business. You got that?"

"Moe, if you think you can make the same dough with young white boys on your stage, then you know nothing about the business of the Blues. You best get your kitchen cranked up. You're gonna have to sell a hell of a lot more spaghetti to make up for that loss."

"Look Wallenberg, if you're stupid enough to play hard ball with us, why don't you come visit us in person so we can see what you look like?"

"Gladly, I'll be there at 8 o'clock."

"Can't wait!" announced Moe as he hung up the phone. "Sonny, give the Lugg Brothers a call. Tell them we need their presence a bit early tonight."

"Good idea, Moe!"

Directly overhead, the floorboards creaked with the activity of a full house. In the middle of the madness an idea descended into Miguel's head as if on angel's wings. He turned toward Rue and shared.

"Hey man, I know this Japanese guy from the neighborhood, who comes in here. He's an electronics freak from M.I.T. I bet he could install a hidden recording device in here, and we could do some serious reel to reel without anybody knowing."

The thought of that stopped Rue in his tracks. "Miguel, that's a fabulous idea! Just as long as we got music worth listening to around here."

"You got a bad feelin' about all this?"

"I don't know man. It's just that I know the music doesn't mean anything to them. If this new deal hurts the cash flow, they're bound to do the wrong thing."

The kitchen had completed the first turn of the evening, and the dining room filled right back up again. Frankie had barely caught his breath when he clutched a thick, new satchel of dupes in his warm hands. It was destined to be one of those nights—a veritable rock fight.

"We're nothing but whores!" he howled. Do it as long as you can, as fast as you can, and pretend you're enjoying it!"

"Move, move, move," Patrick Phelan pleaded with himself, trying to keep pace with the night. But he felt like he was standing knee deep in mud. The exchange with Elena had shaken his focus. His movements were inefficient and out of sync. Soon his dishes weren't coming up on time. Frankie was calling for orders two and three times, until he lost it and snapped.

"Phelan, if this is what getting laid does for you, maybe you should think about becoming a fucken priest!"

Stella Madeira, waiting impatiently for her food, let out a sarcastic laugh aimed like a poisonous dart at the beleaguered pasta cook. Patrick was sinking deeply into the weeds, as he entertained the thought that he'd made a bad career choice. An oil rig in the Gulf of Mexico sounded pretty good right now.

The chaos of the night raged on, until the screen door opened up, and to everyone's surprise in walked Alabama Al McGuirk. He was dressed in mahogany brown, his white cowboy hat rested stately on his head. Accompanying him was the fellow who had shared a booth with Big Mama Thornton the previous night, swamp fox hat on his head, a briefcase in his hands.

"Howdy boys," bellowed the Bluesman. "I hope y'all don't mind us comin' through the back door?" He stopped at the dish machine and looked at the pale white boy with the ponytail, scrubbing pots.

"You the Turk?" he inquired.

"Yes sir."

"Hey man, I bin' hearin' 'bout you out on the chitlin circuit. Folks be sayin' that dishwasher at Sonny's Place is a motherfucker harp player."

He reached out and they shook.

"Thanks Al," smiled the Turk. He was knee deep in slop and dirty dishes, and on such a hard night it was comforting for him to hear that his musical reputation was growing.

Alabama Al bid everyone adieu and led his companion through the swinging doors and out to the front of the house. Rue was surprised to see him, and he waved them down the bar to two empty stools.

"It's nice to see you, Al, but do you have your dates mixed up? We got Hound Dog Taylor and the House Rockers here through the weekend."

"Hey Rue, don't you know I'm a Hound Dog Taylor freak?" Then motioning to his left, he introduced his friend. "Rue, I'd like you to meet Harvey Wallenberg."

"Ahaaa!" spoke Rue shaking, hands. "Now I'm getting the picture."

Alabama Al's big cow eyes got gently serious. "Rue, have y'all been briefed on our visit?"

"Well Al, I didn't know that you were involved in the negotiations. And I don't think the two meatheads downstairs know either."

"Yeah? Well, they be findin' out real soon."

Just then the front door opened and in walked the Lugg Brothers, sporting two freshly wiffled craniums. They lumbered on up to the service bar. "Lugg Bothers, you guys look spectacular," exclaimed Miguel. Rue, don't the Luggs look like they're ready for Hollywood?"

The Lugg Brothers half smiled back. They were flattered, but suspicious. Rue was noncommittal. "We'll have two Gallianos on the rocks," they sang in unison. Miguel iced down a couple of rock glasses and poured three fingers each out of the piss yellow bottle with the giraffe neck.

"Sweets for the sweet," he proclaimed plunking down a couple of stirrers into their drinks.

The Luggs surveyed the room as they sipped their Italian mountain dews. Then they gave each other a wink and a nod, as they headed down the back stairs to Sonny's office. Moe Venti looked up at them and smiled as if they were prime rib.

"Hey, you guys look super!"

"Thanks boss," they blushed.

The Luggs always directed their attention toward Moe, rarely acknowledging Sonny. It was their way of tormenting him. They enjoyed letting him know to whom they truly answered. They'd been on Moe Venti's payroll for some time now. Their menacing bar presence had been known to meet tit for tat, on sidewalks or back alleys, where rearranged noses and broken limbs filled their portfolio. Moe didn't waste a second in giving them the overall scheme.

"No rough stuff yet boys, but when this Jew lawyer comes in here, I want you to give him the look of the fucking way far gone."

The Luggs smiled and ground their teeth in readiness. They knew that if mayhem ensued, there'd be some extra green in the next envelope. Moe was always good about dishing out the sugar after a bloodletting. The four of them sipped their drinks and lay in wait for one Harvey Wallenberg.

"Are those Luggs down there waiting for us?" queried Alabama Al from directly overhead.

"Absolutely."

"Yeah? Well, they gonna be real sorry if they fuck with me. They don't know my rage. See Harvey! I told you they'd bury you in the cellar if you came here alone!"

"So, Al, who are you in this scenario?" prodded Rue. "The Blues Player Representative?"

"Yeah man, that's exactly what I am! Harvey here is our lawyer. We met back in Chicago, years ago. Harvey be goin' to Law School at the time, but he be spendin' all his time in the juke joints instead of the library. I educated him on how bad the Blues musicians bin' gettin' fucked over through the years. We always talked 'bout doin' somethin'. And now we be here to even the score. We ain't movin' from this town 'til we get what we come for."

"Why don't we get together later on after Hound Dog's Show, and you can clue me in to what's gonna happen. You guys know I'm in your corner. I'll do anything I can to help."

"Thanks, Rue. We appreciate that," offered Harvey. Rue got on the intercom.

"Sonny, Harvey Wallenberg here to see you."

"Send him down!" barked Sonny.

"OK boys, you can start frothing!" announced Moe Venti. The Luggs needed little provocation to attain that state.

Alabama Al gave a firm knock to the office door and entered with Harvey right behind him. The Luggs rose in unison looking generally jumpy, panting flecks of saliva in their direction.

"Don't you Luggs dare breathe on me," bellowed Alabama, "or you be pickin' up your teeth with a broken arm!"

"McGuirk? What are you doin' here?" asked a confused Sonny.

"Well, howdy, Mr. Sonny. I'm here as the Blues Player Representative, and this here is our attorney, Harvey Wallenberg."

Harvey kept his swamp fox hat on as he stepped forward extending a hand in Sonny's direction, but his eyes told Harvey not to bother. Moe stared back at the two. Then he spoke.

"Gentlemen, for the past two months my business partner and I have put our capital investments on the line to open up a Blues venue here in Cambridge, where previously none had existed. Is this the way you show us respect and consideration?"

"Mr. Venti, these musicians show their respect and consideration every night by filling up all those empty seats you had when you purchased the Sportsman's Tap."

"Damn right!" echoed Alabama Al.

"And if you care to open up your books to us, I think we'll both see how disparate the financial rewards are between you and my clients."

"I have no intention of opening up our books to you."

"Mr. Venti, these musicians are disgracefully paid in comparison to the money they generate."

"You're damn right!" shouted Alabama.

"I'm not paying these musicians a dime more than I paid yesterday," asserted Moe.

"Alright Mr. Venti, we figured you might go this route. I've warned you that we will be striking and picketing this establishment until our demands are met."

Moe burst out laughing at them as if they were a couple of fools. Sonny and the Luggs joined right in. Their laughter triggered a rage, which erupted from the pit of Alabama Al's gut. He leapt to his feet, pointed a big black finger at the four of them and shouted, "Y'all better be ready for a tango, cuz we be comin' after you! There be a debt that's owed here. Bin' owed for a long, long time. And we be here to pick it up!"

"You're unemployed, McGuirk!" said Sonny.

Harvey had all he could do to wrestle him out the office door and up the stairs.

"Al, we have to get on to Plan B. This is going to be a rocky road at best. You have to control your emotions."

Controlling one's emotions was the antithesis of the Blues. Yet somehow, he knew that he had to heed that advice. "You're right, Harvey. I know you're right."

They walked up the back staircase, arms around each other, united in purpose. Once at the top they stopped for a moment to see the one and only Hound Dog Taylor getting ready to take the stage. It was a perfect visual reminder of their mission. They wandered back to the bar and plunked themselves down on the stools that they'd left.

"How did the powwow go?" inquired Rue.

"Mr. Sonny says I'm unemployed," spoke Alabama.

"So, what's next?"

"I have to presume they're going white," assessed Harvey.

Rue could only shake his head in disgust. He iced down a boozy blend, strained four glasses full and called Miguel down to his end of the bar.

"So, what's the story?" asked Miguel.

"Looks like we're goin' white," responded Rue.

"Don't give up hope," pleaded Harvey. "We still have a serious hand to play out."

They chinged their glasses and toasted to the power of the Blues. But the two dispensers of the spirits couldn't hide their disappointment.

"I feel like I'm looking at the two saddest bartenders on the planet," said Harvey. "Don't feel so bad. We've just begun this fight. If Spiro Agnew can go down, so can Moe Venti and Sonny Bolla."

They all smiled at the logic of that. They kept on smiling as Hound Dog Taylor plugged in his scratchy, squealing slide guitar. The HouseRockers got behind him, and once again that sound began to fill up the room and everybody remembered why they had come.

Back in the kitchen, the crew was well into their nightly cleanup. The onslaught of the evening's dinner rush left them worn out and drained. Frankie turned to Patrick and motioned him to the back porch. Patrick followed him out, fearing the worst. Frankie pulled out some herb and they smoked down a little in silence. They breathed in the cool fall air and calmed themselves into recovery mode.

"Patrick, do you know what hell is like?" asked Frankie Pope.

Patrick shrugged and looked down at his feet.

"It's where we were for the last three hours," assessed Frankie.

"That sounds about right." Patrick agreed.

"What happened to you? You were three steps behind us all night."

"I know, Frankie. I'm sorry."

"Did it have something to do with you and Elena?"

"Yeah."

"Something to do with you scoring that blonde last night?"

"Yeah."

"But you and Elena haven't had anything going on, have you?"

"Well, no, not exactly."

"Then what the hell is the problem?"

Patrick Phelan couldn't explain.

"Look man, this cooking life ain't no day at the beach" said Frankie. "You have to learn to keep your focus no matter what, or you'll get buried for sure. And if you go down, you take everyone down with you. Got it?"

"I know, Frankie. I'm sorry."

"You gotta leave your troubles out in the street. You can't bring them in here, or we all suffer. Understand?"

"Yeah Frankie, I do. It won't happen again."

"OK. Let's get changed and have a cold one."

A handshake put it behind them. They were stapled at the hip night after night. This had been their first bump in the road. The two cooks changed into their street clothes, headed through the swinging doors and out to the bar. Miguel served them up a couple of cold beers, and soon their trying night became a memory.

"Have you guys heard the word?" asked Miguel.

"Word about what?" Frankie wanted to know.

"The Black Blues musicians are striking after tonight. They're bringin' in only white bands starting tomorrow."

"You gotta be shittin' me."

"Nope. After Hound Dog tonight, the Blues are gonna be white as snow."

"Fine by me," chimed in one of the Luggs, who had bellied up to the service bar for a refill. "The white boys play better anyway."

The insanity of that remark sent Frankie off his stool, and into a coughing spree. It took him a moment to gather himself. Patrick flagged down Rue for more details.

"I'm getting together with Alabama Al and his lawyer when we close tonight. Then I'll have a better idea of what's to come down. They're gonna fight it, but what chance they have, I can't say."

"A Blues club with only white musicians? How could this be happening?" implored Frankie.

"Just remember who's place it is" reminded Rue. "It's Sonny's Place. That tells you all you need to know."

It didn't take long for the word to spread from table to table throughout the club. Shock and disbelief were the prevailing emotions. It made no sense to anyone. When word reached the ears of the heartsick Elena Madeira, her sadness turned to anger. Her first instinct was to find Patrick and talk to him about it. But then she remembered she wasn't talking to him anymore. She found Rue at the service bar and pleaded for an explanation.

"It's just money, honey" he told her as he ruffled a twenty between his fingers.

"Is there something we can do?"

"I'll know more tonight," he promised her.

Outrage continued to spread throughout the house, and as Hound Dog Taylor took to the stage for his second set, the crowd rose to its feet for a standing ovation. His face beamed at the reception, and he held out his arms in an open embrace like a Baptist minister in front of his flock. He wasted no time in bringing the Turk on stage to join the band. Then he cranked up his slide guitar, and in no time the whole joint was jumping.

Down in their bunker, Sonny and Moe were toasting each other on a job well done. "Moe, you really put it to those two!"

"Yeah, well a hymie and a sambo aren't gonna be taking down a couple of paisans."

"No fucken way," Sonny cackled greedily. "But Moe, what are we gonna do if they start some trouble tomorrow night?"

"We'll have the Luggs dust them off."

"Yeah Moe, but that McGuirk is one big fucken hombre!"

"Sonny, why do you think we got two Lugg Brothers?"

"Moe, you got everything figured out."

"Let's get out of here and go somewhere for a pop."

They got their coats on, headed up the stairs, and out the front door, where Moe's silver Cadillac was parked. They hopped in, hooked a left onto Cambridge Street, and headed up around the Cambridge Common, pulling over across from the Sheraton Commander. They headed into Dertad's, the cozy hotel bar. Looking around for a comfortable nook, Moe's eyes fell upon an Egyptian style tent that took up a small corner of the room. They ducked inside and rested their bones down on some cushy velvet pillows. Drinks were soon delivered, and they kicked back, posturing like a couple of sultans.

"Hey Moe, where's the broad that peels the grapes?"

They thoroughly indulged themselves in spite of the fact that real trouble was brewing in Paradise.

23: FORTUNE COOKIES

Hound Dog Taylor and The House Rockers, with the Turk in tow, had finished their night's work, setting the room ablaze with their special brand of the Blues. By 2:15 the Lugg Brothers had emptied the room of howling satiated Blues fans. Miguel wiped down the bar and poured the Luggs closing cordials. Rue counted the night's receipts and deposited them downstairs in the safe.

There was, once again, a deafening silence about the room at closing time. The fury of the night's music had built and built, then there was nothing. The final four finished their drinks, turned out the lights, locked up the shop, and left the strange quiet of Sonny's Place behind them.

Rue and Miguel said good night to the Luggs and hung out on the sidewalk to decompress for a few minutes. They watched the two tough guys waddle down Hampshire Street and disappear into the night. Soon they felt reasonably replenished by fresh air and the clear October sky. They headed on into the Tortoise Café, which was typically jammed with buzz and chatter.

Ted caught Rue's eye and waved him over to the counter.

"I can't believe what that prick Sonny is doing!"

"Believe it Ted. It's happening."

"I just talked to Alabama Al and his lawyer friend and told 'em they could run the strike right out of here if they want."

"That's awful nice of you Ted. Just keep an eye out for those Lugg Brothers. If they picket and strike, I know enough about Moe Venti to promise that he'll play rough."

"Yeah, well the real Blues might be the only thing left worth fighting for."

"I hear you brother. Just watch your backside."

Rue spotted Alabama and Harvey at a booth. They wandered down to join them.

"How's it goin' boys?"

"Good, Rue," began Alabama. "Mr. Ted here just offered us the room to run the strike out of, and we talked to a lot of folks that came out of the bar tonight. Damn well feels like we got plenty of support."

"Yeah, I'll tell you what," said Rue. "The word spread quickly tonight, and the people were genuinely outraged. It was something to feel good about."

"It was an excellent start for us," said Harvey.

Rue felt a bit claustrophobic in the tight confines of the diner. He suggested that they cross the river into Boston and grab a bite in Chinatown. They all agreed and as they got up to go, Alabama Al let loose with a shrill whistle.

"Listen up y'all! The picket line and strike of Sonny's Place will commence at high noon tomorrow. We need the support of everybody here. So please come down and git behind us! See y'all tomorrow!"

The contingent in the Tortoise howled, whistled, and stomped their confirmation. The four of them headed out to the street and climbed into Harvey's Electra. They drove south on Hampshire Street and over the Salt and Pepper Bridge. The Boston city skyline stretched out like a long twinkling arm up the banks of the Charles River.

They stopped at a red light on the Boston side of the bridge and Alabama looked across the way at a sign that read "Buzzy's Fabulous Roast Beef". Beyond it was a cascading wall, topped with a huge swath of barbed wire.

"That the stir?" he asked

"The glorious Charles Street Jail," confirmed Rue.

Alabama shook his head and sighed, "Man, the smell of that greasy food must drive the fellas mad."

The light turned green, and Harvey hooked around the jail onto Storrow Drive, and up onto the expressway headed south. They pulled off at the Chinatown exit, and maneuvered on over to their destination, Moon Villa.

Over wonton soup, Alabama retold the story of how he and Harvey had met some years earlier in a Chicago Blues club. Harvey was just your basic Blues fanatic, going to law school in the windy city. His passion for the music drove him beyond the role of spectator. He felt compelled to give something back to the musicians that inspired him.

Late night chats with the Blues greats clued Harvey into the rough and tumble milieu of the Blues, a world where record executives and promoters manipulate the artists, pitting them against each other to ensure maximum financial gain. Naïve, sometimes illiterate musicians signed legal contracts that would bring them a mere pittance of the money they generated, leaving them a life of action on the open road as itinerant troubadours. It was a life for some that would lead to bitterness, not to mention a dependency on drug and drink. Nights spent on stage gave way to sleep in a cheap motel room, followed by a day of travel on the road—an endless stream of one-night stands.

"It's like being on a merry-go-round that don't stop," explained Alabama. "Now boys, I'm a Bluesman, and I swear I got nothing against the merry-go-round. I kinda dig it. Ya know? But me and Harvey wanna get inside the control booth and make the ride a little sweeter for us all. So this is where we make our stand. We be goin' from town to town 'til we put an end to this shit!"

Alabama's eyes looked glassy and violent. Rue couldn't help but notice. Having made his point, he picked up his huge frame and headed for the men's room. Harvey took that moment to explain something.

"Guys, there's something you need to know about Al McGuirk. The very night he opened up Sonny's Place in August, his house in Montgomery burnt to the ground. Al lost his wife and two daughters in the blaze."

That news left a chilly silence at the table. Rue and Miguel could only look at each other. "I think it's best not to bring it up," continued Harvey, "but I think it's important for you to know. He was close to cashing in his chips after it happened. He felt completely responsible because he wasn't home. He's carrying around a truckload of anger and guilt, and he's latched on to this mission with a vengeance. I think it's the only thing that's keeping him going right now."

The Bluesman returned to the table. A spider web of quiet unease hung in the air. The silence broke when a waiter arrived with more food. They got busy eating, and that filled in the empty space.

"One thing that's important," began Harvey, "is that you and your co-workers not get involved with this strike. We don't want anyone losing their jobs over this, no matter how strongly they feel. The people on the picket line won't be harassing them."

"I'll make sure everyone understands," spoke Rue.

Soon their plates were empty. Their waiter cleared the table and returned with the check and four fortune cookies. Alabama Al reached over, grabbed one in his huge hands, cracked it open, and munched down the sweet. Then he smiled as he read his fortune aloud.

"Stand by your beliefs, and never give an inch!"

24: THE ICE CREAM DATE

Patrick Phelan was waking up to the roar of Mildred's vacuum cleaner outside his bedroom in the hallway. The wheels of her Fuller squealed as she dragged the machine from one end of the house to the other, being vigilant not to miss a square inch of rug

He lay in bed for another five minutes to celebrate his day off. Dinner with Liza Jane was his only commitment. Thinking of her made him think of Elena. They seemed to be flip sides of the same coin. He shook off that complexity when he realized he'd be spending the night with Liza and had to come up with a good excuse for his mother.

He pulled his shorts on and wandered out to the kitchen. His parched throat yearned for a glass of juice. He drank that down, and as he poured a refill, Mildred descended upon him. She turned off the vacuum, lit up a smoke, and began to put the lean on her one and only.

"Are your pipes a little dry, son?"

Patrick didn't speak and pretended not to hear.

"I say, are you a little parched son? You do know, I know what that means?"

"Ma, would you please back off?"

"Patrick, are you drinking too much? Do you drink every night? You do, don't you? You know there's never been a man in this family who could handle the booze?"

Patrick thought about reaching below the sink and waving that bottle in her face, but he didn't want to deal with the repercussions of such an act. He looked out into the living room at Jim. He was in his Lazy Boy, stretched out in a deep zombie sleep. A clickety-clackety rattle churned from the back of his throat.

"There he is," declared Mildred, "from one end of the day to the other: boob tube blaring. If I turn it off, he wakes up and tells me he was watching it," she grumbled in frustration.

Patrick poured himself a cup of coffee and retreated to his room. Not more than a few minutes passed before he heard a quiet knock on the door.

"Could I talk to you for a minute?" requested Mildred in a solemn tone.

"Come in Ma. What's goin' on?"

Mildred was still in her bathrobe. She sat down on the bed next to Patrick, turning to meet his eyes. "Son, he's driving me crazy, and I think to an early grave." Her brown eyes were pained and defeated.

"I'm sorry Ma. What can I do?"

"There's nothing that anyone can do."

They shared a silent moment digesting that fact.

"And you know I don't mean to complain."

"I know Ma."

"It's just that sometimes I feel like we're walking down a long tunnel, and things are just getting darker."

She began to sob, and Patrick put his arm around her. "It's alright Ma. It's alright," he whispered to her. Mildred let herself cry in her son's arms for a minute. Then she stopped to dry her eyes with a Kleenex she carried.

"Sometimes it gets to be too much," she confessed.

"I know Ma. I know. Say why don't we sneak out of here for a while? I'll take you into the square for a hot fudge sundae at Bailey's. What do you say?"

Through her crying eyes, Mildred smiled a little girl's smile that told Patrick it was a good idea. They could leave Jim for a little while and get out. He showered, dressed, and within an hour they were heading for the door.

"Jim, we're going into town for a little while," Mildred announced. Jim opened his eyes for a moment and gave them a trembling nod that sent them on their way.

"What car are we taking?" inquired Mildred.

"Ma, I asked you out for an ice cream, didn't I?"

"Yeah."

"Then we're goin' in the Dart."

"In that thing?"

"Yeah, in that thing."

Patrick walked over to the passenger door and opened it up for Mildred. Mother and son hopped in and drove down to Harvard Square. They parked in front of the old Brattle Theatre and crossed the street to Bailey's for a treat.

"Thanks for bringing me down here, son," said Mildred. A good cry, and the prospects of an ice cream date with her son seemed to lighten her mood.

"My pleasure Milly. Besides, what is there about life that a little ice cream can't cure? Right?"

"Right."

They stood in line at the soda fountain, waiting for their turn to order. Mildred eyed the long glass case of chocolates. She definitely had a thing for the sweets. Their turn finally came and the old timer with the funny paper hat gave Patrick the nod.

"One hot fudge sundae, no whipped cream, but with extra nuts, and a coffee frappe for here."

The frappe hummed away on the old pale green Hamilton Beach blender, and the old timer dug deep for the sundae. Patrick forked over five dollars and waited for his change. Mildred looked into her sundae and inquired with a disappointed tone, "Say mister, what's the matter? Don't you have any nuts?"

The old timer blushed with embarrassment, and as soon as Mildred realized what she'd said, she turned to her son and burst into uncontrollable laughter. Everybody's face turned red as they watched the nuts get shoveled into the sundae. They took their treats over to the tiny round tables with the uncomfortable coat hanger chairs. By now Mildred was lost in a full-scale belly laugh. She wasn't making much noise, but she was writhing out of control. Patrick soon caught the contagion and couldn't keep a straight face.

"Mildred, you're awful!"

"Oh stop! Stop or I'm gonna pee my pants!" she feared, still in a rip roar.

"Mildred, if you pee your pants, you're walking home!"

Mildred took a deep breath and tried to pull it together. The fear of losing her bladder in public was the appropriate motivation she needed to stop laughing.

"The lovely Mrs. Phelan," taunted Patrick.

"Stop it!" she demanded as she tried to maintain control. Soon they fully focused on the ice cream, and occasionally made giggling eye contact.

"Well, that was good. Thank you, son," she spoke as she pulled a cigarette from her bag and lit it up.

"Ma, can't you wait till I'm done?"

"Oh balls!" she growled as she stomped out her smoke. She impatiently flossed her teeth with the edge of her match box till Patrick finished his frappe.

"OK Ma, I'm done. You can start pounding those nails in your coffin, now."

Mildred gave him a cold discerning look as she relit her cigarette. Then she redirected the conversation. "Son, tell me about being a cook. Are you enjoying it?"

"Yeah Ma, I am. It's no day at the beach. It's a lot of work, but maybe for the first time, I feel like I'm doing something real."

Mildred seemed to hear that, nodding silently. "Well, I still think you should be getting a college education. I don't understand you turning your back on that opportunity."

"Ma, you don't know how much bullshit college is."

"Son, don't ever belittle an education. It's a dog-eat-dog world out there, and a diploma will open doors for you. But if you don't want to go to college, what about a top-notch culinary school?"

"Ma, I don't feel like I need to go to school to learn how to do this stuff. I'm learning now and getting paid for it. Guillermo, the chef at Sonny's Place never went to school. He's been working in kitchens since he was a kid. Frankie Pope, the guy I work under never went to school either. They learned to cook in kitchens while they got paid."

"I'll bet the chefs with degrees get paid more."

"I don't know Ma. I really don't know about that."

"Well son, I want you to think about it. You know we don't have a lot of money. Your Father had the last twenty years of his working life taken away from him. But if you want to go to a crackerjack culinary school, I'll come up with that money, by hook or by crook."

"I know you would Ma. I appreciate it. But at the moment I feel like I'm in the right place."

"Patrick, I'm only asking you to consider it."

"OK Ma. I will."

They left Bailey's and wandered back out to Brattle Street. There was a thoughtful quiet in the Dart on the ride home.

Mildred spoke as she stepped out of the car in front of the apartment, "Son, I just want you to have the opportunities I never had."

"I know that Ma. By the way I'm not coming home tonight."

"What do you mean you aren't coming home?"

"I'm not coming home tonight so don't worry about me."

"Where are you going to be?"

"A friend of mine is roasting a pig overnight in his back yard, and I want to learn how to do it."

"Roasting a pig?"

"Yeah. I love you, Mildred. I'll see you tomorrow," he yelled out the window as he pulled away.

"A whole pig?" she petitioned in a tone of disbelief.

25: SONNY'S PICKET LINE BLUES

Down at the Tortoise Café, the clock read high noon. A solid consensus of Blues fanatics had congregated a bit bleary eyed amongst Harvey and Alabama Al. There was a definite tension in the air. Off in the corner a couple of protesters were finishing up their picket signs. Everyone seemed ready to hit the street. Alabama let loose with a whistle that got everyone's attention. Harvey Wallenberg stood up to review the rules of the game one more time.

"First, I want to thank everyone for coming down today to start off this strike. We've got a great turnout and we'll be grabbing their attention right away. Remember violence is a no-no. We have to be orderly and calm, but that doesn't mean we can't be vocal. Today the picket line will run for twelve hours from noon 'til midnight. I know a lot more people will be joining us in the late afternoon, when they get out of work. So, let's keep the pressure on them!"

Shouts and hollers from the strikers filled the room as Harvey and Alabama led everyone out onto Hampshire Street to begin their strike. A procession of picket signs and chants filled the sidewalk out in front of Sonny's Place.

"HEY HO, HEY HO, THE BLUES WON'T GO, THEY JUST WON'T GO"

Patrick Phelan parked his car on Antrim Street and as he turned the corner in front of the fire station, he could hear the strikers' call. He crossed the street and headed over to his place of employment. The crowd was edgy. He felt uncomfortable about heading in to pick up his check. Stopping for a moment, his heart told him to join the march. Alabama Al read his uncertain posture and left the line to speak with him.

SEAN MICHAEL DANEHY

"Good afternoon, chef," bellowed the Bluesman, extending his hand for a shake. Patrick felt his hand disappear in Alabama's.

"Christ Al, you guys really got things going here."

"Yeah, we sure do chef."

"Al, I feel caught in a bind here."

"How so?"

"I feel like I should be picketing with you."

"Don't even think about it, chef. We don't want none of Mr. Sonny's workers involved in this. It's not necessary you riskin' your job over this. We be fine without you."

"Alright Al, thanks for taking me off the hook. I'm with you all the way, and I hope you put it to 'em."

Alabama Al rejoined the picket line, and Patrick headed for the front door of Sonny's Place, and he was met with a chorus of boos. "He's alright," shouted Alabama. "He's one of the cooks."

Patrick walked through the front door of Sonny's Place to find Diamond Lil standing idly at her bar. In front of her, twenty empty stools. Behind her, an empty tip jar. The look of disgust on her face told the story. She'd gotten all painted up for nothing.

"Lil, does Sonny know what's going on outside?"

"He's downstairs. If you're going down there, give him the word."

He didn't savor this opportunity, but he needed his check, so he descended the stairs and gave the office door a knock. "It's open," growled Sonny. Patrick entered, and ambled up to the desk, where Sonny was knee deep in paperwork. He glanced up briefly to see who it was, then he brought his eyes back down to the numbers.

"Whadya want, Irish?"

"I'm here for my paycheck, boss."

"Oh, you are, are you?"

"Yeah, I just can't seem to get by without those greenbacks."

Sonny went into his drawer and flipped through the stack till he came to Patrick Phelan's check, and handed it over. "Sonny, I guess you should know that there's a bunch of people with picket signs marching up and down in front of the house."

"What the fuck?"

He slammed down the pen, raced out the office door and up the stairs. Lurching open the front door, he stormed out to the sidewalk. The strikers came to a halt, showering him with boos and hisses. Sonny was caught off guard. After looking back and forth from the picket signs, to Harvey, to Alabama, he made a hasty retreat back into the bar. The picket line erupted into a thick chorus of hoots and hollers.

"Did ya see the look on his face?" bellowed Alabama as he let out a wild cackle.

Back inside, Sonny got on the bar phone, calling his partner in crime.

"Moe, it's me. We got trouble here. The Jew, McGuirk, and about fifty of our fucken patrons are marching up and down in front of our place, carrying picket signs, screamin' and hollerin'!"

"I'm on my way over. Give the Lugg Brothers a call and tell 'em to get their asses right in there!"

"I'm on it Moe!"

The arrival of noontime brought the regular lunch crowd drifting down Hampshire Street. with intentions of dining Italian. What they came upon was an angry, vocal picket line. They would stand and watch the commotion for a few moments, then head off to dine elsewhere.

After one inning the score was Blues Strikers 1, Sonny's Place nothing!

The tension level drew Sonny to the bar. He flagged down Diamond Lil and ordered up a Bloody Mary. He stirred up the drink and took a nervous chomp out of his celery stick. The chanting of the picket line seeped through the wall, providing background music.

"HEY HO THE BLUES WON'T GO. NO, NO, THEY JUST WON'T GO"

Patrick couldn't resist the intrigue of all this. He had no place to go, so he pulled up a stool and ordered a beer. Sonny looked over and noticed he had company.

"Ya know somethin', Irish? We came out of nowhere, opened up a Home of the Blues, and this is what they do to us. We should make 'em all swim back to Africa, with a Jew under each arm!" he added for punctuation.

Diamond Lil wasn't concerned with the politics of the matter. All she knew was that she had only two customers at her bar. One of whom didn't tip.

"Sonny, why don't you call the police and get them off the street," she suggested.

"Moe's on his way over. We'll wait till he gets here."

"Oh, I forgot. We don't do anything around here without Moe Venti's approval."

"Just have your bar ready for business, honey. And leave the thinking to us," barked Sonny. He pointed to his glass for a refill. "You ready, Irish?" he asked, pointing to his beer. He was only halfway done but had no intentions of passing on a freebie from the boss. "And another bud for the mick."

Lil cracked a beer, poured a Mary, and headed to the ladies' room. They watched her backside sashay off to the horizon. It didn't cost anything to look.

"You like?" Patrick inquired.

Sonny took another belt of his Mary and licked the residue off his pencil thin mustache. "Yeah, not bad at all, Irish. I plan on putting the boots to her real soon. And if the bitch doesn't show some respect, it could turn out to be a real grudge fuck."

"What's a grudge fuck?

"A grudge fuck? Well Irish, that's when you got a woman in bed that you'd just as soon strangle. You give her a real good goin' over. Then you toss a ten spot on the bed and thank her for everything."

Patrick wasn't sure how to respond. The combination of potency and loathing confused him. Nevertheless, talking about sex was suddenly far more entertaining since he'd become a full-fledged member of the club. It made him feel much more a part of the world.

Just then the Turk came up behind the bar to pour himself a ginger ale. The bathrooms were spic and span. The floors swept and mopped. His morning duties were complete. He leaned on the bar for a moment, listening to the ceaseless chanting of the picket line as it warbled through the blurry glass block by the front door. "Well, if the black players get shipped out there won't be any reason for me to hang around. Duane Allman's dead, and there ain't another white boy around here that can show me anything about the Blues that I don't already know."

"Look Turk, your heroes are finished here, and if you wanna leave with 'em, the door's right over there."

"I think I'll hang around and see what happens, Sonny. Besides they seem to be winning so far. It's 12:15, and where's your lunch crowd?"

Sonny fumed in silence until his rage was interrupted by Moe Venti's entrance through the front door. Boos and hisses bombarded him from the picket line. He looked fit to be tied.

"Moe, what's the story?"

"I called Milligan down at Police Headquarters. He told me they filed their papers. They've got a legal picket line going on out there."

"There's nothing we can do?"

"Nothing lawful. Did you call the Lugg Brothers?"

"They're on their way."

Moe turned around to see an empty dining room. The lonely moose head on the wall stared back at him with concern. "Nobody's crossing the line to come in and eat?" he inquired about the obvious. He bit his lip, walked out into the dining room, and kicked over a few chairs.

"Calm down Moe," pleaded Sonny. "Have a drink," he said motioning Lil to do some pouring.

"I don't want a fucken drink! Christ, we should have had the Luggs bury those two in the basement when we had the chance. Nobody would've known."

Sonny looked around, realizing that this conversation shouldn't be heard by anybody. He'd never seen his partner so unraveled. "Moe, let's go downstairs," he said, grabbing him by the arm, and leading him away.

Moe's outburst stunned everyone. A general air of unease filled the room. By this time Guillermo and Helen were wondering where their lunch crowd had gone. Nobody had bothered to tell them. They wandered out through the swinging doors of the kitchen to find Patrick, Lil, and the Turk sitting amidst an empty dining room.

"Where is everybody?" whispered Helen.

"Just take a look out the front door," suggested Diamond Lil.

Helen took Guillermo by the arm, and they walked out the front door into the light and stood on the sidewalk in disbelief. Helen read the picket signs and began to put one and one together. She tried to help him understand but couldn't find the shared vocabulary to explain this. Guillermo remembered the big black man with the cowboy hat, and he watched him lead this brigade of white folks in a circular march up and down the sidewalk in front of Sonny's Place. The only thing clear to him was that he had nobody to cook for. He worried that he wouldn't be able to bring his family over by Christmas.

Soon the Lugg Brothers made their appearance to a chorus of catcalls. They thought of themselves as bad guys anyway, so they rather enjoyed the reception. They headed downstairs to the office and found Moe Venti seated at Sonny's desk, cleaning his Luger.

The actual sight of the weapon made Sonny squeamish. He sucked down his Camel as if the smoke was what sustained him. Moe continued to clean his pistol, and when he had finished, he closed the barrel. He held it in his hand, feeling its weight, admiring its steely shine. Sonny watched on as Moe gave the trigger a light, feathery touch with his index finger. The trace of a smile on his face came out of some episode of *The Untouchables*. Moe finally acknowledged the arrival of the Lugg Brothers with a nod of his head. The Luggs nodded right back.

"OK boys, tonight we start playing hard ball."

Those words brought a smile to their faces. Moe picked up the phone and called his "go to" vigilante friend, Lefty Martell. "Hello Lefty, it's Moe Venti. Not too bad, yourself? Good, good to hear it. Listen Lefty, I need you to round up a small crew for tonight. ... Nah, they don't need to be armed. We're dealing with a bunch of lily-white liberals, who are trying to stop us from doing business. ... Yeah, you got it, when the first drop of blood gets spilled they'll be running for the hills. ... How big a crew? About a dozen will do. Great! Be ready for a 7 p.m. curtain call. I'll give you a jingle at 5:30 just to firm things up. OK pal, I'll talk to you then. Thanks Lefty."

Moe Venti, man of action, turned to the Luggs, "OK boys, tonight we clean house when the sun sets. I'm assigning you to the big fellah. I want to see some of his blood on the sidewalk, and I want him carried away, not walking away. You got me?"

"We got you, Boss."

"What about me, Moe," asked Sonny, who was feeling a bit left out.

"Sonny, you're the figurehead here. You're out of the picture. I want your hands clean. And one last thing, the Jew's mine, and mine only. Understood?" Moe inquired.

Back at the bar, Patrick and the Turk discussed the implications of Moe Venti's disconcerting outburst. It was a side of him they'd never seen, so careless and out of control.

"I've never seen him be anything but a cool cucumber," said the Turk, "but you know Dr. Jekyll has a Mr. Hyde, and maybe that bulge in his pocket is more than a prop."

"Turk, what do we do about what we just heard?"

"I guess we should warn Alabama. It beats sayin' nothin'."

"Yeah, we can't say nothin'" spoke Patrick Phelan as he finished off his beer. He realized that he'd spent enough of his day off in the shop. However, the intrigue could not be denied. There were plenty of words to describe life at Sonny's Place. Tedious was not among them.

Patrick said his goodbyes and headed out the front door. He caught Alabama Al's attention in the picket line and waved him over by the front door of the Tortoise Café.

"What's up, chef?"

"Al, I feel obliged to tell you that Moe Venti seems out of control."

"Good."

"But what I'm saying is that I believe he's planning some physical retaliation."

"Good all over again!"

"But Al, he ranted that he should've had you and Harvey bumped off from the get-go."

"Chef, he'd probably be doin' me a favor. Besides that, skinny ginny couldn't dig a hole big enough to put me in!"

"But Al, you know he carries a gun."

"Chef, that don't make me no never mind."

"OK Al, I just felt like I had to warn you. Be careful. I'll catch you later."

"Thanks chef. We appreciate the concern."

Patrick headed out. The only things to be done were to cash his check, and then do a little shop for his dinner with Liza Jane. So, he decided that today he wasn't going to worry about anything, not his Father's condition, not the Blues strike, not Elena Madeira, not a thing.

He would cook dinner tonight for Liza Jane and continue his course of study in Romance 101.

26: RUE'S BLUES

Rue Morley poured himself another cup of coffee. It was midafternoon, yet he was still in the process of waking up. By now his sleep cycle had been fully taken over by the Blues life; late to bed, late to rise. His wife Leslie fell asleep early and was up with the sun to go to school. They'd become ships passing in the night. Their son Arlen, a pendulum that swung between them, somehow kept them tethered.

The blame game had fully commenced. The move to Cambridge, which they made with the hope that it would jumpstart the marriage, seemed to have driven a deeper wedge between them. Leslie missed Carolina and her family. Rue was consumed by the spectacle of Sonny's Place. The Blues had taken him over, and there was no place else for him to be. Rue lit up a smoke as he heard his wife's car come up the driveway. His discontent simmered. Their love life had diminished to uninspired, monthly episodes. Just last night he'd come home from the Chinatown run feeling frisky. He climbed into bed, and attempted to engage Leslie, but was rebuffed. Playing footsies led to a nibble on the ear of his wife, who had her back to him. She awoke in anger, complaining to Rue that she was exhausted and needed her sleep. Rue grabbed his pillow, a quilt, and gave the bedroom door a spectacular slam on his way to the living room couch.

As a dispenser of spirits at the Home of the Blues, Rue was getting flashed the green light by no small number of attractive women. This wasn't helping things. He'd kept himself on the straight and narrow, but just barely. There had been a time when he couldn't pry Leslie off himself with a crowbar. The physical frustration of it all harvested a festering bitterness.

Where did it all go? He blamed her. She blamed him.

As Leslie's key opened the front door, Rue zeroed in on his newspaper, choosing not to acknowledge her presence. She stood silently in their doorway; her arms full of books. Rue sipped his coffee while he locked in on the headlines of the Globe.

"NIXON WILLING TO GIVE UP SUMMARY OF TAPED CONVERSATIONS"

"Rue can we talk?"

"Talk about what?"

"Rue, look at me please."

He looked at her but made no effort to mask his contempt. Then he brought his eyes back down to his newspaper headlines. Leslie began to cry.

"And now you're gonna start bawlin'? Well that's just fucken great!"

"What's the matter with us, Rue?" she pleaded.

"What's the matter with us, Leslie? We don't have sex anymore. That's what the matter is! I remember a time when you couldn't get enough. Now you don't even want to touch me."

"Rue, we never have any time together anymore. I come home from work, and you're headed out the door. How are we supposed to have a relationship? You come home at three in the morning, drunk and high, smelling like a smoky barroom. And you expect me to be turned on? I have to be up at six, and I work a long hard day."

"I remember a time when you used to get high with me, and you didn't mind missing a few hours of sleep to make me happy."

"Rue, that was before we had Arlen. We were partying then. We have a family now."

"So that means I don't get laid anymore?"

"Rue, I want you to get out of the bar business and get a day job so we can have time together and live a normal life."

"A normal life? Shall I wear a shirt and tie? A fucken monkey suit? Carry a briefcase? What do you want me to be Leslie? I was a bartender when you met me!"

"I thought you'd change, Rue! I thought you'd change!"

"You thought I'd change?" he asked incredulously. Why did you think that?"

An anguished, defeated silence filled their kitchen. They both looked up to see their smiling son stroll in from playing in the backyard. He was the dazzling incarnation of their finest moment.

Arlen looked back and forth at his mother and father. His smile vanished as he realized they'd been at it again. He could smell the venom in the air. Leslie could see the scared look on her son's face. She retreated into the bathroom crying.

27: SISTER OF MERCY

Stella Madeira stood wearily over a sink full of dishes. She turned at the opening of the front door, where Tisha was returning from a morning class at UMASS Boston.

"Hi Stell."

"Tish," she whispered.

"Where's Elena?"

"She's still in bed."

"Still in bed?"

"I gave her a shout at 10:30 and haven't tried since."

"But Stella, she's probably sick up there."

"Look Tisha, she's not the first one to get her precious little heart stepped on."

"But Stella, she's really hurting."

"Tell her it's her turn to cook Papa's dinner."

Tisha chose not to engage Stella any further. She knew that was futile. Stella had little patience and even less compassion when it came to Elena. There was no miracle worker alive who could pull the monkey wrench from the machinery of that relationship. Stella Madeira was a world wearied beauty. The burden she carried left a silent cursing darkness in her brown eyes. She did what had to be done, and she wasn't going to put a happy smile on her face for anybody.

Tisha pulled a little bed tray out of the cupboard and opened its legs. She prepared a breakfast of fresh fruit salad with yogurt and honey, a cup of coffee and a glass of juice. One-handing the tray, Tisha climbed the stairs that led to Elena's room. She knocked softly and heard a muffled "come in."

"Good morning little sister."

"Isn't it afternoon yet?" sighed Elena, the groggy excess of sleep etched into her face.

"Yeah, I gotta be honest, it's almost two o'clock, and you know what that means?"

"It's time for our story?"

"That's right Elena, and today you get to watch our story while having breakfast in bed."

Tisha opened the shades, letting some light in to the room. Then she turned on the little black and white television that rested on the bureau. Propping up Elena with a pillow, she brought over her surprise, and laid the tray in at her waist.

"For me?" Elena smiled.

"For you!"

Tisha curled up next to her in bed. They traded kisses and looked so comfortable, the way only two sisters can. "Jeez Tish, what a sweet thing to do. The fruit salad looks gorgeous." Elena took a big sip of coffee as she took in the healing colors of the fruit. A deep breath made her feel a little better.

"I missed our story yesterday, Laynie. What happened?"

"This dirtball right here, the smelly lookin' one with the pack of cigarettes rolled up in his sleeve, just found out that he's the bastard son of Richard Hollyfield, the town millionaire, from a tryst with Charlotte Creed, the old town pump. Now he's headed over to Hollyfield's house to claim his rightful name."

"He's so gross."

"Yeah, and he thinks he's such a bad ass. Speaking of bad asses, how's things with you and Miguel?"

"Real good Laynie. I can't complain."

"Papa hasn't noticed anything?"

"Nope, not yet, thank God."

Just in the last week Tisha and Miguel had surrendered to their curiosities about each other. In her desire to wake up in the arms of her new boyfriend, she had created a means for herself. She'd come in from work with her sisters late at night. They'd knock on Enrique's door to inform him that they were home. But then Tisha would go out her bedroom window and shimmy down a tree until she reached freedom. Miguel would be waiting down the street with his engine running. Then they'd be off to the Kokomo.

"Jeez Tish, I hope Papa doesn't find out. He'd blow a gasket."

"He sure would. I wish we could just be ourselves around here. We humans need to be touched. I don't think he wants to face the fact that we're sexual creatures."

"Tish, you're so lucky. I wish I had someone to love."

"Your time is coming Laynie."

"I hope so. I'm tired of whipping up the hollandaise by myself."

"Yeah, it means more when someone is whipping it up with you."

"But I tell you something Tish. I hope Mr. Right comes along for Stella first, because she's gonna be tough to deal with if we both have boyfriends, and she doesn't."

"No shit."

Just then they heard Stella's footsteps coming up the stairs. They shared a wink and a nod, terminating any further discussion of her. She knocked on the door and entered.

"Get enough sleep today, Elena?"

"Oh Stella, give it a rest," pleaded Tisha.

"Elena, it's your turn to cook Papa's dinner. There're pork chops in the fridge."

"OK Stell, I'll get right to it in a few. Come on in and sit down with us."

"You two are still watching this crap?" she inquired pulling up a stool. Stella didn't like to admit that the soaps held any pleasure for her, although she could get involved in a heartbeat.

"Who's that pig?" she inquired. "He's gross. Reminds me of Sonny."

"That's Stephen Hollyfield's bastard son from an affair with the town trollop. He's just pulled into town to demand his piece of the pie," explained Elena.

"He seems like the kind of guy that would expect you to go down on him without reciprocation," assessed Tisha.

"The only reason to go down on a man like that would be to cut his nut sack off with a grapefruit knife."

"Oh Stella!" the sisters chimed in horror.

"Yeah, well it's true," she confirmed.

"Speaking of Sonny, can you believe Lil wants to marry him?" inquired Tisha.

"Lil's a complete idiot," spoke Stella.

"Any word on the Blues strike?" asked Elena.

"We'll find out soon enough," spoke Stella. "In the meantime, you've got to get up and make Papa's dinner."

"OK Stell, I'm on it," surrendered Elena, who finally pulled herself from the sanctuary of her bed. The three sisters all got into motion, doing what needed to be done around the house before heading off to work.

Enrique's girls all chipped in and kept up a nice home for him. Stella ran the show and assumed the traditional responsibility for everything that her Mother would have done. Her sisters never questioned it and pretty much did what Stella told them to do.

Enrique had never found a woman to replace his wife Ria after her death. He'd begun having affairs about a year after her passing, but chose to keep them separate from his daughters. After sex, he always came home to sleep in his own bed like Luca Brassi. If a woman couldn't handle that, Enrique would just move on and find someone else. It was that simple. He never spoke to his daughters about his trysts, just as they never spoke to him about theirs. If they were his sons, it might have been different, but they weren't. They were reflections of the lost love of his life. Enrique kept it all separate.

In a short time, the sisters had completed their domestic assignments. Donning their autumnal wraps, they took the walk into Inman Square. Just in front of the Haberdasher, they ran into Rue Morley crossing Cambridge Street. The four of them turned the corner onto Hampshire together and stopped dead in their tracks. What they saw and heard was a crowd of very familiar Blues clientele; stomping, hooting, and hollering about an injustice.

"Holy shit," exclaimed Rue. "Check 'em out!"

"Not a bad showing!" exclaimed Elena, who was thrilled by the distraction.

The picket line needed no introduction to these four people. Being the dispensers of spirits, they were as recognizable as the performers on stage and thus very important people in their world of the great indoors. The strikers cranked up the volume to show Rue and the sisters how they felt. Alabama Al, his toothy smile spread from ear to ear, conducted them like an orchestra. His eyes shone as he opened the door of Sonny's Place for them in gentlemanly fashion.

Elena was the last one to the door. Looking back, she stopped when she noticed the handsome, bearded man, who had sat down with Big Mama Thornton the previous night.

She looked straight at him, and he looked straight back.

Once inside the four encountered a glum, solitary Diamond Lil. Both the bar and her tip jar were empty. Her ashtray full of half-smoked cigarettes.

"Lil, are you alright?" asked Tisha.

I had two customers all afternoon long. And Sonny doesn't fucken tip," she moaned. "I'm going home to get stewed," she announced, reaching for a bottle of the bar vodka. Rue grabbed her arm and took the bottle back. Lil was about to tell him where to go, when he reached over, plucking a full bottle of Stolichnaya off the shelf that he slipped into her bag.

"Lil, if you're gonna take something, go top shelf. If you get caught the punishment's the same."

Everybody got busy readying the house for the evening that wouldn't happen. They polished silver and glasses, refilled the salt and pepper shakers, jammed butter into ramekins, and filled the bin with folded napkins.

"Do you think anybody will cross the line tonight?" wondered Tisha.

"We didn't do a single cover at lunch," announced short Helen. She looked both shocked and bored silly. "Guillermo's really upset. He wants to bring his family over here by Christmas, and now he's afraid there won't be anybody to cook for."

The impending economic reality was beginning to dawn on everybody. The house had already lost a full day of lunch receipts. The night ahead seemed destined for the same disastrous results. "It's a good thing I don't get paid by the plate," assessed Helen. "One way or another it better straighten out soon."

Rue decided to duck downstairs and replace the bottle of Stoli he'd handed off to Diamond Lil. He walked by the office door, which was open a crack. Inside were Sonny, Moe, and the Lugg Brothers. Rue could hear Moe Venti on the phone. It stopped him in his tracks.

"Hello, I'd like to speak with Sargent Milligan please. Yes, tell him it's Moe Venti calling."

Rue couldn't resist as he inched up to the door to get within an earshot of this conversation.

"Yeah Milligan, I need to talk business with you. Tonight, at seven o'clock I've got some muscle coming in here to take care of this picket line. We're just going to send these people back from whence they came so that we can run our business. You'll probably be getting a 911 shortly after seven. I need twenty minutes before you arrive. Just stop off for a cup of coffee somewhere. Rest assured I'll sweeten the pot for you and your boys. That's right Sargent, it's what we call good business. I appreciate your cooperation. Great, I'll see you about 7:30 tonight. Thank you, Sargent."

Rue grabbed the bottle of Stoli and slipped up the back stairs without making a sound. He went directly to the payphone and dialed up Ted next door at the diner.

"Tortoise Café."

"Ted, it's Rue."

"Hey, what's shakin'?"

"Trouble. I just heard Moe Venti on the phone with one Sargent Milligan. Moe's bringin' in a fleet of goons arriving at 7 p.m. sharp to clean house on the picket line."

"Yeah?"

"Yeah, and when Milligan gets the 911, he's gonna take his boys out for a slice of pie before they drop in to clean up the mess. Ted, can you pop out front and give Harvey and Alabama the heads up?"

"They're gonna hit us at seven?"

"Right at seven."

Ted put away his daily receipts and checked his watch. It read 5:15 p.m. The thought of ensuing violence made his stomach rumble and tighten with tension. Ted was just an old hippie. He hadn't had a fight since the fourth grade. He considered for a moment the pugilistic potential of the strikers. They had Alabama Al, who could surely handle himself. Harvey? Maybe?. There were a couple of other formidable fellows in the contingent, but this surely looked like a stacked deck.

"We're fucked," Ted spoke out loud. "They're gonna bury us."

Having thus accepted the reality of a physical thrashing, he tried to calm his nerves with a bong hit. The smoke filled up his dusty office. Ted's mind searched for something that could even up the score. Another bong hit later, and an idea surfaced. He pulled down the yellow pages from his shelf, dialed up the number for the local television station Channel Four, and asked for the news dispatcher.

"Look pal, I've got an exclusive over here for you. If you can get a camera crew down to Sonny's Place on Hampshire Street in Inman Square, Cambridge at 7 p.m. tonight you'll be able to capture the essence of great live television. I'm talkin' sordid violence with a racial slant. Now are you gonna send a crew down, or do I call Channels Five and Seven? Great! And when it's all over ask for Ted from the Tortoise Café. I'll let you buy me a drink. That is if I'm not spitting my teeth out. OK, see you at seven."

Ted hustled up the stairs and out onto Hampshire Street. There he found the picket line howling as another person crossed the line and opened the front door of Sonny's Place. It was none other than Enrique Madeira. The jeers of the strikers left him unaffected.

"I drink a beer here every day after work. Today's no different," he let them know with a half-smile, half sneer. The boos and hisses funneled into the bar as Enrique slammed the door behind him. Everyone inside looked up at the commotion.

"Papa," shouted Tisha. The three sisters hustled over to greet their father. "Papa are you alright?"

Enrique pooh-poohed the attention, stomped right up to the bar, and ordered a beer. "They didn't even ruffle my feathers. What's the story with these assholes parading up and down the street?"

"It's the Blues strike, Papa," explained Elena.

"Blues strike? Give me a break."

"But Papa …"

"Don't Papa me. Find me an ashtray," he commanded.

He settled into a beer and a smoke. The sisters scurried back to their side work. They knew when to leave him alone.

Back in the street, Ted waved Harvey and Alabama off to the side to break the latest news. "Fasten your seat belts boys. Rue just called to tell me that he overheard a phone conversation between Moe Venti and Sargent Milligan of the Cambridge Police."

"Yeah?"

"Yeah, and it seems that at 7 p.m. tonight, they're bringing in some vigilantes to team up with the Lugg Brothers to wipe us off the map!"

"I'll eat those Lugg Brothers for dinner," promised Alabama Al.

"What's with the cops?" wondered Harvey.

"They're gonna take their time getting here after the 911."

"Wow," spoke Harvey with concern. "I thought it might come to this. Maybe we should let everyone know and get the women off the line."

Alabama Al directed all of the strikers into the Tortoise for a closed-door meeting.

"We've just received word from an inside source," began Harvey. "It appears that in an hour and a half we can expect some trouble on the picket line. Word has it that Moe Venti is bringing in some vigilantes to break up our strike."

A chorus of indignant utterances filled the room, forcing Harvey to speak over the chatter. "As a result, we want all of you to know that we don't want or expect anybody to get in a fist fight over our strike. In addition, we're asking all the women involved to take a break and leave the line for the next few hours."

"Wait a second Harvey! Hold it right there!" shouted a tough looking gal in the back of the room. A brown leather cap covered her short, cropped hair, a motorcycle jacket, tight black jeans, and a pair of steel toed boots filled out the rest of her wardrobe. "If you think us ladies are gonna take a hike just because things might get rough, you better think again! I'm Cookie Jones and I'm here with a good dozen of us from The Sisterhood, Cambridge Chapter."

"The Sisterhood?" asked Alabama Al. "What's that?"

"We're here in spirit for Bessie Smith, Ma Rainey, Billie Holiday, Memphis Minnie, and all the other women who sang their Blues in every bucket of blood gin mill from here to Tuscaloosa, not knowing if they'd get cut by a razor, or have a beer bottle thrown at them. So, if you think we aren't tough enough to hang, or if you think the Blues is just a man's game, you better keep a good twenty feet away from me. Cuz that's about how far I can spit!"

The Tortoise erupted with whistles and cheers. Harvey was left speechless. He knew that this was a stunning watershed moment that could only have happened in Cambridge at this very time and place. It infused a defiance into the spirit of the strikers as they headed back out on to Hampshire Street to pound the pavement in front of Sonny's Place.

"'HEY HO THE BLUES WON'T GO. NO, NO THEY JUST WON'T GO"

"HEY HO THE BLUES WON'T GO. NO, NO THEY JUST WON'T GO"

28: A MOUNT AUBURN CEMETERY SLUMBER

Patrick cashed his paycheck at the Cambridge Trust in Harvard Square before heading up north to the corners of Concord and Huron. There he bought an Italian sub at Armando's, and a cold beer around the corner at the Mannix Liquor Store before driving to Mount Auburn Cemetery. He found a comfortable knoll off of the reflecting pool, a ways away from any tombstones, and enjoyed a solitary lunch.

Putting his head back to rest, he fell into a deep graveyard slumber. It was then that a subconscious demon took hold. He was back in college again, and it was time to take his Western Civilization final exam. Of course, he hadn't been to class in a month. He'd procured a hit of speed, borrowed a friend's notes, and stayed up all night memorizing the salient facts of a few thousand years of the story known as the History of the Planet Earth. That wasn't so difficult.

The tough part was twofold. First, sneaking in the back of the class without the professor seeing him. Second was keeping a tight sphincter post exam until he could find a toilet and send the salient facts back out to the Atlantic Ocean.

As he groaned his way back into consciousness it took a long moment for the October sun to cut through the nightmare. It felt so real and left him feeling like a fraud. Finally, relief came when he realized that he didn't go to college anymore.

"I'm a cook now," he said aloud. "I'm a cook."

He sat up, caught his breath and wiped the torment from his eyes. He looked down through the tombstones and trees to where the silver light hit the reflecting pool. The visual brilliance cleared his head. Another deep breath and he let it all go. Rising to his feet, he dusted himself off and took a slow walk back to his car. Then he headed over to the Fresh Pond Market on Huron to pick up the ingredients for tonight's dinner with Liza Jane.

When the family lived on Sparks Street, Mildred would often send him there to pick up some odds and ends. He entered the market and wandered over to the meat counter. He was happy to see old Mr. Blake still there. Though he had a neck condition that twisted him up like a pretzel, Mr. Blake always had the warmest smile.

"Patrick Phelan!"

"Hi Mr. Blake. How are you?"

"Not bad. I haven't seen you in a long time. Look at you. You're all grown up."

"Yeah, I guess I am."

"Why yes you are. So, tell me, how's your Dad doing?"

"Not so good, Mr. Blake."

"Oh, I'm sorry," he lamented, silent for a moment, sharing that sadness. "Please give him my best."

"Thanks, I will."

"So, what can I get for you?"

"A half pound of veal cutlets, and a quarter pound of prosciutto."

"Ah, we're fine dining tonight," he spoke with a grin.

"Yes, we are," confirmed Patrick. He watched on as Mr. Blake shuffled around the meat chest and slicer. Behind him on the wall hung a sign that read "It's hard to soar with the eagles, when you work with turkeys."

Patrick said goodbye to Mr. Blake. Then he grabbed some vegetables, pasta, wine, and headed over to Liza's on Upland Road. Once there, he gathered his provisions and shut the car door. Immediately he heard the percussion of a dribbled basketball. He walked over to the fence and peered down into his old hoop court below. There he saw a skinny teenager he didn't know shooting lonely jumpers as the sun sank. The basketball echoed off the sky as if coming through a wall of time.

There were years when he lived on that court day in and day out—passing the time like Steve McQueen's "Cooler King" in *The Great Escape*. He ambled up Liza's front steps, wondering why it had been so long since he'd shot a basketball. Patrick rang her doorbell, and she welcomed him in with a hug and a kiss.

"Well, it must be dinner time."

"Yeah, it's dinner time. I hope you like veal."

"Sure do! Give me that young stuff any old day!"

"Young stuff?"

"That's right. Give me a young man so I can shape him and mold him into what I want him to be," she giggled, pulling him close and getting him lost in a kiss. Patrick put down his bags, wrapped his arms around her, and got lost a few more times before a question rose to the surface.

"Should we go upstairs before I cook you dinner?"

"You're gonna cook me dinner. There's plenty of time to go upstairs," she smiled.

Patrick picked up his groceries and headed down the hall to Liza's kitchen. She poured two glasses of wine, pulled up a stool and hovered around the chopping board where Patrick got busy with dinner.

"What are you making with the veal, Patrick?"

"Veal saltimbocca on a bed of linguine."

"Yum! Hey, suppose I take you out to the movies after we eat?"

"What's playing?"

"There's a double bill at the Harvard Square Theatre, *The Maltese Falcon* followed by *Casablanca*."

"Wow, a Bogie blockbuster! What time does it start?"

"Seven o'clock."

"Let's do it."

29: THE RUMBLE

Rue Morley looked nervously at his watch. It read 6:45. Miguel walked down to the service station of the bar to bum a smoke. Enrique Madeira, still seated, was the only patron to have crossed the line all day.

"Is it time Rue?"

"Almost."

"Rue, check out Enrique," requested Miguel as he took an apprehensive drag from his cigarette. Rue looked down the bar at him.

"Yeah, what about him?"

"Well, every once in a while, I catch him staring at me with this wild fucken look in his eye. I think he knows about me and Tisha."

"She's been keeping it a secret?"

"Yeah, trying to."

Rue squinted his eyes as he took another good look down the bar at Enrique.

"Miguel, he looks at everybody like that."

"You sure man?"

"I ain't sure of nothin'. Maybe he knows and he's just biding his time before he makes a castrati out of you."

Downstairs in Sonny's office, the phone rang, and Moe Venti picked it up immediately. "Lefty, everybody ready to go? Good. Let's synchronize our watches. In five seconds it will be 6:50. Check. We hit them at seven on the button. See you in ten minutes." Moe hung up the phone and began emptying the chamber of his pistol. Sonny began to pace nervously at the mere sight of Moe's piece.

"Moe, you're gonna use your gun tonight?"

"Just the butt end, to whack some sense into the Jew's head."

The Lugg Brothers broke into hyperactive giggles. They ground their teeth and cracked their knuckles in anticipation.

"You boys ready?" asked Moe.

"We're ready, Boss!"

"Remember, the big cotton pickin', porch monkey is yours. The Jew's all mine."

"We got it Boss!"

The Luggs leapt to their feet, headed out the door and up the back stairs. Moe followed behind, when he was interrupted by Sonny.

"Moe, what am I supposed to do?"

"Stay in the bar, Sonny. Your name is on the sign out front. I want your hands to be clean."

Outside the picket line had taken on a peculiar quiet. They continued to march, but the chanting had ceased.

"What time we got, Ted?" asked Alabama, his big cow eyes intently surveying the scene.

"It's just about time, Al. Everybody be ready," warned Ted.

A fierce looking Cookie Jones glanced over her shoulder to see some frightened looks on the faces of a couple of her girls. "Don't worry babes. Just stay right behind me. Everything will be cool," she promised.

Inside Rue saw the Luggs come up the back staircase with Moe Venti right behind. He knew it was time. Sonny straggled behind, taking a seat at mid bar, a half a drink in front of him. Moe stood by the front door with the Luggs eyeing his watch.

Just then a large van came screeching to a halt out on Hampshire Street. A pack of goons exploded onto the sidewalk, and the rumble ensued.

"OK now!" screamed Moe Venti as he and the Lugg Brothers burst out the front door and into the fracas. The muffled sounds of shrieks, moans, and well landed punches filtered through the façade of Sonny's Place. Everybody's head turned to hear the trouble outside.

"What's going on out there?" shouted Elena as she headed for the door.

"Don't Elena!" screamed Rue. But she was out the door, and in a shot, he was over the bar and out the door after her.

"Elena!" screamed Tisha, who flew out the door, and with that Miguel was over the bar and out the door after her with Enrique Madeira on his shoulder. Stella saw this and not relishing the thought of being alone with Sonny, headed for the street as well, shutting the door tight behind her.

The sounds of the melee that Sonny heard outside were muffled and strangely distant. Just then somebody's head came crashing through the glass block, shattering a huge hole in the foggy façade. The sound of the struggle outside became more real as it poured unabated into the barroom.

Sonny jumped off his stool, ran up to the hole and peaked out at the fight. What he saw was a Popeye cartoon; a blur of dust, arms, legs, and bodies entangled. Countless punches were being thrown, some landing, some not. Sonny squinted his eyes and saw the Lugg Brothers on Alabama Al, one behind him with a strangle hold, the other in front landing some serious body blows. Then he saw some big striker tangling with Enrique Madeira, having perceived him as the enemy. His daughters frantically coming to his aid.

Farther down the sidewalk, Sonny saw Moe Venti in the middle of the pack, making his way toward Harvey Wallenberg. Moe, pistol in hand, wound up his arm and commenced his downswing toward Harvey's head, when a bright klieg light came out of nowhere to shine down on the blindsided assault. All this was caught on camera like a witch riding her broom across a full moon on Halloween night.

The blow caught Harvey flush on the side of the head, dropping him like a sack of potatoes right at the feet of Elena Madeira. His face hit the sidewalk with a loud, ugly slap. The presence of a television camera crew sent Lefty and his boys scattering like tenement house cockroaches. They weren't making enough dough to be caught on the evening news.

"What the fuck?" screamed Moe Venti, blinded by the camera lights.

Ted of the Tortoise was on one knee, tasting a bloody nose, when he saw Moe Venti headed for the television cameras, intent on destroying the evidence. Pushing his own pain aside, Ted made a running leap at Moe, dropping him on the sidewalk a few feet away from the crew. Moe squirmed and rolled trying to break free from Ted's sizeable mass. It was all in vain as Ted had him pinned. The cameras kept rolling.

In moments the sounds of police sirens filled the air. Sonny could only hear them from inside, where he was beginning to feel rather lonely. "I better get out there," he thought to himself. He put his best foot forward, headed out the door, breaking into a trot as he hit the sidewalk. Directly in front of him was Cookie Jones, who sensed an attack from her backside. As Sonny came running into the camera light, he saw Cookie Jones quickly pivot, thrusting off her left foot.

"She wouldn't," thought Sonny in the millisecond he had to protect himself.

But she did. Cookie followed through with her steel toed trucker boot, landing full and square on the Bolla family jewels. It was a crisp, clean shot that would've put a big smile on the face of Marie Bolla.

Sonny tried to scream, but nothing came out. He closed his eyes and saw a red neon sign that had the letters P-A-I-N flashing on and off. He crumbled, kissing the sidewalk just outside his front door. Covering his stricken groin with his two hands, he cursed the day he was born with a pair.

Seconds later three police cruisers came to a screeching halt. Their party lights pulsated Hampshire Street in dizzying flashes of red and blue. Sargent Milligan hopped out of his squad car and was stunned to find himself in the lights of the television cameras. He stepped over the bodies of Harvey and Sonny, making a quick decision.

"Arrest them all!" he shouted to his crew. "Disturbing the peace!"

His officers began pulling the bodies apart, beginning with Ted and Moe Venti. The cameras kept rolling.

"We had a deal Milligan," muttered Moe as he was being led away.

"Yeah, we did Moe. But you didn't tell me you were bringing Metro Goldwyn Mayer in on it," barbed Milligan pointing to the cameras. "The deal's off!" he stated flatly. "Get the paddy wagons down here, pronto," he screamed at one of his boys. "And an ambulance too!"

"What about the women?" inquired one cop of Milligan.

"Forget 'em," he ordered.

"Forget 'em?" screamed Cookie Jones, who proceeded to spit on the Sargent.

"Cuff that bitch!" he screamed at his crew. It took three of the boys in blue to get the job done. They handcuffed her cussing and kicking, then dragged her off to the squad car. The paddy wagon pulled up and soon to follow were Rue, Miguel, and Enrique Madeira. The two bartenders went peacefully while Enrique fought every inch of the way, calling Cambridge's finest every name in the book. Stella and Tisha tried to intervene, but it was no use.

As Elena hovered over Harvey Wallenberg's frightfully still body, she saw blood trickling from his ear. She screamed for the ambulance, which was pulling up. EMTs checked his vital signs and lifted him on to a stretcher. Instinctively, Elena took hold of his hand, and climbed into the ambulance alongside him for the ride up to Cambridge City Hospital.

As the cops disentangled what remained of the combatants, they found Alabama Al on his knees at the bottom of the pile. He had each Lugg Brother by an ear, as he coco butted them into submission. They fell to the sidewalk crying like newborns. The cops descended on him. Having dispensed with the Luggs, he offered them no resistance. His shirt and pants were all torn up. Blood dripped from his elbows and knees. He was led to the paddy wagon, when he saw Harvey being lifted into the ambulance with Elena at his side. "Harvey! Harvey!" he screamed in desperation, trying to break from the grips of the Cambridge Police, his hands cuffed from behind. He watched the ambulance pull away, siren blaring, lights flashing. A peculiar hush came over the street as the ambulance disappeared out of sight. Two paddy wagons were jammed full and already on their way to the Central Square lockup.

Sonny Bolla was still squirming on the sidewalk, unable to move. His pain had subsided to the merely intolerable. He pleaded in a whisper for an ambulance too. It arrived shortly, and Sonny grunted and gasped as he was lifted onto a stretcher and into the wagon. He looked out the window to see Milligan being interviewed by a reporter on the now empty sidewalk in front of the shattered glass block façade at The Home of the Blues.

None of that really fazed Sonny. He only had room in his brain to discern the throbbing agony emanating from between his knees. He covered his testicles with his hands as if to protect them from the outside world and cursed every pothole they encountered on the way up to the Cambridge City Hospital.

30: THE CLUB CASABLANCA

Up on the big screen of the Harvard Square Theatre, Bogie had just pulled out his gun and shot a Nazi, who was attempting to prevent the escape of Ilsa Lund and Victor Laszlo from the airport in Casablanca. Claude Rains had sent out the order to "round up the usual suspects" as he and Bogie headed out for a nightcap toast to their wonderful friendship.

Patrick felt Liza reach over and grab his hand. He glanced over at her and saw a lonely teardrop slide down her cheek. "It's such a sad movie," she whispered. "They couldn't be together."

The screen went blank. The curtain closed. The house lights came on.

They grabbed their coats, angled their way out toward the aisle, stepping over empty cups and popcorn containers. Then they made that silent, emotion filled walk up the ramp, through the theatre lobby and out into Harvard Square. There they found life to have gone on uninterrupted; honking cars zipped by, headlights glared, and the October breeze whistled. They stood idly on Mass. Ave., savoring the magic of that great movie.

"What do you want to do?" asked the pretty blue eyed one.

"This way," he spoke after thinking about it. "There's a place I want to take you."

He led her up Church Street, and over to the Brattle Theatre. Down a staircase they walked through a long hallway beneath the very first American Repertory Theatre. A dark bar with a great jukebox marked their destination.

"What's this place?" she asked.

"Welcome to the Club Casablanca," smiled Patrick.

He opened the door and led her down the bar. Directly in front of him was a huge black and white etching of Rick and Ilsa drinking champagne, looking out their hotel window in Paris before the Occupation.

"Wow," she sighed, duly impressed.

"Isn't that the way we should think of them? When they had Paris?"

Liza gazed at the picture a while and smiled. "You're kind of a romantic guy, aren't you?"

"I've been feeling like one lately."

She grabbed him by the collar and gave him a kiss. Then a bearded bartender with dark bespectacled eyes made his way over to them.

"Patrick, how are you?" asked the smiling tender before dropping down two beverage napkins, and giving him a shake.

"Good Reggie, and you?"

"I'm just ducky."

"Reggie, this is my friend Liza. Liza, Reggie."

"Pleased to meet you. What can I get for you?"

"Maybe a little cognac for a chilly night," Patrick suggested. Liza gave a nod of approval and pulled a cigarette from her bag. Reggie put down a couple of snifters in front of them. Then he retreated through the beaded curtain into the backroom, returning with a pot of hot water to warm their glasses. He emptied the hot water into his sink and poured them a few fingers of Remy each.

"Cheers," said Reggie.

"Cheers," they sang back.

Patrick and Liza chinged their glasses under the Casablanca's red and white striped awning. Then they toasted to Rick and Ilsa, and took in the dark, warm atmosphere of the 'Blanca. It wasn't long before Dooley Wilson's voice, singing "As Time Goes By" came resonating out of the jukebox.

"There they are in Paris," said Patrick, "not knowing what was about to come down."

"It's such a sad story," she said once more.

When Reggie got a moment, he wandered back down their way to chat, resting his hands on the bar in front of them.

"It's kind of quiet for a Saturday night, heh Reg?"

"Yeah, well the Harvard–Yale game was down in New Haven."

"Who won?"

"Who cares?"

"Good point, Reg."

"Well, I feel it in the pocketbook, but sometimes a quiet Saturday night is fine by me."

"How do you feel about our Celtics this year, Reg?"

"Last year they were the best team in basketball. If Havlicek hadn't ripped up his shoulder against the Knicks, it would have been ours for the taking."

"I agree, Reg. It still hurts."

"Yeah, it still hurts," agreed Reggie as he slipped away to pour some drinks.

"I like this place," spoke Liza, fitfully comforted by the fire of a little cognac.

"You think this is a nice place?"

"Yeah, I do."

"Well believe it or not, I saw a guy get murdered in here about a year ago."

"Murdered?"

"Yeah, murdered."

"What are you talking about?"

"I'm talking about a guy who got murdered right here in this bar. My pal McDougal and I were having a beer right over there by the piano, when it went down."

Liza stared back in silence, taking a long, slow drag of her cigarette. "What happened?"

"Well upstairs is a salt and pepper dance club. It's an unusually integrated scene, and it's known for that. A guy named Van was the manager. Well one night Van had a beef with a dude, and he threw him out of the Club. The cat went home, got his piece, came back here and blew Van away."

"Where in here did it happen?" she asked, looking around the room.

"He got shot right outside that door we came in. Then he stumbled into the Club and died right on the floor over there by the men's room."

Simultaneously they reached for their snifters and took a sip. Patrick reached over and touched her leg to lighten the mood. She looked back at him with a half-smile. Then Reggie came back down the bar to continue their conversation.

"How's your father doing, Patrick?"

"Not so good, Reg. It just keeps getting worse. There's just no hope with it. You know?"

"Yeah, I'm sorry. Give him my best, will you?"

"Thanks Reg, I will."

"Patrick, what's the matter with your father?" asked Liza, happy to get off the subject of murder.

"Well," he began, taking a deep breath. He's got Parkinson's disease. He's been sick since I was a little boy."

"Parkinson's? Isn't that when their hands shake?"

"Yeah. It affects the mobility center of the brain. His hands tremor, sometimes uncontrollably, and his feet drag when he walks. Sometimes his legs will freeze up on him in mid-stride, and he'll just fall face first."

"And there's no cure?"

"No cure, and it takes its sweet time taking you down. My Dad had a big dental practice in town, and got diagnosed when I was ten, and his career was finished. A lot of people in town thought he was a drunk because his hands shook. But he was just real sick."

"That must have been terrible for you as a little boy."

"It's not so great right now. It feels like my family has had a dark cloud following us around for as long as I can remember."

Reggie turned on the television as it was just about time for the eleven o'clock news. Patrick and Liza were finishing up their drinks and getting ready to leave when the night's lead story came forth.

"Good evening. In a shocking and unprecedented move, President Nixon has fired Watergate Special Prosecutor Archibald Cox."

"How the hell can he do that?" asked Patrick.

This news drew patrons out of their tables, and up to the bar, crowding around the television.

"In the aftermath of this, Attorney General Elliot Richardson has announced his resignation from office. The president has discharged Cox from his position and has ordered the F.B.I. to seal shut the Prosecutor's Office."

"How does he get away with firing this guy?" Patrick asked again.

"Hey, Cox has been breathing down his neck, demanding those tapes," someone said.

"Yeah, but can he get away with it?"

"Nixon's the big tomato. He thinks he can do whatever he wants."

"Yeah, and it leaves no doubt that he's up to here in this mess!" spoke another.

Interviews with Cox and Richardson ensued before they broke to a commercial. The bar was buzzing with this news. For the first time, Nixon was beginning to act truly desperate. Now there was blood in the water for sure.

Patrick and Liza said their goodbyes, leaving Reggie and the dark warmth of the Club Casablanca. They headed arm in arm down the long basement hallway and out onto Brattle Street. But back inside the Club, the news had returned with a story that hit closer to home.

"There was violence tonight outside a Cambridge barroom. The melee apparently broke out between supporters of striking Black Blues performers and the owners of Sonny's Place in Inman Square, as well as other yet unidentified assailants. One man, Harvey Wallenberg is unconscious and in serious condition tonight at Cambridge City Hospital, when he took this blow to the head, captured by our own news cameras from an assailant unofficially identified as a co-owner of the club, Attorney Moe Venti of East Boston."

"At this moment Cambridge Police are reviewing our own exclusive footage of the brawl. Mr. Venti is now under police custody pending further investigation. Seventeen others were also arrested for disturbing the peace. Another person identified as co-owner of the establishment; Mr. Sonny Bolla of the Back Bay was taken to the

Cambridge City with what one hospital official described as a 'lower abdominal crisis.'"

Unaware of all this, Patrick hopped into his car on Church Street with Liza Jane and kicked over the engine. They drove back to her place on Upland Road to get re-entangled.

31: THE AFTERMATH

Deep, deep, deep in a dream, Patrick Phelan was flying like a hawk through the Cambridge sky. He hadn't flown like this since he was a child. It was pure exhilaration. People in the streets stopped and looked up at him. He flew high. He flew low. He flew wherever he chose, from the steeple of St. Paul's then across the river to the top of the Prudential.

He gazed down at the Boston Harbor coastline and saw the silvery light of the sun reflecting off it. In that moment he wanted to go higher, so naturally he did. Straight toward the ball of fire he flew. Soon the glare became blinding, and the heat began to disintegrate his clothes. A jolt of panic shot through him when he realized that he was completely and utterly irretrievable.

Patrick wanted to turn back but couldn't. He sensed that this flight was coming to some sort of conclusion. It was then that he began to feel a rhythmic pounding on his body from head to toe and a tickling sensation flailed across his face to the beat.

He awoke to see long blonde hair dangling in his face. Parting the locks with his hands revealed Liza's face, her eyes closed. He was full and inside her, and she rode him like a posse was on their trail.

She grabbed his hands, brought them to her breasts and began to zero in on their destination. Her utterances became desperate, and he followed her sensing his own imminent arrival coming from the base of his spine. They flew into the sun together, entangled and thrashing until all their energies had been exhausted.

In time they came back to earth. Liza disengaged. Patrick gasped mournfully to be leaving that place. She rolled to his side and pulled the covers up over them. Patrick laid there panting. He tried to hold on to what he could of the dream that preceded his fleshy awakening.

"I woke up and I was inside you," he whispered barely believing.

"That was so good, Patrick."

Her words were honest and magical. They were the words that all men yearn to hear. Patrick was consumed, totally under the influence. Something powerful had been provoked from deep within. He was alive in a way that was unimaginable a mere week ago. She pulled him close for a long, still kiss. They laid there for some time. The only want in his head was to keep looking into her beautiful blues. In time she whispered to him.

"Ready for some coffee?"

"Sure."

Patrick Phelan watched her shimmy bare bottomed across the room like a fair haired Morticia Addams. Liza stepped into her fluffy slippers, donned her bathrobe, and headed down to the kitchen. He reached over and peaked out the blind to find a grey Sunday. Yet it did not dim the internal light that had been switched on inside him. He got dressed and headed downstairs to the kitchen, where Liza poured him a cup of coffee.

"Patrick, why don't you grab the Sunday paper off the doorstep."

This he did, bringing it back to the kitchen table. The front page exploded with the news that was being dubbed "The Saturday Night Massacre." Photos and allegations filled the paper above the fold. Patrick went straight to the sports page to learn that the Washington Bullets had handed the Celtics their first loss of the season. Liza sipped her coffee as she scanned the front page. Down below the fold some headlines caught her eye.

"TROUBLE IN A CAMBRIGE BAR—18 ARRESTED, ONE IN CRITICAL CONDITION"

"Patrick, look at this!"

He glanced over to see a photo of the front door of Sonny's Place with a big hole in the glass block façade. He grabbed the paper and scanned the article for the essential details. It sounded really bad. Patrick grabbed the phone and quickly dialed Rue's number. It rang three times before a dour Leslie Morley answered.

"Hello."

"Hi Leslie, it's Patrick Phelan calling. Can I talk to Rue, please?" She handed the phone off without a word.

"Yeah?"

"Rue, it's Patrick. What the fuck happened over there last night?"

"It was mayhem. Harvey Wallenberg's up the Cambridge City in a coma. He got gun butted in the head by Moe Venti, but some news guy was there with a camera, and caught the assault on film."

"Holy shit!"

"Yeah man, you missed a pretty wild scene. We all got arrested for disturbing the peace. I had to call the old lady down to Police Headquarters to spring me, so she's in a hell of a mood."

"Is everybody else alright?"

"As far as I know. I'm leaving soon to go up to the hospital. Alabama and all the strikers are down there trying to keep the flame burnin' for Harvey."

"Is he gonna make it?"

"Who knows? I'm leavin' in five minutes. You wanna meet me down there?"

"Yeah, I'll meet you there," affirmed Patrick.

Rue Morley hung up the phone, took one last drag of his morning smoke, and finished the dregs of his coffee. Leslie was positioned in the living room rocking chair keeping a steady, pensive beat as she awaited their next altercation. Rue put on his coat and stood before her. Leslie looked out the window. Having to drive down with Arlen to the Central Square lockup last night to spring her husband was a humiliation. Rue was going to pay for that.

"Leslie, I gotta go up to the hospital to check in on Harvey."

"I thought Sunday was supposed to be a family day, where we do something together—as a family."

"Well then, let's go to the hospital as a family to check in on my friend Harvey, who is in a coma."

"Rue, I've had it with this life you live, where everything is based on a barroom. It's a sickness, Rue. Can't you see it?"

"Harvey is a person. He's a friend of mine. He might never wake up. Do you understand that?" his voice rising in a crescendo.

After a long silence she got up from her chair and said, "Leave Arlen here." Then Leslie left the room. Rue grabbed his keys and headed out the front door.

Young Arlen was on the floor in his room tinkering with his collection of toy soldiers. He'd heard the loud punctuation of a slamming door as well as the verbal exchange. Arlen had been hearing everything for some time now. It left him frightened and unsettled.

Rue got in his car and kicked over the ignition. As he waited for the engine to warm up, a jolt of anger erupted in his gut. His clenched fists lashed out at the steering wheel in front of him as if it were a speed bag in a boxing gym.

"You miserable bitch!" he screamed at the top of his lungs. Then he looked at himself in the rear-view mirror, shouting an indictment. "You stupid bastard! You married a miserable fucken bitch! How could you be so fucken stupid?"

The reality of that stark assessment hit raw bone and nerve. It produced a cocktail of evil feelings. He took a deep breath, put the car into drive, and headed up to the Cambridge City Hospital. He arrived to see Patrick parking the Dart across the way by the Coady Florist Shop. There was no hiding the look on Rue's face.

"Are you alright?" inquired Patrick.

"No."

"Domestic strife?"

"Yeah."

Patrick made no further inquiry. They checked in on Harvey's whereabouts at the front desk and were told to head upstairs to Intensive Care. They rode up on the elevator, walked out into the hallway, and found the benches filled with the Blues Strikers, some of whom looked pretty beat up. One of them was Ted from the Tortoise, who sported a broken nose and a fat lip.

"You alright?" asked Rue.

"I'm OK. But I guess I'll be living on coffee frappes for a while."

"What's the word on Harvey?"

"No change. Did you hear about Moe Venti?"

"No, what?"

"He got released this morning on $50,000 bail."

"Woah! Did you drop the dime on him to Channel Four?"

"Absolutely," he smiled.

"Ted, does anyone know who tipped you off?"

"Nobody," he stated firmly.

"So, it's just you, me, Miguel and Phelan here?"

"Correct, Rue."

"Patrick, you better believe that Moe Venti's gonna be pumping people for info. Nobody knows. You got me?"

"Nobody knows," Patrick agreed. But he felt the tension rise as he understood the seriousness of all this.

"Are you guys gonna go up and visit Sonny?" asked Ted.

"What happened to Sonny?" Patrick wanted to know.

"Cookie Jones laid him out cold with a boot to the root," explained Ted.

"You're shittin' me?" begged Patrick.

Just then a somber Al McGuirk came out of Harvey's room and into the hallway. His face exuded worry. The cuts around his eyes and mouth incurred during the altercation with the Luggs shone from the overhead lights. He spoke to the strikers around him.

"Now everybody be gettin' a chance to spend a few minutes with Harvey. The Doctah done told me that we gotta be talkin' to him when we visit, cuz he just might be able to hear us. So talk it up."

With that he led Cookie Jones and a couple of her girls from the Sisterhood into the room to visit Harvey. When he came back out, he came over to greet Rue and Patrick.

"Thanks for comin' down fellas."

"No problem, Al" spoke Rue. "So where does Harvey stand?"

"Doc says Harvey took a mean blow to the head, and his chances of makin' it are fifty-fifty. At best he could wake up in ten minutes with a bad headache. At worst he dies or stays like he is for the rest of his life."

Alabama's head hung after he spoke those words, and he looked away unable to mask his despair. "Elena be in there with him."

"Elena Madeira?" inquired Patrick.

"Yeah, Elena Madeira. She rode in the ambulance with him, and bin at his side ever since."

The mere mention of her name made Patrick uncomfortable.

Alabama looked at Rue and his eyes welled up. "I can't lose Harvey this way. If I lose Harvey, I don't know what I'm gonna do."

"Have a little faith, Al. Things might work out alright."

"I don't have any faith left, Rue. And if he goes, I don't know what I'm gonna do."

Cookie Jones was coming out of Harvey's room, so Alabama Al motioned them in. Patrick hesitated, knowing that Elena would be there, but Rue gave him a look that made him walk on. Harvey was on his back, eyes closed, head bandaged, an I.V. in his arm. Elena sat in a chair up by his face. She said hello to Rue and gave an indifferent nod to Patrick. A tape recorder was playing some quiet Country Blues.

"Harvey, we got some mo' friends here to visit. Got Rue, the bartender, and Patrick the cook, here. Rue says we owe 'em bail money for getting' him locked up in the pokey last night."

"Yeah Harvey, I go getting' myself involved with you guys and I got another blemish on my rap sheet."

Harvey didn't answer of course. The two newcomers felt the odd vibe of talking to a body that didn't answer back. The cassette tape ended and clicked off.

"Whadya wanna hear now, Harvey?" asked Alabama. "I'll put on Mance Lipscomb. He's one of Harvey's favorites. He loves them ole Country Blues. 'Kitchen music' he calls it. Mance, Mississippi John

Hurt, Son House, Fred McDowell. All them old Blues before they made it up to the big city."

"Trouble in Mind" began to waft out of the tape player, quietly filling the room. In Mance Lipscomb's voice one could hear the early thread of the Blues that ran from the twenties to the present. From Charley Patton to Big Bill Broonzy. Robert Johnson to Buddy Guy. It was all connected by one endless, mournful heartbeat. Rue could see it all in Alabama Al's sleepless, bloodshot eyes; fear and hope hooked up in a knockdown, drag-out, muscle tussle.

"We'll be back tomorrow, Harvey," spoke Rue. "Get some rest. Your job's not over yet."

They left Harvey's room in the ICU, heading back out to the hallway, where a worried hush hung in the air. The Blues Strikers were a somber looking lot.

"How'd he look?" asked Ted.

"Quiet and still," assessed Rue.

"You goin' upstairs to visit Sonny?"

"Yeah, I guess we should. I'm sure nobody here has sent up any bouquets."

"That's a fact. Here, take my Sunday paper so he can see his name in print."

Rue took Ted's Sunday paper, then he and Patrick headed down the hallway to the elevator and up to the third floor to see Sonny. They found him in room 320, stretched out on the bed, his head propped up on a pillow. Appearing both pained and disheveled, he stared out his window unaware of his visitors.

"Hey Sonny, how they hangin'?" inquired Rue with tongue in cheek.

"Yeah, big fucken joke, heh, Morley?"

"Sorry Boss. How're you managing?"

"Oh, just dandy! Except my balls look like a couple of pomegranates."

Sonny pulled back the sheet and lifted up his jonnie to reveal the state of the state.

"Jesus Christ!" they both gasped in unison. His penis shriveled and lifeless lay doornail dead aside his testicles, which were blown up to a frightening proportion.

"How the fuck do you like that?" he inquired as he held up the sheet with his right hand.

"Enough Sonny!" Rue begged, waving his hand for Sonny to cover himself up. Patrick Phelan was overcome with a wave of nausea. It was a ghastly sight, but Sonny would not relent.

"I bin lyin' here all night long, wondering if my machinery will ever work again. That fucken dyke! I'll have her skewered and grilled if it's the last fucken thing I do!"

Finally, having made his point, Sonny covered himself up with the sheet and bummed a smoke off of Rue. A couple of drags of nicotine and he coughed violently, sending a jolt of agony from his groin to his brain. "Oh, fuck me!" he grimaced, smoking down the cigarette despite himself.

"Has anybody been by to see you?"

"Nobody."

"Do you know what actually happened last night?" Rue pushed further.

"Yeah, I got my onions shattered last night! That's what happened!"

Rue pulled out the front page of the paper and handed it over to him. Sonny's cigarette bobbed in his mouth as he half muttered the words he was reading. His eyes bulged with each ensuing paragraph. He'd been lying in his hospital bed, all Saturday night and Sunday morning, virtually in the dark. Cookie Jones' crotch shot and the bumpy ride to the hospital were all he remembered.

"The Jew's in a coma? Moe might be up on a murder rap? What the fuck is going on here? How did they catch all this on camera for the fucken evening news?"

Seconds later his bedside phone rang. It was Moe Venti. "Hello, Moe? Are you alright? Yeah? Morley and Irish are here with me. Yeah, I just read the paper. Moe, I can't fucken believe it! $50,000 bail? Who coulda tipped off the television station? I have no fucken idea! An inside job? Who woulda done that?"

Rue felt a nervous, sweaty tingle trickling down his armpit. He hoped his tracks were covered.

"Moe, we gotta pray that the Jew comes out of it! If not, we're fucked! Right Moe, I know you're fucked big time. But I'm in this too. You should get a gander at my condition. It looks like I'm draggin' a couple of volleyballs around between my knees," he proclaimed, lifting up the sheet to take another look.

"Moe, I know it doesn't stack up to a murder rap. I know! I know! Look Moe, I gotta second cousin, she's a Carmelite Nun. We'll send some cash up there, and get them sayin' some fucken Novenas for the Jew. … He's gotta come out of this Moe. He's got to! You got a lawyer? He's the best? Moe, he's gotta be! I am Moe. I'm prayin' as we speak! OK Moe, call me if something breaks."

Sonny hung up the phone. A panicked pallor came over him as the blood left his face. He coughed hard again, as a barbed wire agony rocketed through his groin.

"Jesus Christ, Mother of fucken mercy!" he petitioned.

He gathered himself once again and wasted no time in bumming another smoke from Rue. "This is like a bad dream. It's gotta be a fucken bad dream. Everything was goin' so smooth. Now the Jew's in a fucken coma, and Moe has to lay down 50 large just to see the light of day?"

"Where the hell did he get fifty grand on a Sunday morning?" wondered Patrick.

"Whadya shittin' me? Moe Venti's Big Time."

"Yeah? Moe may be Big Time, but if Harvey doesn't come around, he's gonna be poundin' big rocks in the hot, hot sun!" offered up Rue.

"The Jew's gonna wake up," insisted Sonny. "He's got to!"

Just then a doctor in a white coat with a stethoscope around his neck and a clipboard in his hand knocked and entered the room.

"Mr. Bolla, I'm Dr. Eberman. I'm here to look you over."

"Eberman? Another fucken Jew? Just what I need."

Dr. Eberman stared back at him in seething silence. "Could you gentlemen step outside please?" he requested. Rue and Patrick obliged and listened from the hallway.

"Mr. Bolla, I'm going to write you up a prescription to manage your pain. There's nothing more we can do for you here. When you get home if you experience any complications, give us a call."

"Give you a call? I can't even stand up and you're sending me home?"

"Mr. Bolla, we need these beds for people that are truly sick. You got kicked in the groin. There's nothing more we can do for you here," he said, putting a script in his hand. Sonny crumpled it up into a ball and threw it back at him.

"Eberman, I wouldn't let you get near me with a fucken Percodan!"

"Good luck with your convalescence. Start getting dressed. The nurse will be up soon."

"Fucken quack!"

The good doctor breezed by the boys outside the door. They kept a straight face until he got down the hallway. Then they crumbled into laughter. There's nothing Sonny could do or say that would surprise them. But when they witnessed a stranger having his virgin Sonny experience—it was as if they were meeting him for the first time, too.

"He's sending you home, Sonny?"

"Can you believe it? Maybe they got a fucken wheelbarrow around here I can rest my testicles in before I push 'em over to the Back Bay. Irish, gimme that script on the floor. I'll probably need it."

"Boss, you want us to give you a lift home?" offered Rue.

"Jeez, wouldya?"

"Sure Boss. What are friends for?"

The boys got Sonny out of bed, into a chair and dressed. Soon the nurse arrived with a wheelchair, and in no time, they were loading him into the front seat of Rue's Camaro.

"Uh, uh, ohhh, easy, easy now!"

32: MORE AFTERMATH

As Sonny rested precariously in the passenger seat of the Camaro, Rue drove a block north to the Skenderian Apothecary to pick up his medication. Having completed that bit of business, he banged a U-turn and headed toward Boston.

"Rue, why don't we breeze by the shop, and grab some provisions?" requested Sonny.

Rue hooked a right in front of the fire station on Hampshire and found a parking spot in front of the Shamrock. They gazed across the street at The Home of the Blues. The hole in the glass block stared back at them.

"Whadya want, Sonny?" asked Rue.

"There's a piece of plywood in the basement. See if you can brace it up and cover that hole. Grab a bottle of scotch, and Irish—make us some sandwiches to bring back to my place. I'm fucken starving."

"There's nothing like a good kick to the nuts to rouse a man's appetite," quipped Patrick.

"No lip, Irish. Just go!"

They hopped out of the car and crossed the street. Patrick hadn't been around for the big fight, so this was his first glimpse of the battlefield. The sidewalk was blood stained and strewn with broken glass.

"Looks like I missed a real party."

"You did, pal."

"Rue, how did you know it was gonna happen?"

"I went downstairs to replace a bottle of vodka, and I overheard Moe Venti chatting it up with Milligan about an assault that was to take place at seven. Moe was asking Milligan to take a slow drive over here

234

after the 911 came through. So, I tipped off Ted and he thought up the rest. The television crew was waiting in the weeds to catch something for the eleven o'clock news."

Rue unlocked the front door, and they ambled into the dark, silent bar. He went down into the cellar to secure a bottle and some plywood. Patrick headed into the kitchen to rustle up some grub. Rue came back upstairs to find him laying down some mortadella, prosciutto, mustard, onions, and chopped olives onto a big Italian loaf.

"Hey man, that's makin' me hungry."

"You know what Rue, I bet Guillermo doesn't even know what's going on. He's been off the last two days."

"You're probably right."

"Was Frankie arrested too?"

"Nobody in the kitchen even knew what was happening. Frankie walks out into the dining room about eight o'clock, and the place was empty. He sees the big hole in the glass block, walks out the front door, and sees the sidewalk stained with blood and glass."

"When did you talk to him?"

"He ended up down the lockup last night, raising bail money for people."

"Christ, what a night!"

They shut out the lights and left the kitchen. Then they slapped a piece of plywood over the hole in the façade, propping it up with cinder blocks and two by fours. Patrick looked into the room and lamented.

"Rue, this could be finito—the last time we're here."

"I don't know. I got a funny feeling that this adventure is just beginning."

"You do?"

"Yeah, I do."

"Why?"

"It's just a feeling. Some places have a life of their own. Some joints live on 'til they're blown up, get burnt down, or the ball and chain takes 'em."

"You talkin' about fate, or destiny?"

"Fate? Destiny? I don't know. I think it's more about a life force. Even right now, when there's nobody in this place, I can feel some sort of buzzing, crackling presence. And I don't get the feeling that it can be frightened away by a picket line, or court room litigation, or even an attempted murder. No man, I think this story is just beginning. I think the table has merely been set."

Patrick found that concept appealing. They stood there feeling the vibe of the room for a good minute, then Rue locked up the front door. They crossed Hampshire and hopped back into the car. Sonny was stretched out trying to give his swollen entities some breathing room.

"All locked up, Rue?"

"All locked up, Boss."

Rue headed over the Longfellow Bridge, down Charles Street and past the Public Garden on his way to the Back Bay and Sonny's pad on Fairfield Street. Sonny was beginning to feel a bit more comfortable until Rue hit a pothole on Beacon Street that sent another shockwave of agony through his fragile being.

"Mother of fucken Christ, Morley!!!"

"Sorry Boss."

"There's a spot, right in front of my place."

Rue pulled over and they helped jimmy and pry Sonny out of the front seat, and up the steps of his apartment. He pulled out his key and unlocked the door. "Wanna come in for a drink?" he offered meekly as if he expected them to say no.

"Sure, let's have a drink," obliged Rue.

"Come on in," he offered, happy not to be left alone in his empty bachelor quarters. Down a hallway, through a door, Sonny flicked on a light, and waddled into his living room. The place was strewn with assorted man cave trash—old pizza boxes, empties and half empties, an overflowing ashtray, and numerous Penthouse magazines. The boys looked around taking in the scene—the outer manifestation of the inner Sonny. They could see into his bedroom, which looked like a legitimate disaster area. An unmade bed surrounded by numerous piles of dirty clothes that rose to knee level.

"The bar's over there. Help yourselves."

"You got any brews, Sonny?"

"Yeah, on ice in the kitchen. Grab me one too."

Rue came back with three Heinekens and handed them out. Sonny was fiddling with his big color television, tuning in a clear picture.

"Do we watch the Patsies boys?"

"Sure."

Soon the New England Patriots vs. The Chicago Bears showed up clear as a bell. The Monsters of the Midway sporting their demonic black jerseys and helmets zeroed in on the Patriots quarterback with bad intent.

"Fucken Pats," bellowed Sonny. "Besides Hog Hannah, their offensive line is a slice of fucken Swiss cheese! Plunkett's gonna end up in the fucken Mayo Clinic, learning how to walk!" Sonny lit up another smoke and quickly launched himself into one more extended coughing session.

"Hey Sonny, instead of lighting up another smoke, when you get the urge, why don't you just go over to that electric socket and stick your pecker in it," suggested Rue.

"That'll be enough out of you." Sonny shimmied in his chair in search of comfortable. "Jesus Christ, I gotta take off these boxer shorts. They're as tight as a fucken jock strap!"

He waddled off to his room penguin style, cigarette dangling from his lips, his face contorted into a relentless wince. He returned moments later, carrying a big fluffy pillow into which he gently laid his expanded appendages. He oohed, ahhed, and nestled his way into the pillow searching for the most favorable angle.

"Rue, what was the name of that dyke?"

"You mean the one that drilled you?"

"Yeah, that one."

"Cookie Jones."

"Yeah, well you guys please pay witness. This Cookie Jones, this man hater, this chick with a dick has got a big-time payback comin'. I'm talkin' a big-time fucken payback!"

Just then Sonny's phone rang out. He reached over from his chair and picked it up.

"Hello. Yeah Moe, yeah, I'm back. Released me? The Jew doctor threw me out. He claimed they needed the fucken bed! Anything new with Wallenberg? Still out cold? Moe, he's gotta wakeup. Yeah? Yeah? Fifteen minutes? I'll be here. I ain't goin' nowhere, not without a forklift anyway. Alright Moe, I'll see you here in a few."

"Venti?" Rue inquired.

"Yeah, he's on his way."

"Is he flipped out?"

"What the fuck do you think? He's lookin' at a murder rap. But he says he's gonna find out who dropped word to that TV station."

"Yeah, and what?"

"They're dead in the fucken water, that's what."

"Who does he think could've done it?"

"He didn't say. He's comin' over to talk about it."

"Well, we're gonna let you two have some time together," spoke Rue as he downed his beer. Patrick followed suit.

"OK boys, don't mind me if I don't show you to the door, and thanks for the ride home."

"Alright Sonny, keep us posted," urged Rue.

"Hope you're feelin better, Sonny," pledged Patrick.

"Thanks Irish. I'll be in touch."

They left Sonny's apartment and walked silently down the dark hallway without exchanging glances. Once out on to the sidewalk, they stopped and eyeballed each other with deep concern.

"Whadya think?" asked Patrick.

"I think I want another drink."

Rue found his way back to Mass. Ave. and pulled over in front of the Newbury Steak House. Then they headed across the street to the Eliot Lounge, where a friendly, mustachioed bartender named Tommy poured them a couple. They pushed their worries aside for a time to watch the Patriots pull out a 13-10 victory over the fearsome Bears. It provided a brief distraction until reality came back around.

"When I woke up this morning, I only knew of one person in the world that wanted me dead. Now there's two," assessed Rue.

"Your wife and Moe Venti?"

"Correct."

"But Moe doesn't know you dropped word on him."

"So far, he doesn't know. But that could change."

"How?"

"Well, he's probably figured out that somebody overheard his conversation with Milligan. He's gonna know it was somebody inside the shop. I'll be suspect Numero Uno."

"What are you gonna do?"

"Deny, deny, deny."

"Then what?"

"Then he's gonna bring everyone else, one by one down into the office for a grilling, hoping that someone spills the beans."

"Just me, Ted, and Miguel know?"

"Just us four."

"You don't have to worry about me, Rue."

"Just be prepared, Patrick. Be prepared because Moe Venti's gonna put you under the microscope. Rest assured of that."

"I'll be ready for him. He won't get a peep out of me."

"Make a move?"

"Sure."

They settled their tab with Tommy, wished him well, and headed back over the Mass. Ave. Bridge to Cambridge. "Alright Phelan, let's drink our way up Mass. Ave. till we get to the Lexington Green!"

First stop was Father's in lower Central Square. This was followed by stops at The Bradford Café, The Paddock, Ken's Pub, The Cantab Lounge, and on to The Hi-Lo, which was darker than Sonny's Place.

"The 'Hi-Lo' —mostly low," Rue evaluated.

"Yeah, but the price is right," proclaimed Patrick upon examining the change he got back for a ten spot. They drank in silence, floating in the darkness of The Hi-Lo.

"It's like drinking in a movie theatre, but the movie never comes on," figured Rue. "One's enough here. Let's check out The Plough and Stars. They drank them down and moved on. They were feeling no pain as they shuffled up Mass. Ave. to their next stop on the hit parade.

"There's one thing about "The Plough," said Rue. "There's gonna be about ten bar flies in there, sittin' in the same fucken seats they were in a month ago when I last imbibed here. And they're all gonna give us that 'Who the hell are you to be walkin' through my living room' look."

Patrick opened the door for Rue and followed him in. Sure enough, they felt a dozen pairs of eyes giving them the once over. They made their way down the bar to a couple of stools, not far from where "Marie's Sunday Brunch Buffet" was being broken down. The boys ordered up a couple of pints, and it didn't take long for the Blues fans in attendance to inquire about last night. It started with the bartender, who served up their brews, and waved off his Jackson in lieu of some news.

As Rue began to tell his story, Patrick looked over his shoulder to see a small gathering of Blues freaks had surrounded them. Amongst them, two gals of premium appearance. He recognized them all as regulars of Sonny's Place. They crowded around to hear the account of the last twenty-four hours.

It was clear that Rue's tough chiseled features had become well recognized in the Blues community. So, he gave his assessment of the situation, and his audience was left shaking their heads in disbelief. They all wondered if this was the end of the Blues in Cambridge.

Eventually the bartender went back to pouring, the Blues fans went back to their seats, and the attractive ladies hung on to chat. Rue knew them both and made with the introductions.

"Patrick, this is Amanda and Mia, a couple of our loyal patrons. This is Patrick, one of our fine cooks down at Sonny's."

"Nice to meet you both," spoke Patrick, giving them a polite handshake and a smile.

"So, what do you think is going to happen, Rue?" asked Mia.

"It's anybody's guess. I'm just hoping that Harvey comes to. Then we go from there."

"Well, a bartender like you won't have any trouble finding a gig," she cooed, giving him a pinch on the cheek.

"Thanks sweetie," smiled Rue. They watched the two lovelies sashay down the bar and out the door.

"Torment. Pure torment," muttered Rue.

"Monogamy got you down, pal?"

"Monogamy means you're having sex with somebody. It's Mary Palm and her five sisters that I've come to loathe."

"Rue, what happened? How did things get this way for you and Leslie?"

"Hey, who the fuck are you? Hedda Hopper?"

"You must've loved her at some point. Arlen didn't show up on your doorstep."

Rue lit up another smoke and sighed. "Yeah, there was a time when we had a real hot thing going on. Then Leslie got pregnant. We decided to roll with it. Get married, have the baby and that was the beginning of the end. Don't get me wrong, I wouldn't trade Arlen for a pot of gold, but Leslie became another person after we got married."

"How so?"

"She wanted me to become something that I wasn't."

"Meaning what?"

"A straight shooter, I guess. Wear a suit and tie? Carry a briefcase? Get up at seven, come home at five? Become a Republican? Grow zinnias out my ass?"

"How long have things been bad?"

"A couple of years now. I talked her into moving up here, thinking the change might help. But things have only gotten worse."

"What do you think will happen?"

"I don't know. I don't know anything anymore, except that I want another beer."

"Have you been faithful?"

"Hey! There you fucken go again, man."

"I'm sorry. I know it's none of my business. I'm just trying to understand."

"You're a real pisser Phelan. But you know, I look at your homely Irish mug, and I can't even get mad at you. The answer is 'No.' Not once have I fucked around. Although lately I've been thinking about it twenty times a day."

"What stops you?"

"Arlen, I guess."

That comment finalized the discussion for a while. They drank on, gazing about at the sights The Plough had to offer.

"You know what I mean about these cloistered stew bums that call this place 'Home'?"

"I'm learning."

Just then the front door of The Plough opened and once again everybody in the joint turned to see who was coming in. It was a solidly built, handsome Black man, pushing a two-wheeler with half a drum kit on it. "It's Bunny Smith," whispered Rue, who gave him a playful elbow to the ribs as he passed by.

"Hey Bunny, you workin' on the Lord's Day?"

"Hey Rue, man I gotta take what I can get. Hey, what the fuck happened down your place last night?"

"Chaos."

"Yeah, I saw the whole thing on the news this mornin', and I drove by there on my way here and saw the place all boarded up. And that lawyer's in a coma?"

"He's still out cold."

"And the owner's on the hot seat for layin' him out?"

"A news crew caught the assault on film, so he's goin' away for a long time if Harvey doesn't come to."

"And in the meantime, you ain't got a job."

"The joint's all shut up tight."

"And that place was just startin' to cook!"

"That's a fact."

"Let me set up, Rue. First number's for you."

"OK Bunny."

Bunny Smith and His Sweet Things got busy setting up their stage at the far end of the bar in front of the restrooms. A trip to the men's room would require one to duck under the bass player's axe coming and going. It made for an up close and friendly listening experience. It didn't take long before they broke into a version of "Caledonia." Bunny on the vocals gave Rue a wink from behind the traps.

SEAN MICHAEL DANEHY

The music managed to infuse some life into The Plough and all the livers that were marinating on this Sunday afternoon. The boys were wading chest high into the comfort zone by this time, and they hung in for a set of music until Patrick noticed a restless look in Rue's eyes.

"Wanna head out?"

"Yeah."

They waved their goodbyes and headed for the door. They hung for a moment on the corner of Mass. Ave. and Hancock, stretching their legs, breathing in some fresh air. The sun was setting, darkness fast approaching.

"One more?" inquired Rue.

"Where to?"

"Jack's."

They walked the block down to Jack's in silence, enjoying the cool October winds.

"There's something lonely about Sunday night," Rue philosophized. "The promise of the weekend is coming to its conclusion. Most of the world is headed back to the merry-go-round of work and school. Night is falling. Winter's on the way."

"That from the Book of Morley?"

"I guess."

Rue stopped outside the door of Jack's before entering. "Ya know the one thing I hate about this dump?"

"Nope."

"It's the smell of the urinals as you enter."

Rue opened the front door. They entered, and Patrick nodded in agreement.

"You gotta drink your beer straight from the bottle in Jack's."

Things inside were kind of subdued. They sat at the bar, ordered up and watched the west coast football game—Rams versus the Forty-Niners in the Coliseum. Rue looked behind them at the empty stage.

"Who's playin' tonight?" he asked the barkeep.

"Peter Johnson and The Manic Depressives."

"What time are they on?"

"9 p.m."

"I hear that band's hittin' its stride. But I'll be in bed by then," yawned Rue. "Check that, I'll be on the couch by then."

They drank up and decided to call it a night. Rue brought Patrick back up to the Cambridge City to pick up his car. "Christ, I don't wanna go home," he muttered in a voice filled with defeat.

"Where does the love go?" asked Patrick.

"I don't fucken know, man. But remember one thing. Moe Venti's coming after you. Be ready for him."

"Don't worry, Rue. All he's getting' is my name, rank, and serial number."

33: BODY LANGUAGE

Patrick woke up the next morning in his white room to the sound of a ringing telephone. Three times it rang over the drone of Jim's television set before Mildred picked it up. Then he heard the pitter patter of Mildred's footsteps coming down the hallway to his door. Two knocks were followed by her stern voice.

"Patrick, telephone for you."

"Right there Ma."

Patrick rolled out of bed and opened the window shade to find the day dark and rainy. Then he headed out to the kitchen to answer the phone.

"Hello."

"Irish, it's Sonny."

"Hi Sonny, how're you feeling."

"Better, thanks. Look Irish, when can you come down here to the restaurant?"

"What's up?"

"Moe has some questions he wants to ask you."

"Questions for me? What does he wanna question me about?"

"Just when can you get down here, Irish?"

"About an hour."

"See you then."

Patrick hung up the phone, and in seconds he could feel the tension rise in the pit of his belly. Jim Phelan could see the look of concern on his face.

"Is that work, Son?"

"Yeah, that was Sonny, my boss down at the restaurant."

"Are you in any kind of trouble down there, Son?"

"No Dad, everything's alright."

"We saw what happened on the news down there Saturday night. They say that lawyer with the Jewish name might be dead."

"He's in a coma."

"Son, is this Venti fellow involved with the Mob?"

"I don't know Dad. He owns a few barrooms, but I can't say if he's in with the Mob."

"I'm worried about you working down there."

"Don't be worried, Dad."

"If anything happened to you, I don't know what we'd do." Jim began to shake, and a tear ran down his cheek.

"I love you, Dad. Don't worry about me."

Patrick got down on one knee and gave Jim a hug and a kiss. Then he went back to his room to get dressed. He grabbed an umbrella from the closet and headed for the door.

Mildred turned to see him walk down the hallway. His buttocks caught her eye as she took a drag from her cigarette. She walked a few steps forward to take a better look at his backside till he was out the door and gone. Then she turned to Jim.

"Did you notice his rear end?"

"His what?"

"His rear end!" she raised her voice. "Did you notice his rear end?"

"No."

"It's not so rigid and tight looking. He's strutting around loose and bouncy."

"So what?"

"So what? Don't you know what that means?"

"No. What?"

"It means he's been having sex!"

Jim's Parkinsonian mask disintegrated, and his old face reappeared briefly, as he laughed like he might shatter into pieces. Mildred took another drag from her cigarette and glared at him.

"And you think that's funny, Jim? Now the whole can of worms starts anew!"

*****

Patrick decided to make his way down to Harvard Square for a quick stop at The Tasty. He found an empty stool down the counter in front of Mr. Charlie.

"Good mornin' Chief, what'll it be?"

"Good mornin' Charlie. Regular coffee and an English muffin, please."

"English and a regular, comin' right up Chief."

Mr. Charlie poured him a cup of coffee and laid down a napkin, a knife, and a spoon as Patrick watched him do his breakfast thing. The Tasty was a tight spot to work out of, but Mr. Charlie was a smooth old pro. He could've run that counter blindfolded. Patrick sipped his coffee and glanced at the newspaper headlines an old timer was reading.

"PRESSURE FOR NIXON IMPEACHMENT MOUNTS"

"Charlie, what's gonna happen to our President?" the old timer wanted to know.

"I believe he's in some hot water, Chief."

"He's goin' down!" proclaimed a young Harvard kid in the corner.

"Put him in jail!" another demanded.

"Where are all the god damned people that voted for him?" Patrick wondered aloud. "The piece of shit was elected in the biggest landslide in American political history. Now you can't find anybody around that's got his back!"

"Good point, Chief," spoke Mr. Charlie.

Patrick remembered well, election night 1971. He'd gotten himself to the polls in Cambridge by closing time. He cast his vote for George McGovern, headed back to the Dart, and turned the radio on in time to hear that the networks had declared Nixon the winner by computer forecast. This was three full hours before the polls were closed in California. It left a bad taste in his mouth.

He finished his coffee and muffin, leaving them all to ponder Nixon's fate. Patrick had his own problem at the moment. Moe Venti would soon be putting the lean on him. "Deny, deny, deny," he repeated Rue's advice as if it were a mantra. As he drove down to Inman Square, he could feel his stomach rumble. Parking the Dart on Hampshire, he ran into Frankie Pope, who was coming out the front door. They hadn't seen each other since the whole fiasco had come down.

"Hey Frankie, what's the word?"

"The word is unemployed. The word is I'm broke. I gotta come up with a rent check in a week."

"It's hard to believe what's happened."

"No shit."

"Did Sonny call you in?"

"Yeah, he called me in so that Moe Venti could do his Gestapo number on me. He had me down there with the Lugg Brothers trying to scare some info out of me. The guy's come completely unwrapped. I can't believe this gig is over. Everything was so ripe."

"Have you seen Guillermo?"

"I saw him yesterday. He's pretty upset. He was hoping to have his family here by Christmas, but now he doesn't know what to think. But I've got to pull a resume together and find a job. It's that simple. I can't wait."

Patrick felt unsettled by Frankie's words. It was Guillermo's kitchen, but Frankie had been his mentor, taking him under his wing, generously sharing his knowledge, and simply being his friend. Now it looked like Frankie was out the door, if a door was there at all. Sonny's Place had become the center of their lives, but just like that, it seemed to be slipping out of sight.

"Where you gonna be looking, Frankie?"

"I don't know—downtown, the hotels maybe. Someplace with some fucken stability, man."

"Frankie, I'm starting to feel lost. I was just getting a handle on things here."

"I know man. It really sucks. Sometimes this business is for the birds. Anytime things are going well, it means things are about to turn to shit. It's best to just keep moving. There's always another joint opening up right down the block."

"Not another joint like this one."

"That's for sure."

"Maybe we should try to get Guillermo and the crew together for a little fiesta."

"Good idea. Let's do that. I'll call you in the next day or two. Hey man, it was fun while it lasted."

"Maybe it's not over."

"Don't count on that, Patrick."

They shook hands and Patrick watched Frankie shuffle down the block and out of sight. He felt his heart sink. As he headed inside, he heard a pair of boots clomping up the back stairs. It was the Turk, and he looked hassled.

"Hey Turk."

"Hey Patrick. Your turn to be grilled?"

"Yeah, Sonny called me in. Did they give you the third degree?"

"Third degree? Moe essentially accused me of setting him up. He's out of his mind down there. How this guy ever got involved with the Blues is beyond me. I think we can kiss this place goodbye!"

"Don't say that, Turk."

"Sorry man, but I think it's a done deal."

"I guess I better go down and face the music. Turk, I'll be in touch. Frankie and I wanna get the crew together for a party."

"Sounds good, Patrick. Watch out for yourself down there," he admonished. The Turk pulled his harp from his shirt pocket and wailed a mournful sound as he headed for the street.

Patrick took a deep breath, approached the office door, and gave it a knock.

"Come in," he heard Sonny shout out.

He opened the door and entered the office to see Sonny stretched out on the sofa, still searching for comfortable. Moe Venti was seated behind Sonny's desk, leaning back with his hands behind his head. His eyes evoked a smoldering panic. Patrick said his hellos then looked off to the right, where the Lugg Brothers sat, looking like a train wreck.

"Christ, what happened to you guys?"

The Luggs were a composite of bruises, black eyes and broken teeth. The tops of their crew cut heads were laced with wide scrapes as if someone had taken a belt sander to their heads. They looked back and said nothing.

"Irish, do you know why we called you in here today?" asked Sonny.

"No," he lied sheepishly.

As the denial fell off his lips, Moe Venti leaned forward in his squeaky chair, resting his clasped hands on the desk in front of him. Patrick felt the heat rising. The toes in his sneakers squirmed with tension.

"Well, to be honest," he began again, "I just bumped into Frankie and Turk on the way in here. So, I do know why you want to speak to me."

Moe Venti arched his brow, and a succession of taut parallel lines creased his forehead. It was as if a door had opened for him. Patrick Phelan could feel Moe's switch blade eyes cutting through him as his heart began to really pound.

"But I don't have any idea how that television crew got tipped off on Saturday night. Moe, I understand that you're on the hot seat, but I have no idea how that happened."

Silence filled the office, as eight eyeballs bore in on him. Frankie and the Turk spoke of Moe Venti ranting and raving out of control. But now he wasn't making a sound. He just sat in his chair smiling as if he were reading Patrick like a newspaper. Finally, Moe spoke.

"Well Patrick, I'm sure that if you uncover the identity of the person who set me up, you'll let us know."

"Yeah, sure Moe. If I find anything out, I'll let you know. Is that it?"

"Yes, that's it," he smiled.

Patrick Phelan got up, headed out the door and closed it behind him. Sonny and the Luggs listened to him scamper up the back stairs as Moe Venti began pointing his finger in Patrick's direction and nodding his head.

"No Moe! Not Irish! Not the kid!" insisted Sonny.

"He might not be the one who blew the whistle on me Sonny, but he knows who did. It's written all over him."

"You want us to get it out of him Boss?" inquired the battered Luggs.

"We'll hold off on that for the moment. I think that scared little pissant will spill the beans without a beating. I don't like getting sloppy about this kind of thing."

Sonny lit up a nervous smoke. He liked talking tough, but when it got around to really taking care of someone, the blood would leave his face and that cold pizza he had for breakfast would flip flop in his tummy.

Patrick was panicked. He walked down Hampshire, hooked a right on Cambridge, and headed directly through the front door of the Inn Square Men's Bar. It wasn't even noon, yet there was an expansive cast of regulars and graveyard shifters on their stools. Patrick ordered up a Pickwick Ale and headed out back to the pay phone to call Rue Morley.

"Hello."

"Rue, it's Patrick."

"What's up?"

"It's eleven o'clock and I'm drinking a beer."

"Good for you. What's the problem?"

"I just squared off with Sonny and Moe."

"You didn't tell them anything?"

"No, nothing."

"So, what's the problem?"

"I got a bad feeling. I ran into Frankie and the Turk on the way in. They said that Moe was ranting and raving, giving them the third degree, practically accusing them of setting him up."

"Yeah?"

"Well, when I got down there, all he did was stare at me like I was a piece of modern art."

"What did you do?"

"Deny, deny, deny."

"Then what?"

"Then nothin'. Moe just kept staring at me like he was reading my mind. He had a cocky little grin on his face. Rue, I'm worried."

"I think you're reading too much into it."

"I hope you're right, but I got a bad feeling. Have they called you in?"

"Yeah, I'm due in at noon."

"Good luck. By the way, what the fuck happened to the Lugg Brothers? They looked like a couple of shattered windshields."

"They double teamed Alabama, and he made 'em pay."

"Wow! The Luggs eating humble pie? Go figure."

"I wouldn't have believed it if I hadn't seen it with my own eyes. Sometimes you give a bully a good shot to the chops, and he don't know how to respond."

"It's too much. Well good luck in there and be careful with those guys."

"I'll talk to you."

Patrick hung up the phone and felt no better. He was plain worried. His sneakers walked him right back to the bar to fill his empty schooner.

34: THE VIGIL OF ELENA MADEIRA

Miguel, the Chicano from Four Corners and Tisha Madeira had just finished up some fun in the afternoon. Together they lay, Tisha holding him close as she always did after disengaging. Miguel felt she was clinging as he stared up at the ceiling. Wishing to be alone was a brand-new feeling in their exchange, and he couldn't push it aside. Retreating to the bathroom, he sat down on the toilet to just be by himself for a moment, assessing his preliminary pangs of restlessness.

More than love, the scene at Sonny's Place had kept Miguel in Cambridge. Almost three months of the Blues, night after smoky night had only whetted his appetite. The curiosity to know who'd be driving their van down the alley to the backdoor of Sonny's and hauling their equipment through the kitchen and out to the stage persisted. The excitement of that was only getting stronger.

But the music had stopped, and he didn't feel much hope about the situation straightening out. That being the case, he knew that very soon he'd be down the road, and down the road alone. Miguel cared for Tisha more than a little, but he was beginning to resonate to the distant whistle of a Hank Williams freight train. He thought about broaching this reality with her but chickened out. Instead, he walked out to the living room and rolled up some herb for them to smoke.

Tisha got off his newly purchased mattress, shook out her long brown hair, and pulled it behind her head in a momentary ponytail. She ambled over to where Miguel was lighting up. They gazed down onto Antrim Street from their third-floor perch. School kids on their way home freckled the street and sidewalks, filling the air with the sounds of joyful release. They smoked a little herb, smiling as they watched and listened to the segregated little clusters of boys and girls giving each other the business as they made their way home for milk and cookies.

Looking out through the half bare trees, Tisha could sense that old man winter was stalking them from beyond the edge of town. Soon it would be time to break out the scarves and mittens. Tisha felt happy. She was in love.

"Honey, have you enjoyed your first autumn in New England?"

"Yeah, it's been a trip."

"Winter's coming Miguel. The holiday season, some good snowstorms. I want you to come over to our house for Thanksgiving and Christmas dinner."

Miguel took a hit of herb, held it in silently, and heard that lonesome whistle blow.

"Don't you want to come over to our house for the Holidays?"

"What about your father? You're gonna clue him in to us?"

"Well, I have to sooner or later."

"Why?"

"Well, he's my father. I can't hide this from him much longer."

"Why not?"

"Miguel, are you afraid of my father?"

"Absolutamente! Hombre's got a crazed look in his eye, and he ain't gonna take to the idea of us doin' what we do."

"You're a Chicano Loco, Miguel!" she teased.

"Maybe so, but I don't like the idea of him knowing about us. I think he might snap if he found out."

"But I want him to know about us. I'm proud to be with you. I don't want to hide it anymore."

"Tisha, relax. Put your Papa thing on the back burner for now."

"OK, OK," she relented.

Soon a velvety, buzzed air overtook them. Miguel felt his separation dissipate. The piercing whistle of Hank's freight train fell out of earshot for the time being. Soon they got lost in each other again, and danced their dance to its conclusion. Afterwards they rested at each other's side.

"Miguel, I've got to go to the hospital and check in on Elena. Come along with me?"

"Is she still over there with Harvey?"

"Yeah."

"Strange."

"Yeah, it is strange. She doesn't even know Harvey, but she can't leave his side. When he got hit, he fell right at her feet, and she's been with him ever since."

"Why?"

"She says that if she leaves the hospital, she's afraid he's going to die."

"Why does she feel so responsible?"

"She tends to go that way. You see my mother died in labor, giving birth to her. She's prone to feeling like she's to blame. Stella and my father don't exactly knock themselves out trying to make her feel welcome. Stella feels she was robbed of her childhood, being a mother to the two of us. My father lost his wife, and I don't think he's ever gotten over that, and he takes it out on Elena in ways he's not aware of. So, she's had it pretty rough. She had a real crush on Patrick too, and it really hurt her when she found him dating that blonde he's taken up with. So, she's got a few reasons for acting strangely."

They rose to their feet, got dressed, and descended the three flights of stairs. Tisha took Miguel's hand, walking him down Antrim and up Cambridge Street to the Cambridge City Hospital. They took the elevator and found a despondent Alabama Al sitting on the bench outside Harvey's room. A handful of the strikers were seated on either side of him. His big, dark, cow eyes looked up, and he rose to greet them. Tisha gave him a big hug and a kiss on the cheek. Miguel offered his hand and felt it disappear into Alabama's.

"How are you doing, Al?" asked Tisha.

"Oh, we be hangin' in there. Nothin's changed. The doctah says that Harvey's stable, but he can't say what will be. So, we be sittin' here, hopin' against hope. D'ya know?"

"Yeah, we know," she spoke for the two of them. "Is Elena inside?"

"Yes Tisha, I bin' after her to go home and get some rest in her own bed, but she won't budge. That lil' girl is some kinda stubborn, I'll tell you."

"Al, I'm gonna try to talk her into coming back home with me tonight. There's only so much she can do."

"You be right Tisha, but don't count on her budgin'. You might just as well put this here hospital on your back and carry it home!"

"Thanks for the warning, Al. Is it alright for us to go in?"

"Yeah, I'll come in with you," he spoke, holding the door open for them. "Hey Harvey, we got some mo' guests here to see you. We got Elena's sister Tisha, and Miguel the bartender."

Elena looked up from where she had been reading aloud. She rose out of her chair and gave her sister a big hug. Then she smiled her first and only smile of the day.

"How're you doin' little sister?"

"I'm OK," she whispered. "I've been reading to Harvey."

Miguel hadn't seen Harvey since the rumble. All this talking to a man lying flat out on his back made him uncomfortable. Alabama picked up on that fast and gave him a nudge. "Talk to him, Miguel. He can hear you."

Miguel coughed to clear his throat "Buenos Dias, Harvey. What's happening, pal. How're you feelin'?"

Silence.

"Harvey, you gotta wake up soon, man," begged Alabama. I don't know how much mo' of this hospital slop I can eat. The last plateful I had; I wouldn't have fed to my dog!"

"Bad?" inquired Miguel.

"Badder than bad! Harvey, we gotta get outa this joint and head back to Chinatown. What was the name of that spot we hit, Miguel?"

"Moon Villa."

"Yeah man, off we go to Moon Villa. Lil' chow mein and a couple of cold ones!"

No answer. Just Harvey's lungs doing some light breathing. They hung on a few more minutes talking up a storm as if they were at some house party. But the chatter dried up pretty quick. Elena told Harvey that she'd be right back. Everybody else said their goodbyes and headed for the hallway. The Madeira sisters started a slow walk down to the water bubbler. Alabama Al followed several strides behind to lend some support.

"Elena, you know that I have a lot of respect for you staying here with Harvey and trying to do everything you can to bring him back."

"Yeah Tish, but what?" asked Elena pointedly before she held back her long black hair to take a slow drink of water.

"Honey, I'm not trying to tell you what to do, but I think you need to stand back and get a little perspective on this. I think you should come home tonight and get some rest in your own bed. Harvey's life and death don't hinge on you being here. You're not responsible for any of this, Elena."

"She be right, Elena," slipped in Alabama Al. "Listen to your sister, now."

"Has Papa noticed that I haven't been home?"

Tisha's silence answered that question. Elena's tired eyes looked away and over their shoulders. She folded her arms and looked ahead. Then took another drink of water and left them both at the bubbler.

"I told you she's some kinda stubborn," chimed in Alabama.

Tisha nodded in agreement as she watched her little sister head down the hallway and back to the bedside of Harvey Wallenberg to maintain her vigil.

35: THE KILKENNY PUB BY THE DUMP

Patrick Phelan had set out to Castle Island in South Boston to pass a few hours of nervous concern. A flock of seagulls squawked and chattered above him. The wind, speckled with mist, blew back his curly brown hair. A steady procession of steel birds rose and descended as the arrivals and departures made their way to and from Logan Airport.

The worrying hadn't stopped since he'd left Sonny's Place. If Moe Venti was on his way to jail for murder, why wouldn't he relish getting even with whomever he believed had set him up? What would he have to lose? Patrick's inner monologue spun around in circles like a freaked-out dog chasing its flea bitten tail. By the time he made it back to the Dart, parked near Kelly's Landing, he was cold, wet, and fearful.

It was midafternoon and time to drop in on Uncle Liam at his barroom in North Cambridge. Celtic tickets in exchange for moving a fridge. Besides, Patrick needed a chat with his uncle right about now. The Dart found its way onto the Mass. Pike, into Cambridge, up Memorial Drive, over to Sherman Street, and the front door of The Kilkenny Pub by the Dump. Although he had seen and spoken to Liam several times, this was the first visit to the bar since he'd returned from Louisiana.

Patrick felt a bit self-conscious as he opened the front door, expecting to see a lot of faces that he'd have to explain himself to. But it was midafternoon, and most of the regulars were still on the clock. Uncle Liam was behind the bar, holding court with a couple of the retired elder statesman of the neighborhood: Misters Finnerty and O'Brien. They heard the front door open and looked over their shoulders to see him shuffle into the bar.

"Lo and behold, Liam. Look what the cat dragged in!" proclaimed Mr. O'Brien.

"Better card him, Liam. He's not old enough to drink!" estimated Mr. Finnerty, smoking a smelly old cigar, his dog, Goldie, asleep at his feet.

Patrick smiled and shook hands all around.

There was something timeless about the Kilkenny. Liam wasn't keeping up with any fashion trends. The décor was bare bones—seven four-top tables and chairs, eleven unpadded barstools, and, fronting the bathrooms, a backroom where Saturday night poker games were a mainstay. Finally, a tight little kitchen just beyond the bar sat idly by, used only when one of the regulars threw a party.

The right-hand wall was filled with formal portraits of the patrons, photographed by Liam. They spanned the generations of the neighborhood. Old world weary five and dimers positioned next to young upstarts with a fire in their eyes. But if you scrutinized the wall closely, in the very middle you could see the photograph of a lean, crew cut, eighteen-year-old man-child, who happened to be the greatest hockey player that the world would ever see.

A friend of the Kilkenny had brought Bobby Orr through for a couple of underaged beers during his rookie season. His money was no good there, and Liam wasn't letting him leave before he sat down for a moment in front of his lens.

Patrick glanced at the black and white of Number Four and felt the subtle, homespun magic of The Kilkenny Pub by the Dump. It served as a medicated womb for the working men of North Cambridge. Their wives and girlfriends knew that they were drinking, but at least they knew where. When asked to describe his bar, Liam always said, "We've got geniuses sitting next to idiots, and they talk for hours!"

"What can I get you, sailor?"

"Bottle of Bud."

"That's on me, Liam," spoke Mr. O'Brien. "Tell me Patrick, how's your dad doing?"

"Not so good, Mr. O'Brien."

"I'm sorry, son. I love your father. Give him my best, will you?"

"I'll do that," promised Patrick.

"Christ, I'll never forget the time," started old man Finnerty, "that your Father called up Liam here and pretended to be the Internal Revenue Service."

"That son of a bitch!" recalled Liam. "He called me up here, disguised his voice, and said that the bar was being investigated for tax fraud. Tells me there's a court date set for the following Monday. I start sweatin' bullets. So, I pull out all my records on the table over there, and I'm trying to figure out what's what. Twenty minutes later I hear someone giggling over my shoulder. I look up and it's Jim Phelan. Now he's laughin' so fucken hard, I can hear his bones rattle. It took me another second to realize it was him on the phone. I chased his ass out the front door, and halfway down to the fucken dump!"

"And oh, what a dancer!" recollected Mr. O'Brien. "On Saturday nights we'd all go out with our dates to The Westminster Roof or The Totem Pole to hear the swing bands. Well, we'd all do our best two-step. But your father? Your father could really dance!"

"The Fred Astaire of Cambridge we used to call him."

"The Fred Astaire of Cambridge," sighed Patrick—a sweet, unfathomable notion. When Jim's old friends spoke of him, they painted a portrait of a vibrant man bubbling over with humor and life. He imagined a young Jim Phelan swinging a beautiful gal, not necessarily Mildred, around a crowded ballroom to the sounds of the old Dorsey Band—Jim inspired and in control, his date wide eyed thrilled, anticipating his next move. Couples would instinctively back off a bit to give them the room they needed to operate. Some stopped dancing altogether, then stood back and watched.

Patrick Phelan held on to that notion until it began to hurt. Then he looked around the bar and thought of the many times Jim brought him here as a young boy. Their old tradition was that after the 11:15 Mass at St. Peter's they would drop Mildred off back at the house on Sparks Street to get the Sunday roast in the oven. Then he'd take his young son down to the Kilkenny to visit Liam. Jim would lift Patrick up on a barstool, set him up with a ginger ale and a bag of beer nuts. Then they'd watch the New York Football Giants: Y.A. Tittle, Rosey Grier, Frank Gifford, and Sam Huff.

Jim would smoke a Sunday cigar, knock back a couple of Narragansetts, and give the business to all the regulars. Those were happy memories that would never vanish, but it felt bittersweet to be back in Liam's bar.

"Are you ready for some heavy lifting, sailor?"

"Yeah, let's do it."

Uncle Liam led Patrick down the bar, through the little kitchen, and out to the back stoop. A lowboy fridge sat solo in the rain atop Liam's flatbed truck.

"This won't be too much trouble," assured Liam. "I saw it at an auction last week and the guy practically paid me to take it off his hands. Besides, you never know when yours' is gonna shit the bed."

They both climbed up on the truck and swiveled the cooler down to the edge of the tailgate. Then they hopped back down, got their hands underneath, and carried the fridge into the kitchen, grunting and shuffling all the way.

"Careful sailor. We don't want you poppin' a plumb!"

They wrestled it inside and slid it nicely under a shelf. Liam reached into his pocket and handed over the prize; two tickets for the Celtics/Knicks game a week and a half away.

"Thanks Liam. Wow, promenade seats!"

"Remember those seats your father used to get?"

"Yeah, we'll be breathin' in Red's cigar smoke."

"I got 'em from the same guy—Mr. Peabody. He'll be dropping in soon for a drink."

"I remember him. Big guy, well dressed, smokes Havanas?"

"That's him. Been coming here for years. He's got season tickets. Goes to about half the games and drops a lot of tickets on me."

"The kind of guy we like to know. So, what do you think, can we win it all this year?"

"We had the best regular season record in the N.B.A. last year. We would've won it all if Havlicek hadn't ripped up his shoulder."

"He pushed the fucken Knicks to seven games with one arm! Afterwards I read that Auerbach said, "the great ones" can play on one leg, and they're still better than everyone else."

"Yup. And this kid Cowens, he ain't Bill Russell, but I tell you what—he's the kind of guy I want to go to war with. He doesn't give a fucken inch. I don't care who he's up against—Chamberlain, Jabbar, Lanier, Reed, Thurmond. He fears nobody. I like that about him. It makes me think they can beat anyone."

"He muscles them for every square inch on their end, then torments them with eighteen-foot jumpers on our end."

Having dissected their dreams for World Championship Number Twelve, it didn't take long for Patrick's troubles to surface. Liam could see worry on his face.

"You seem a bit distracted, sailor. Is there a problem?"

"Yeah, there's a problem."

"Does it have to do with all the trouble I've been hearing about down where you work?"

"Yes."

Liam pulled up a couple of stools. Then Patrick walked him through the whole panorama: the Blues Strike, Moe Venti, Harvey Wallenberg, Alabama Al, Rue, Ted from the Tortoise, the TV cameras, the arrests, and this morning's meeting with Sonny and Moe.

"But Venti can't be certain that you're involved, right?"

"I denied it up and down, but I felt like he was seeing right through me. He might be going away for murder. If he has a notion that I'm involved, what's gonna stop him from putting the screws to me? I have to think he might get some satisfaction out of it. Liam, I don't feel safe. I think he's gonna send someone after me."

Liam nodded, rose from his stool, and silently paced about the kitchen, taking in all that he had just heard.

"Do you think I'm crazy for being worried?"

"You're not crazy if you feel danger. You gotta listen to your instincts, sailor."

"What should I do, Liam?"

"I'm thinking."

Liam paced the floor of his kitchen for another minute until he heard the front door of his bar open. In walked a refrigerator of a man wearing a Stetson, a long tweed overcoat, smoking a big Havana.

"There's someone who can help us."

"Mr. Peabody?"

Liam nodded and stepped back behind his bar to pour Mr. Peabody his usual.

"Good afternoon, Arnold."

"Liam."

"Arnold, I'd like you to come back to the kitchen, and meet my nephew, Patrick."

"Jim's son? Gladly."

Arnold Peabody took his stinger on the rocks and gave it a stir with the swizzle stick that looked like a light beam in his huge hands. He sucked the stirrer dry, tossed it in an ashtray, and walked the length of the bar through the swinging door of Liam's kitchen.

"Patrick Phelan, Arnold Peabody."

Patrick rose and they shook hands.

"You're Jim Phelan's son."

"Yes sir, I am."

"Call me Arnold."

"OK Arnold," smiled Patrick before letting go of their shake.

"How is your dad doing, son?"

"Not so well, Arnold."

"I'm sorry. Please tell Jim I was asking for him."

"I will."

"Years back your father knew I was going through some tough financial difficulties, and when I sent my children to him for some dental work, he refused to send me a bill. That's the kind of man he is," spoke Arnold glancing over at Liam with a nod.

"Arnold, Patrick thinks he might be in some danger."

"What kind of danger, son?"

"Arnold, I cook down at Sonny's Place in Inman Square."

"Moe Venti's joint."

"Correct."

"Moe's in some deep shit right now."

"Yeah, he's up on a possible murder rap, and the place has been shut down."

"Too bad. I've eaten there. Try the veal," he affirmed to Liam, "It's the best in the city. Even though he's propped up that bonehead Sonny to front the place. So why would Moe want to hurt you, son?"

Patrick took Mr. Peabody through the entire scenario that he'd just explained to his uncle. Arnold sipped his drink and took a couple of puffs off his cigar while he listened. He nodded when Patrick had finished.

"Well Patrick, I happen to have done a lot of important work for a man that Moe Venti has to answer to. Where's a phone Liam? I'll nip this right in the bud."

Liam brought the extension over, and Arnold dialed the number right off the top of his head. He took a slow hit off his Havana and blew some smoke up to the ceiling while the phone rang in the North End.

"Hello Gennaro. It's Arnold Peabody. Very well thank you, and yourself? And the family? Good, good. Gennaro, do you recall last year when I straightened out that problem you had in Charlestown, and you told me that you owed me one? Good. I'd like to call that favor in if you don't mind. A very close family friend of mine believes that our colleague Moe Venti may be pinning blame on him for the mess he's in. If you would, Gennaro, I'd like you to tell Moe that he's not to harm a hair on this young man's head. No problem? That's great, and I owe you one. No? I guess you're right. You owed me one!" Arnold laughed. "Yes, you'd think he would have hired a pro for that kind of thing. The young man? His name is Patrick Phelan. Oh yes, he's a mick. Yeah, they do have funny names, don't they?" Arnold winked and smiled, looking back and forth from uncle to nephew.

"OK Gennaro, I appreciate your help with this. We'll talk soon" and Arnold handed the phone back to Liam.

"Son, you won't be having any problems with Moe Venti. We'll just call this payback for the good turn your father did me many years ago. Don't forget to give him my regards."

"I won't Arnold, and thank you so much."

They shook hands again, and Mr. Peabody headed back to the bar, leaving uncle and nephew alone. Patrick breathed in and breathed out as he felt a mighty weight come off his shoulders. But he didn't understand what had just taken place.

"Who did he call up? Who is Gennaro?"

"Don't ask."

"Well, who is Mr. Peabody?"

"Do you remember when Arnold said that Moe Venti should have hired a pro?"

"Yeah."

"Well, let's just say that Arnold is one of those professionals."

"You're shittin' me?"

"Hey sailor, we're not playin' Dominos here. This is the fucken Kilkenny!"

"Yeah, I got it."

Patrick stood up and put his arms around his uncle in thanks. Liam returned the hug, slapping him on the back heartily a few times.

"Hey sailor, that's why I'm here."

They looked each other in the eye and shared that moment. Liam was a rock and Patrick felt lucky to have him. They left the tiny kitchen and headed back out to the bar. Patrick took a seat between Mr. Peabody and Mr. O'Brien. He took a long haul off his beer and felt the tension of the day dissipate.

"Thanks again for your help, Arnold."

"It's my pleasure to help you out, son. Your Father came to my aid that time without even being asked. I'm happy to reciprocate. And I don't want you worrying about Moe Venti. Trust me, from now on he will fear you."

"Fear me? I have a hard time imagining that. I don't think I've ever been feared."

"Hey, you might grow to like it," laughed Arnold.

"Yeah, I just might get to liking it," confessed Patrick.

All the worry began to leave his mind. He felt like he'd been delivered to some agent of mercy found within the womb of his uncle's bar. He thankfully dropped a twenty down and bought a round for himself and his cohorts of the moment: Peabody, O'Brien, and Finnerty.

Arnold clenched and reclenched his Havana between quips and stinger sips. But he got his deadly serious face on when he said, "Trust me, son. He'll be viewing you differently since he got that phone call."

"How does that work, Arnold?"

"Well son, it's actually quite simple. We all have to answer to somebody—you, to your parents, and maybe your girlfriend. Your Uncle Liam—to his wife Delia and the tax man. Moe Venti and I? We answer to Gennaro, the fellow I called on your behalf."

"Who does Gennaro answer to?"

"The Man Upstairs? That is if there's anybody up there," he spoke in a dubious, nonchalant tone before returning the Havana to his clenched teeth.

Patrick considered all that for a quiet Kilkenny moment till the calm was broken up by a shriek at the front door.

"Where is he? Where is that nephew of mine? There you are!" Delia wailed, grabbing him from behind with her meaty washerwoman hands in a grand display of mock strangulation. "You've been home for almost three months, and it takes you this long to come down here and see me?"

"Get him Delia! Show no mercy," crowed the peanut gallery.

Delia was just getting started as she got her forearm square up under Patrick's Adam's apple and yanked him around some more.

"How's this Arnold? Is this how it's done?"

"That's how Delia!" he roared. He's yours! You own him!"

Having made her point, Delia's choke hold slid down around his shoulders and arms, turning into a warm embrace. Patrick laughed to feel her big bosom pressed against his shoulder blades. She whispered only for him to hear.

"It's so good to have you home. We missed you so much."

Her words made him wrestle free so that he could swivel around and return her embrace. Delia and Liam had no children of their own.

So, Patrick held a special place. He was Delia's child along with all the other scallywags and rogues that inhabited their barroom.

If Delia had a quarter for every time she forked over fifty bucks to one of her boys to keep the gas and electric from being shut off, she'd be able to sail off into the sunset. She gave and gave. Never asked for anything.

"Thanks Delia. I missed you and Liam too."

"And Liam tells me you have a sweetheart in town?"

"Yeah, I've been seeing a girl who lives around the corner on Upland."

"Well, aren't we getting all grown up. When are you bringing her by so I can meet her?"

"I don't know if she's ready for this place."

"What's the matter with this place?"

"Are you serious? This is the outpatient clinic for the North Cambridge/Irish-America Insane Asylum."

"Yeah? Well, you may have something there. Now listen Patrick, I gotta go run errands, but I don't want you being a stranger around here anymore. Understand?"

"I won't be Delia. I promise." And with that the nephew and aunt gave each other a squeeze goodbye.

"Liam honey, I'll be waitin' for ya upstairs," she announced, pulling up her dress to flash a little thunder thigh. A chorus of catcalls filled the bar.

"You'll be waitin' a long time, sweetheart", muttered Liam. "Ya dried up old prune."

In no time the pace of the Kilkenny picked up as the regulars punched out of their jobs and came in to knock a few back. First it was

Jackie McManus, who drove the Waverly bus out of Harvard Square, followed by Bobbie Duggan, who read the meters for the Commonwealth Gas Company. Then in came Albert Mahoney and Barry Mulray, both Court Officers of Middlesex County. Then the arrival of Joe O'Regan, the mailman. The bluster and blarney commenced.

They were all from the neighborhood—born there, grew up there, ran wild there, got married, and settled down there. The neighborhood was their past, present, and future. It spanned for them to the horizon, and their drudgeries and dreams breathed a continuity of life into the streets of North Cambridge. One by one they came in, ordered a drink, and made their way over to interrogate the long-lost nephew of The Kilkenny.

"Where the hell you been? Why did you quit school? Where you workin'? What the hell's goin' on down there in Inman Square? How's your dad? Geez, I'm sorry. Give him my best, will ya?"

Liam noticed that it was seconds before six, so he turned on the evening news. Everybody had gotten used to Watergate dominating the airtime, but tonight they got thrown a curve ball by the local anchor desk.

"Good evening. This is the News at Six. Today, the High Court in an 18-page unanimous decision has rejected the Boston School Committee's third and final attempt to invalidate the Racial Imbalance Law of 1968. There is no longer any recourse left for the Boston School Committee to pursue. Nonadherence to the High Court will result in a multimillion dollar freezing of State and Federal funds. The future of the Boston School System weighs in the balance."

"I knew this was comin' down for the last month" announced Barry Mulray, Officer of the Middlesex County. They're headed for fucken World War Three. There's speculation that they'll have to bus kids back and forth from Southie and Roxbury to balance things off. If that happens watch out!"

Everyone took note, but the tone wasn't personal. The Killkenny wasn't taken over by a sudden racial hemorrhage. The city of Cambridge had always been a vortex of colliding cultures. Folks from all over the world had settled in and wrestled over this turf since the beginning.

The guys in this bar grew up with black kids, went to school with them, played ball with them. Had there been trouble? Yes, there'd been plenty of trouble. But for a white kid growing up in Cambridge, rubbing shoulders with black kids was a regular occurrence. The desegregation of the Boston School System would send hardly a ripple through old Cambridge town.

Liam had black friends that frequented the Kilkenny. He wouldn't have tolerated any overt hatred. But that doesn't mean pockets of hate weren't festering.

As Patrick stood up to stretch his legs, he found himself in one of those pockets wedged between Albert Mahoney and Bobbie Duggan. Bobbie closed off their pyramid and whispered only to the two of them.

"Fucken jungle bunnies."

Albert Mahoney nodded in agreement, then he and Bobbie stared Patrick down to see if he was a member of the club. He looked back and forth at the two, holding his ground, and took a deep breath.

"Fellas, where's the love? Bobby Duggan, I used to see you with your family every Sunday down St. Pete's at the 11:15. … Did you receive the Holy Eucharist with that fucken tongue?"

Bobbie Duggan flashed his tough guy posture, but Patrick stood his ground.

"Hey, if I was gonna die on Sunday, I'd wanna spend this Saturday night at Sonny's Place, just so I could see Willie Dixon sing 'Backdoor Man.'"

"'Backdoor Man'? The Doors tune?" inquired Duggan.

"The Doors tune?" Patrick beseeched with incredulity.

He shook his head, side-stepped the venom, and found his barstool next to Arnold Peabody. It wasn't a shock to encounter the ugliness, but it was disappointing, as well as tired and old. The newscaster flashed to City Councilor Louise Day Hicks, who was holding a press conference to decry this turn of events. Other South Boston mothers expressed outrage.

"There's gonna be trouble," predicted one of the mothers. "Mark my words."

The network broke to a commercial, then came back with more Watergate speculation. What did Nixon know? And when did he know it?

"Thank you," thought Patrick. "Let's focus in on someone we can all hate."

The national press was inflicting painful body blows to the machine of Richard Nixon. He had clearly begun to backpedal. America tasted blood in the water. This would be the biggest news the sixties crowd could possibly have imagined. Could this actually be happening?

Amidst this lively bar, Patrick thought of Liza Jane. He rose off his stool, found a dime in his pocket, and went out to the backroom to dial her number. He heard three and a half rings.

"Hello."

"Hi, how are you?"

"A little lonesome."

"Can I come over?"

"Sure. Bring a bottle of red wine, cowboy."

"See you soon!"

"Hey, are you drunk?" she wondered upon hearing the raucous background of the Kilkenny.

"I ain't drunk. I'm just drinkin'."

Patrick hung up and hit the men's room. As he began to pee, he looked down to see the Hanoi Jane Urinal Target that was taped securely into the porcelain, but it was too late to stop now. He finished, flushed, washed up, and came back out. Slipping another dime into the pay phone, he dialed the first phone number that he had ever learned. The phone rang on the other end, and he searched hard and fast for the story he'd tell his mother this time. Like a good sax player with an edge, he wasn't completely sure of what would come out of his mouth. But he felt certain that it would be something good.

36: THE FAREWELL PARTY

Elena Madeira sat at Harvey's bedside for the fourth day, reading aloud, playing Blues tapes, and generally keeping him company. Alabama Al maintained his vigil outside in the hallway with a revolving skeleton crew of Blues Strikers. Their spirits were at an all-time low.

Just that morning Tisha Madeira had received a call from Frankie Pope, who was pulling together a little farewell party for all the employees of Sonny's Place. It was to take place early evening downstairs at The Casablanca in Harvard Square. A good opportunity to say goodbye, good luck, wish each other well, and raise a glass to the premature death of the most happening spot that Cambridge had ever known. There was little optimism regarding a happy ending. Most of the crew had begun a job search. Time marches on.

Tisha decided to swing by the hospital in hopes that she could persuade Elena to leave Harvey's room for a little while to attend the festivities. The elevator door opened, and Alabama Al looked up to see her coming down the hallway. He rose to greet her.

"How're you doing Al?" she inquired, giving him a kiss on the cheek.

"Not so good, Miss Tisha. Nothin's changed, and I fear I could spend the rest of my days waitin' in this hallway for bad news."

"I'm sorry, Al. How's Elena doing in there?"

"She be doin' fine. She be in there readin' to Harvey, talkin' to him like they be on a trip to the Poconos."

"Al, I got a call from Frankie, and he's pulling together a little party tonight for all the employees of Sonny's. I'm hopin' I can get Elena out of here for a while."

"Well good luck if you be tryin' to tell that girl what to do."

"I thought we'd tell her that you could take her place in there even if it was just for an hour or so."

"I'm all for it, Miss Tisha. Let's give it a try."

They headed into the room, where Elena was reading aloud from Ken Kesey's masterpiece, *Sometimes a Great Notion,* a book that was being handed from friend to friend. She heard them come in but finished the paragraph before looking up. Tisha walked around Harvey's bed to give her kid sister a hug that was warmly returned. Then Tisha and Alabama said their obligatory hellos to Harvey.

"Laynie, I got a call from Frankie Pope and there's gonna be a little party tonight at the Casablanca for everybody that worked at Sonny's Place. Do you want to come for a little while?"

"Oh, I don't think so, Tish."

"Now Miss 'Lena," began Al, my man Harvey here is a Blues freak through and through. If he thought that he caused you to miss out on a party, well I believe his heart might just stop tickin'! Now you gotta believe Al McGuirk when he tells you this."

"Elena looked off out the window. "Is crazy Helen gonna be there?"

"Frankie told me that everybody was coming."

Elena looked off out the window. "OK then I'll go for just a little while."

"Alright, little sister, we'll go out and have some fun!"

The big black man and the two Portuguese sisters smiled at each other, smiling at the mere thought of having a little fun.

****

Across the river in Boston, Sonny Bolla was gingerly raising himself out of his bathtub. The daily soak would temporarily subdue his anguish. Carefully he patted himself dry and noticed that the swelling had shrunk from grapefruit size down to orange. Sonny was on the mend.

He slipped into his bathrobe, waddled out to the living room, lit up a smoke, and flicked on the television. A violent spasm of coughing ensued. He cursed the soul of Cookie Jones one more time, and then poured himself a drink.

The News at Noon was on, and the lead story was still the High Court's decision to desegregate the Boston School System. He sipped his eye opener and listened while all sides of the story were once again considered.

"Why of course! Put the mulignans on a bus every morning and drive them to South Boston to go to school. Then take the good children of East Boston, and put 'em on the Congo Cruise to Roxbury every day. Geniuses! Every last one of them fucken geniuses!"

Sonny's editorial was followed by the rattle of his apartment buzzer. He pulled himself to his feet and made his way to the intercom.

"Who is it?" he barked.

"It's me," shouted Moe Venti.

Sonny buzzed him in and stood by the door. He could hear Moe's despairing footsteps coming down the hallway. He entered in silence, his eyes taut and sleepless. Sonny's heart sank at the sight of him.

"Any news?"

"No news."

"Can I get ya a drink, Moe?"

"No."

"Some pizza, Moe? I got some cold pizza in the fridge."

"No Sonny! I don't want any pizza, and I don't want a drink! This isn't a fucken party. I got a murder rap hanging over my head!"

"I know, Moe. I know. Calm down. What can I do?"

"What can you do? You can take me back to last August and talk me out of doing this fucken deal we did. Can you do that, Sonny? Can you do that? That would be fucken helpful!"

Sonny went silent. Moe had never spoken to him this way. Another minute passed without words. He sat on his couch staring out the window.

"How are your balls doin'?"

"They're alright Moe. They're OK. They're comin' around, ya know?"

"Sonny, I haven't slept a wink in days."

"I know Moe. You don't gotta explain."

"Whadya know about this punk, Phelan?"

"Irish? What's there to know?"

"What's there to know? I got a call from Gennaro last night, tellin' me not to touch a fucken hair on his precious head."

"Moe, come on?"

"Sonny, you come on."

"Out of the blue, he calls to tell you that?"

"Yup. How do you figure that?"

"You got me. I don't have a fucken clue. I thought he was just a kid from the neighborhood, but you're tellin' me that he's callin' up the Man to take the heat off? Now I've heard it all!"

"Yeah, well I'm glad I didn't threaten him. If I had, I'd have to offer an official apology to the little shit."

"Patrick Phelan, a made man?"

"Face it Sonny. He's got a lifeline."

"That little mick prick. Who could have figured?"

"Not me. That's for fucken sure."

"Any word from your lawyer?"

"Yeah, he's hoping to get the rap down to manslaughter if the Jew doesn't wake up. After all I didn't shoot him with the fucken gun, I just whacked him with it."

"Moe, the Jew's gonna wake up. He's got to!"

"Unfortunately, Sonny, the Jew doesn't have to do any fucken thing. He could lie there like a clam in a shell for the next forty years."

They stared out the window in silence, breathing in a shared sense of doom. This isn't the way things were supposed to go. The team of McGuirk and Wallenberg had tossed a big monkey wrench into the machinery of Moe's luxury vehicle, bringing it to a grinding halt.

"I'll tell you one thing Sonny—McGuirk—dead. And if the Jew wakes up I'll have him thrown in the same ditch. We'll let some time pass, then I'll hire a pro to take care of it. Mark my words, they're both dead meat, and the world will be a better place."

****

Over on Oak Street, off Inman Square it was early evening, and the Morley family was finishing their dinner of meat loaf, mashed potatoes, and gravy. The fighting had ceased, and an uncomfortable silence filled their home. Rue took note of his wife as he scraped up the last remnant of food from his plate with a cold biscuit. Her presence seemed somewhat robotic. It disarmed him. The yelling and screaming were familiar. This was not.

Leslie got up from the table. Clearing everyone's plate, she brought them to the sink to wash. Rue approached her there.

"Uh, Leslie, a few of the people from Sonny's are getting together tonight. Kind of a way to say goodbye, so I'm gonna be out for a while."

Leslie continued to wash the dishes. Her demeanor revealed nothing. Rue was perplexed by this move into uncharted territory. He turned to his native banter of sarcasm.

"Then after the get together, I'll probably douse myself in gasoline, strike a match and get this thing over with," he added casually.

Leslie didn't blink an eye. Rue stared at her another ten seconds or so before grabbing his coat and heading out the door, which he gently shut behind him. An unsettling walk to his car didn't provide the usual relief of escape. Deep futility seeped in and took hold. He started his car and drove up to Harvard Square, wondering how much more of this two people could take.

****

Tisha Madeira and Miguel arrived at the Cambridge City Hospital to find Elena discussing with Alabama Al the various rituals she had maintained while keeping vigil over the comatose Harvey Wallenberg.

"Now Al, you have to talk to him regularly, calling his name. Remind him who you are, and what happened. In between you can read him the story we're into. The bookmark is in place, and when you're tired of talking, play him some of the Blues tapes. I've been playing him a lot of Son House lately, and I think it's hitting home."

"Miss 'Lena, I hope you ain't playin' him no 'Death Letter'?"

"No Al. No 'Death Letter.' Now the number for the Casablanca is on the pad of paper by the phone. And be sure to remind Harvey that I'm only out for a little while, due back in an hour or so."

"Yes Miss 'Lena. But don't you be rushin' right back here. You go out there and try to enjoy yourself tonight, and that's that!"

"OK Al."

She put on her coat, and they headed out. Once outside the hospital, they hopped in Miguel's old Fairlane and headed off to Harvard Square. They found a parking spot on Church Street just across from the Oxford Ale House.

"It feels good to be outside guys. Thanks for springing me."

"You've been cloistered for days, little sister. Breathe it in!"

The trio crossed Brattle and headed down the alley next to the Café Algiers till they came by the back entrance to the downstairs of the Club Casablanca. There they tromped into the dark barroom to find all their cohorts. They had taken foothold at the pole by the service bar, and they stretched two deep down the length of Reggie's bar. Short Helen saw the Madeira sisters enter the room and she lept off her stool to greet them.

"I miss you guys so much," Helen lamented, giving the sisters a simultaneous squeeze.

"We miss you too, Helen," they cooed in sync.

"Where's your sister Stella?" Helen wanted to know.

"Oh, you know Stella," answered Tisha, "She can't be bothered with goodbyes."

"She can't, huh?" retorted Helen. "Well maybe I'll call her up and tell her to pull that stick out of her ass!"

"Oh Helen! Now you're talkin' honey!" beamed Elena for the first time in days.

"Whadya drinkin' ladies?" inquired Frankie Pope, who was crinkling a Jackson in his hands.

"Hey Frankie's buyin'!" proclaimed Tisha as she and her sister pulled him into their circle with Helen.

"Yeah, I'm buyin'! What are you havin', Shorty?"

"If you're buyin' Frankie, I'll have a Manhattan on the rocks with a twist."

"You got it, Shorty, and how 'bout Las Hermanas Portuguesas?"

"How about a Rolling Rock?" requested Tisha.

"Make it two," chimed in Elena.

Seated at a table was Mouton Duvalier, who brought along his wife and five children, and they were all dressed up for a party. He proudly introduced them one by one to the crew.

"In Haiti," he explained, "for party? We bring everyone!" and he smiled a big Mouton smile.

Miguel wandered down to mid-bar, where he found Freddie DiSavio trying to convince Patrick and Rue that the Big Bad Bruins had it all over the Men in Green. They were having none of that, and Miguel's arrival felt like divine intervention.

"Miguel, what's what? "inquired Rue.

"Oh, just the big adios, I guess."

"Yeah, I guess so," lamented Rue, who pulled a bill from his wallet, waved to Reggie behind the bar, and bought a round of beer for the boys. Soon beverages abounded, and Frankie took note of it. He came up behind Guillermo and gave a shout to announce a toast.

"Hey, it didn't last long, but while we had it, Sonny's Place was the best gig in town, and none of us will ever forget it!"

Frankie put his arm around the Chef's shoulder and they chinged their glasses. In seconds everyone was over to do the same, shouting confirmation. In that moment Patrick and Elena's eyes met. It left him feeling awkward and empty.

As the toasting ended, a somber mood took over the dark bar. This gathering was about saying good bye, and after all, saying good bye is the essence of sadness. Soon talk came around to employment prospects and future plans. Guillermo pulled out his return trip ticket to Italy and flashed it around for everyone to see. There were a couple more hours to drink on, share each other's company, and that would be the end of it.

****

Meanwhile back at the ICU of Cambridge City Hospital, Alabama Al McGuirk maintained Elena's vigil at Harvey's bedside. Ken Kesey's opus *Sometimes a Great Notion* was in his huge hands, his elbows rested on his knees. He forged into the narrative to quickly find that a logger, Joe Ben Stamper, was trapped under a fallen tree: rain pounding, river rising.

Joe Ben Stamper, the happy Caliban in Kesey's rosary of rain— thoroughly reborn in the spirit of Christ—fully surrendered to his mysterious ways. His intentions barely wavering like a flickering flame as an Oregonian river rises up around his neck. Harvey Wallenberg hears this story play out while trapped motionless in the stalled-out vessel of his own body.

"If I could just move my little finger, I'll be alright," he believes.

He notices that the story is now being told by the deep gruff voice of his old friend, not the sweet young voice that had kept him company through the first five hundred pages of this epic tale. But the change in narrators did not bother him. Harvey's frozen exterior belied the fact that the power of this story had literally taken him over.

Now the river has risen over Joe Ben's head as Hank Stamper desperately buys time by delivering air to his cousin, mouth to mouth. Joe Ben perceives a black laughing cancer that's trying to get inside of him, to take him over. He dreams of the smells and tastes of Thanksgiving dinner, only a few days away, to distract himself and keep death at arm's length.

Joe Ben's plight became Harvey's as the tension of this tale sent an overload of emotional charge through the electrical transmitters of his physical being. A surge rising from the base of his spine shot upward toward his neck and skull. The awakening jolt sent his arms and legs flailing. His frozen torso came alive and shot a foot off the bed.

Alabama shrieked in disbelief. Harvey's arms and legs shook as if in a seizure. His respiration left him fighting for breath. Alabama jumped to his feet and let out a holler for all of the world to hear.

"Harvey! Harvey! Nurse! Nurse! Harvey you're back! My God you're back!"

Minutes later the phone rang in the downstairs bar of the Casablanca. Reggie the bartender picked up the phone and stepped behind the hanging bead curtain into the backroom so that he could hear above the clamor. Seconds later he poked his head out through the curtain.

"Phone call for Elena Madeira."

The room quieted down for a moment as Elena walked around the wait station and entered the backroom. Seconds later her head popped out through the beaded curtain.

"Harvey's awake!" she screamed.

The gathering stood silent in disbelief. Elena's eyes beamed back demanding a response.

"You pinheads! Do I talk funny? Harvey's OK! He's awake!"

With that the entire crew, which had come to bury Sonny's Place, leapt off their barstools hooting, hollering, and raising their fists in celebration that the Home of the Blues might well be rising from the dead as well.

"Alright Harvey!" screamed Rue. "Shake off those cobwebs baby!"

Frankie Pope pulled the Globe's help wanted section from his back pocket and began ripping and tearing the pages into little bits, showering Guillermo with black and white confetti. Short Helen was hugging the two of them, jumping up and down like a high school cheerleader doing a pom-pom dance.

Freddie DiSavio bottomed up his tall seven and seven, punctuating this feat with a vile belch, his black mustache frothed with foam. He threw his money on the bar, and hollered at Reggie, "A round on me!"

The Turk pulled his harp out and blew one of those manic Little Walter riffs. Patrick, Rue, and Miguel howled and raised clenched fists into the air, slapping each other five. Miguel looked over his shoulder to see that Tisha was an earshot away, down toward the middle of the bar.

"Hey hombres, let me confess. My bags are packed. I was gone!"

Looking over his shoulder again, he saw a joyous Tisha Madeira making her way toward him for a hug. Rue also saw her coming and gave Miguel a nudge to the ribs.

"Unpack your bags, Chicano. You're a Cantabrigian for a little while longer!"

"I'm a what?" asked Miguel, who was then grabbed from behind by Tisha.

"Patrick, you got a dime?" asked Rue. "I gotta let Sonny know about this."

Patrick fished a dime out of his pocket and handed it over. Rue made his way down the bar to the pay phone just outside the men's room. He popped in his dime, heard a dial tone, and fumbled through his wallet for Sonny's number. Coming upon it, he dialed up the number and heard the phone ringing on the other end, smiling at the joy of the moment.

"Hello."

"Hey Sonny, It's Rue."

"Morley? Speak up! I can barely hear you. Where are you, fucken Times Square?"

"Nah, I'm just at a little celebration. But I was just wondering how your onions are hanging?"

"My onions, Morley, are a little better. And what the fuck is there to celebrate?"

"Sonny, I got good news for you. Harvey Wallenberg just woke up."

"Say that again."

"Harvey Wallenberg just woke up down at the Cambridge City."

"Morley, don't kid around about something like this!"

"This is no joke, Sonny. Harvey's awake, and Moe's off the fucken hook."

"The Jew's awake? The Jew's awake! The fucken Jew's awake! My prayers have been answered!"

Rue heard Sonny howling in utter glee. He imagined Sonny in his smoking jacket, doing a jig, being careful not to enrage his tender fulcrum point.

"Morley, I wanna kiss you!"

"Let's skip over that one, Sonny."

"I gotta call Moe! Thanks for the news!"

"See ya, Sonny."

****

An ecstatic Elena Madeira grabbed her coat, hustled out the back door of the 'Blanca, across Brattle Street and out toward the front door of the Harvard Coop, where she flagged down a cab for the short ride to the Cambridge City Hospital. Her heart pounded as she made her way up to Harvey's room.

She opened the door of the intensive care unit to find Alabama Al and a bunch of the Strikers crowded around Harvey's bed. The room's celebratory chatter dropped to a hush as Harvey's eyes met Elena's. Intuitively, he knew who she was. The entire room stopped in its tracks as they witnessed two worlds merge.

Slowly Elena walked around Harvey's bed till she arrived at the chair by his side. She sat down next to him as Harvey reached out for her two hands, which he held in his own. Speechless, they gazed at each other. It took a few seconds for everyone to realize that they should leave the room. This they did while hardly making a sound.

Elena felt Harvey's eyes burrowing into her lonely heart like a warm mercy. Harvey was lost in the face of the voice that remained at his side throughout this ordeal. He wanted to hear that sweet voice again.

"Could you finish reading me the story?" he asked in a whisper.

Elena nodded and reached for the book, which had been left open face down on the table next to her.

"Can you turn back a few pages? Joe Ben dies," he whispered, feeling the need to warn her.

"Joe Ben dies?" she asked in disbelief.

"Yes."

Harvey gazed at Elena as she began to read aloud, and he tried to recapture a sense of where he'd been for the last few days. Once again, he heard her sweet voice sing the song that had somehow called him back home.

37: NO HARD FEELINGS

Word of Harvey Wallenberg's recovery spread through town, reaching all parties concerned. His hospital room had been a beehive of activity all morning long as many of the Blues Strikers came by to say hello and share in the thanks.

Elena Madeira had spent the night in her own bed for the first time in many days. She came downstairs for coffee and bumped into her father, who was headed out the door to work. He didn't speak a word to her. Equal parts relief and despair beat in her heart.

Sonny had gotten hold of Moe Venti with the good news. Their elation was unbridled as Moe told his family, then sped off to Sonny's pad to celebrate. Sonny felt perky enough to waddle around the Back Bay putting down numerous cocktails with his main man, whom fate had spared.

They hit the Copley for drinks then a bite to eat at The Half Shell. Midnight brought on a trip to the Combat Zone. Drinks at the Teddy Bear Lounge, then over to The Naked i to catch Princess Cheyenne's act before retiring to Sonny's pad, where they drank till dawn. It was almost noontime when they were awoken red-eyed and bleary by the sound of the telephone.

"Yeah, Sonny here," he mumbled.

"Sonny, it's Harvey Wallenberg."

Sonny struggled to his feet, covering the mouthpiece of his phone. "Moe, it's the Jew, he's on the phone! Uh, Harvey, Harvey, how are ya feelin'? We was so glad last night to hear you'd come around!"

"I'll bet you were, Sonny. I'll bet you were."

"Yeah, look Harvey, Moe never meant to hurt you like that, he just wanted you guys off our sidewalk. Ya know?"

"I know, Sonny. No hard feelings."

"You mean it, Harvey?"

"Sure Sonny. Besides life is too short. Say, would Mr. Venti be there with you by chance?"

"Well, uh, yeah he is."

"Sonny, you two aren't dating now, are you?"

"Oh Harvey, you're a chuckle. Hold on, I'll get Moe."

Sonny tiptoed over to his couch, where Moe was trying to wipe the sleep from his eyes. He sat up and took a deep breath searching for the proper salutation. He couldn't find it.

"Yeah?" he mumbled into the receiver.

"Hi Moe, how've you been? It's been a while since we chatted. … Aren't you gonna ask me how I'm doin'? Come on Moe, show a little concern."

"What do you want, Wallenberg?"

"What do I want? Well, that's a good question. Moe, do you realize that your immediate future is in my hands? I talked to the Cambridge Police this morning. Attempted murder isn't murder, but it's what you're looking at."

"No Harvey, I'm looking at assault and battery. I wasn't trying to kill you. That was a love tap."

"A love tap? Moe, the only way you skate off free is by playing ball with me."

"What do you want?"

"I want you and Sonny to come over here and visit me. Show a little concern. We've got a typewriter at my bedside. I'll be writing up an agreement that I expect you to come over and sign."

"What kind of fucken agreement?"

"Don't worry, Moe. I'm not greedy. I just want what we came for. Bring your bifocals with you so that you can read the fine print. And by the way, if we don't strike a deal today, I'm taking this deal off the table, and the toll is going up, if you catch my drift. It's up to you, Moe. I'll be waiting to hear from you."

Moe heard the receiver click, then stared at the phone as if it were a person he hated. "You stinkin', slimy …," which was followed by a violent slam of the receiver.

"What'd he say?"

"He's pushing me to sign an agreement, after which he'll drop all charges. And if we don't sign the agreement today, he ups the ante."

"Christ Moe, that sounds like the kind of ultimatum that we laid on Lou Lopes when we bought the fucken place!"

Moe shot Sonny back a look.

"I'm sorry Moe! I'm sorry!"

38: TRICK OR TREAT

Sonny and Moe pulled themselves together and made their way across the river for the big powwow with Harvey Wallenberg and Alabama Al McGuirk. Moe had indeed brought his reading glasses. The contract awarded Harvey with exclusive booking rights to the club as well as a sweet raise for the musicians. It was no more, and no less than what they came for.

Moe Venti found himself behind the eight ball for the first time in his life. He'd never been manipulated this way. It was abhorrent to him. But he had no recourse. So, he bit the bullet, signed the contract, and promptly left Harvey's room at the Cambridge City. All charges were dropped, and Sonny's Place was rescheduled to open at 9 p.m. Halloween night. The kitchen would reopen November 1st, All Saint's Day.

"Just who we be bringin' in, to open up?" Alabama inquired of Harvey with a triumphant smile.

"Halloween night? It's gotta be the Boogie Man!"

"Hooker?"

"John Lee," Harvey added with a grin.

So, the word rang forth. October 31st brought on a buzz of activity. Moe called in his ace carpenter, Bennie Felice to repair the façade that was shattered in the big fight, not to mention Mouton and the Turk's bleach scrubbing of the blood-stained sidewalk.

Although the kitchen would not be serving food till the following day, Guillermo had the crew in because they were starting over from Jump Street. Over the course of the week, the walk in had become a science project of mold and frothing soups.

"Hey, smell this!" petitioned sulking Freddie DiSavio, his face twisted up in distress.

"Just throw it out, Freddie!" ordered Frankie Pope.

Nevertheless, everybody was thrilled at the turn of events, happy to be back in Guillermo Vitello's Orchestra. Patrick found his return to work both a comfort and a relief. Helen Beech glowed with contentment. The team was back, and this machine was gearing up to feed the City of Cambridge once again.

Sonny and Moe convened downstairs in their inner sanctum. Sonny kept prompting Moe for a good feeling, a mood that was hopeful, upbeat, positive. But it wasn't forthcoming. There was no thanks or relief in Moe's heart. He had revenge on his mind. It was braising in his belly like a violent osso buco. A knock on the door interrupted the hate.

"Come in," shouted Sonny, and in walked none other than Sargent Milligan of the Cambridge Police Department.

"Oh Sonny, look. It's Andy of Mayberry," chirped Moe. "We're celebrating tonight Sargent. We're back open for business. Have you heard?"

"That's why I'm here. Wallenberg dropped all the charges. I'm here to return this to you."

Sargent Milligan laid an object in front of Moe that was tightly wrapped in brown paper. Moe knew what it was immediately. He pulled the wrapping paper off and held the Luger in his hands, measuring the weight of it, lightly fingering the trigger. Feeling whole. Feeling dangerous.

"So, Sargent Milligan, I suppose that you're looking to get back on the payroll?"

"Well Moe, if you plan on living with the maximum capacity that's listed on your permit, I'm not sure that you're gonna be able to pay Sonny enough to keep his Eldorado clean. That concerns me, a dirty Eldorado does."

"Yes Sargent, but what concerns me is that we've been supporting you for three months now, and when things get a little rough over here, you're slapping the cuffs on me like a common criminal."

"Yeah, well you never told me that you were making a fucken documentary about cops and the Blues. If my reputation is ruined, I'm of no use to you. Am I?"

"I get that Sargent," spoke Moe, still admiring his hardware. He continued the observance for a half minute or so before he gave Sonny the nod to pull some scratch from the wall safe. Milligan counted the cash in his hands, his lips barely moving as he mumbled inaudible numerals on the rising side.

"OK gentlemen, congrats on your reopening. I wish you great success!"

And with this Sargent Milligan headed for the door. As he got there the Luggs were heading in. They appeared sheepish and defeated. There was someplace they'd rather be, but they didn't have the guts to not show up for Moe Venti. After all, he had provided them with their identity. They'd been directionless Luggs before Moe had discovered them and helped shape their destiny.

"You ready to open, Boss?"

Moe looked up from his piece and smiled compassionately at the Luggs.

"You boys like a little taste?" he inquired. They nodded in the affirmative.

SEAN MICHAEL DANEHY

Once again Moe looked over at Sonny and nodded toward the office bar. He poured up a couple hard and sweet, the way the Luggs liked it. They sipped their beverages and squinted their eyes like most kids do when taking medicine.

"How are you boys doing?" Moe inquired with genuine concern.

"We're alright, Boss," they spoke, trying to project confidence.

"Now look, I don't want you boys to be feeling any shame for the beating that big baboon administered. McGuirk's a fucken animal. You Luggs are human beings."

"Thanks Boss," they stammered.

"Well boys, we're gonna let some time pass, and then we're gonna take care of those two. You read me?"

"Yeah Boss, we read you."

"How'd you boys like to be there to piss into the ditch before we shovel the dirt back on 'em?"

The Luggs clenched their fists, and their beaten-up bodies twitched at the prospect. Their heads nodded greedily in anticipation.

"Can't we all just be happy that the fucken Jew woke up?" Sonny pleaded.

Back upstairs in the kitchen, Patrick was cleaning squid, when he heard a pounding on the back door. He felt genuine excitement about who was knocking. He opened the door to find John Lee Hooker dressed to the nines, wearing a white fedora and dark sunglasses.

"Tri, tri, tri, trick or treat?" stuttered the Boogie Man.

"Welcome John Lee!" smiled Patrick, extending his hand for a shake.

"Greetings, son. My, my somethin' sure smells fine in heeya!"

Hooker and his crew tromped through the kitchen with all their equipment and headed on out to the bandstand. Patrick looked over at Guillermo, who was peering at the band as if he were staring into a tank of tropical fish. He never got used to this part of the job. He had no reference point for it. This was a slice of pure, raw Americana.

"The Blues is back!" shouted Frankie Pope.

"Yes sir!" affirmed Hooker.

Soon everything was moving into place. A healthy line was forming out on Hampshire Street and there was excitement in the air. Next door at the Tortoise all the Blues Strikers had convened, and a few bottles of champagne were cracked open to celebrate the moment. Harvey was spending one more night at the Cambridge City for precautionary measures. But Alabama Al was there, giving thanks to all the folks that gathered together to make the strike happen. He read a note from Harvey that summed up their collective accomplishment.

"On behalf of Al McGuirk and myself, I want to thank you all for standing with us. It's a great victory for all of us, who consider the Blues to be the most powerful artistic expression of our times. Long live the Blues! Love to you all, Harvey Wallenberg."

The gathering howled in delight with glasses chinging and hugs all around. The mood was sweet and triumphant. Soon they finished their celebration and headed out to Hampshire Street to line up for Hooker's show. Alabama took one look at the line and ventured down the alley to sneak in through the kitchen door. He had no need to show up the Luggs.

Inside the Home of the Blues, Rue and Miguel had their bar stocked and primed.

"Youse guys ready to open?" inquired the Luggs.

"We're ready Teddy," confirmed Rue as he lit up a smoke. Miguel iced down a couple of kamikazes as the Luggs limped out to man the door.

"Y'all got a taste for me?" inquired Alabama Al, who had slunk in through the kitchen and into the first stool at the bar. Miguel poured one for Al, and they chinged their glasses.

"Let the good times roll," affirmed the big black man.

"Let 'em roll," echoed Rue.

Over in the wait station the three Madeira sisters killed some time. There wasn't much setting up to be done with the kitchen yet to open. This provided no consolation for Stella Madeira, who sat in a chair looking out at the room of Sonny's Place like she wanted to spit on it. The combination of beauty and bitterness etched into her face was nothing short of tragic. She was a shiny Thunderbird with a dead battery.

Elena stood over the utility sink scrubbing her cocktail tray clean with a wet rag. Tisha yawned a big one and asked, "You guys want a cup of coffee?"

"Sure," affirmed Elena. Stella didn't answer.

"Stell, you want a cup?"

"No," the dark beauty spoke flatly. Her mood had a way of taking the air out of a room. Elena looked at Tisha and they silently acknowledged it. Tisha gazed closely at Elena's face, almost like a startled parent, who sees their child ripen in front of their eyes. It was as if she'd paid some archetypal turnpike toll and had grown from girlhood to womanhood. It took all the fear out of asking a difficult question.

"Laynie, can you explain this Harvey thing to me? What was the compulsion to be at his side through this? You don't even know him."

Elena gathered her thoughts in an attempt to explain the unexplainable.

"Well, when he first got struck, he landed right at my feet. Initially, I just felt compelled to help him, like you'd help any stranger that had fallen. The EMT driver saw me holding his hand, and probably thought we were a couple because he asked me if I wanted to ride with them to the emergency room. There was no reason not to, so I did. Then, when Alabama Al got released by the Police, he came back to the hospital, and we spent the night at Harvey's bedside. We talked through the night, and Al explained their friendship to me. It was clear how much Al loved him. I began to feel something for him as well. I was taking care of him, and I felt like I belonged somewhere, maybe for the first time," she confessed as she wiped a tear from her eye. "Then I just wasn't gonna let anyone tell me what to do."

"Are you going to see him again?"

"We're having dinner tomorrow when he gets released," smiled Elena. "Then we'll see what happens."

One by one the patrons paid their cover to the Luggs and entered the Home of the Blues, primed in a big way to once again pay witness to those American sounds of pain and ecstasy. The liquor was flowing. "Hooker" was the name being spoken from table to table. The cash register rang out as the jukebox roared out Muddy Waters' "I'm Ready." There was great anticipation in the air.

Patrick and Frankie finished their day in the kitchen with a bowl out on the back stoop. Then they cleaned up, changed, and joined Alabama Al at the bar.

Halloween night brought in a colorful crowd, many of whom had dressed for the occasion. A fellow wearing a Richard Nixon mask walked about the room flashing the peace sign. Another, with a Spiro T. Agnew mask, hung by the jukebox reading the Help Wanted section of the paper. Other assorted witches, pirates, and phantoms cruised the room, filling in all the open spaces.

Downstairs Moe Venti loaded the chamber of his Luger. Sonny paced the office floor. All this talk of revenge made him uneasy because Moe was off the hook. Why couldn't he be thankful for a resolution to his looming incarceration? Why couldn't he let bygones be? The muffled sounds of musicians tuning up above them wafted through the drop ceiling.

John Lee Hooker was ready to come on stage.

"Moe, they're gonna start makin' that fucken racket again. Let's get out of here. Let's go back up to the Sheraton Commander and stretch out in that tent again. Whadya say?"

Moe continued to admire his hardware, then stood up, and slipped it into his pocket. His silent nod said they were out of there. They donned their coats and hats and headed up the back stairs. Halfway up the band broke into "The Motor City's Burnin'." The whole house began to vibrate.

Hooker's lament was followed by shrieks and hollers that held no meaning for the proprietors. They headed down the bar, past the Lugg Brothers, and out onto Hampshire Street. They breathed easier as they put some distance between themselves and the stone club behind them, which was pulsating to a fever pitch that neither could feel.

Climbing into Sonny's Eldorado, they drove past the fire station and took the left onto Cambridge Street. They were too Big Time to notice any of the children, traveling in packs, dressed up for Halloween—their sacks filled with sweet loot.

A little rain began to fall as they drove around Cambridge Common. Sonny proceeded up Garden Street but spotted a parking space right out in front of The Sheraton Commander and hooked a spectacular U-turn, pulling his Eldorado up snug to the curb. They hopped out of Sonny's machine and sashayed on in to Dertad's. Sonny was happy to find an empty sultan's tent across the room. The plump pillows called out to be sat upon.

"C'mon Moe, let's pretend we own one of those oil wells in Saudi!"

Moe followed Sonny into the tent. They both stretched out, assuming their sultan postures. Soon a waitress appeared, and Sonny ordered a couple of stingers on the rocks, figuring that it might lighten Moe's mood. The stingers delivered; Sonny called a toast.

"Moe, I wanna raise this glass to you, to me, to our lifelong friendship, and to our future prosperity!"

They chinged their glasses and took a taste. The sweet boozy fumes rose upwards into their nasal passages like a fog permeating a swamp. The potion tingled and burned on the way down. Still Moe was silent and grim, offering no lyric response to Sonny's toast. Now Sonny was getting frustrated.

"For Christ's sake, Moe! Two days ago your ass was deep fried. Today you're in the clear, and you can't even crack a smile. C'mon Moe. How 'bout showin' some fucken thanks?"

"Thanks? Maybe in November, Sonny. The fourth Thursday in November."

Moe took a good belt from his drink and stared out into the room. If he were a guitar string, he would have snapped by now. "Sonny, nobody has ever fucked with me like this before. As we walked out of that joint tonight, I didn't even feel like we owned it."

"Moe, it's alright. It's just a setback. Think of the positive. Did you hear that cash register ringing again when we left? Just like the Bells of St. Mary's! We're back Moe! The kitchen opens up tomorrow. We're rollin' again. Let those fools think they won something tonight. But just remember—they're getting' pie eyed in our joint, buyin' our booze!"

Glasses empty, they ordered up a couple more. Sonny hoped another round might loosen Moe up. He was correct, the booze was doing its thing, and suddenly Moe felt his intestinal track churning.

"Christ, I don't think I've taken a shit in a week."

"Hey Moe, why don't you go take a fucken dump?"

Moe rose off the pillows, tipped back his drink and finished her off. The two stingers had gotten their claws into him. His eyes were a bit glazed as he spoke of himself in third person.

"Sonny, Moe Venti doesn't like losing. As a matter of fact, Moe Venti doesn't lose. And Moe Venti doesn't forget." He looked down as he spoke, patting the metal monster that lay breathing in his pocket.

He turned and walked out of the bar, down the hallway and into the men's room. Opening one of the stall doors, he went in, did an about face, secured the door, unbuckled his belt and unzipped his fly. Moe began to sit down on the toilet when his pants slipped from his grasp because of the weight of the Luger. The top of the pistol barrel struck his shoe, then the handle hit the floor.

Moe heard a shocking echo rattle off the tiled walls, then felt a piercing flame shoot through his knee and up into his chest. The explosion reverberated through the entire bathroom, and Moe was knocked backward onto the toilet seat. He shrieked in horror as he touched his hand to his knee and chest, where blood spurted freely from both wounds.

The bathroom wall muffled the gunshot, but it was loud enough to pull Sonny off his pillow, running to the men's room. He flung the door open, not knowing what to expect.

"Moe? Moe??"

A wheezing, animal-like sound emanated from one of the stalls. Sonny tried to open the door, but it was locked from inside. He got down on his knees, and his eyes absorbed the nightmare that was Moe Venti's. Sonny's heart pounded to a rhythm of pure panic as he crawled headfirst into the stall and a river of blood.

"Moe! Moe! Christ Moe! What happened?"

Moe was still here in this world as he attempted to utter words pertaining to the hot, smoking gun, still sizzling in his pants pocket, rumpled about his ankles. Hysteria reigned as Sonny unlocked the stall door and picked up his friend in his arms. The blood pumped rhythmically from his wounds as if it didn't care where it was going.

"Hospital! Hospital!" Sonny screamed aloud. Waiting for an ambulance was out of the question. Sonny carried Moe down a hallway and out in the street. He slipped Moe into the backseat of the Eldorado, kicked the engine over, and put the pedal to the metal, then a screeching right on to Mason Street.

"Hang on Moe! I'm beggin' you to hang on!"

Mount Auburn Hospital was a stone's throw away as Sonny ripped through the Stop sign on Brattle, then a furious left on to Hawthorne.

As Moe began to realize that he was leaving his body, he felt a profound need to be touched, held, and to share eye contact. This need expressed itself in a guttural, nonverbal utterance.

Sonny's ears heard it for what it was, slammed on the brakes, jammed the shift into park, and reached into the back seat, pulling Moe as close as he could. They stared into each other's eyes for a few breathless moments. Then Moe's spirit began making its journey onward. Sonny wept as Moe's eyes stared off at nothing, like a fish in a butcher's display case.

"Come back, Moe! Come back!!!"

In moments reality set in. Sonny crawled out of the car, collapsing on the hood of his Eldorado crying like a lost child in the woods. A cruel aloneness enveloped him unlike anything he had ever known.

****

Meanwhile, back at The Home of the Blues, the room was exultant. The whole place reverberated as John Lee Hooker was finishing up his first set with "Boom, Boom, Boom, Boom," and there was still a wild night ahead to be had. The little stone bar in Inman Square shook, rattled, and glowed, unlike any other joint for light years around.

TO BE CONTINUED IN BOOK TWO

"THE TRANSFORMATION OF SONNY BOLLA"

ABOUT THE AUTHOR

Sean Michael Danehy has been a professional cook and a resident of the town of Cambridge, Massachusetts for the last forty-five years. Throughout this time, he has cooked in many fine kitchens on both sides of the Charles River.

Sean writes what he calls "Restaurant Fiction." Stories about the world he has lived in for his entire working life—tales about chefs, bartenders, dishwashers, and despotic restaurateurs.

seanmichaeldanehy.com